CARNAGE IN THE COUNTY

A Sheriff Elven Hallie Mystery

DREW STRICKLAND

www.drewstricklandbooks.com

ISBN 9781964110011 (paperback)

ISBN 9781964110028 (hardcover)

Cover Design by Juan Padrón

For the Johnson County Public Library,
I wish you well

JOIN MY READER'S LIST

Members of my Reader's List get free books and cool behind the scenes information to go along with them.

They're also always the first to hear about my new books and promotions going on.

To be a part of the Reader's List and get your free book, sign up at:

https://drewstricklandbooks.com/mail-list/

CHAPTER ONE

LINDA KUNNEKE HAD WORKED AT THE LIBRARY FOR TEN YEARS and two months. In that time, she had seen just about everything she could have imagined, and plenty of things that never would have crossed her mind. She'd read so many books, but found that some of the people in Dupray could be even scarier, funnier, sadder, and far more outlandish than the imagination of any of the authors' words that her eyes had scanned across.

On a good day, it was a great job. The people who came to check out books, or even read them while sitting in the aisles, were pleasant, kept to themselves, and maybe even added a touch of excitement to her day.

But on a bad day, well, her patience being tried would have been putting it lightly.

The thing about it, though, was that it wasn't the patrons who visited the library who pushed her buttons. She could struggle with them at times, that was for sure, but none of them could come close to the people she worked with.

Her fellow employees were the ones who made her question her sanity, day in and day out.

They put things where they didn't belong, left messes that she had to clean up, and called in sick even when they weren't ill, leaving her to cover their shift on her day off. She liked the library, but even someone's favorite activity needed a break, and this wasn't even close to her favorite thing.

Not all her fellow employees were awful. She could put up with them most of the time. That is, until Phylis came along and got in their ears.

Phylis had worked at the library for just under two years, and somehow, she'd become the higher-ups' favorite person on staff. She had fooled them all. Even Linda had been taken in for a few days at first. But once she worked with the woman for a week, she could tell Phylis wasn't who she presented herself to be. She was a phony who said all the right things, then turned around and gossiped to whoever would listen about whoever she wanted. To Linda, "snake" was the word that fit her best.

Phylis would butter up the bosses and then throw people under the bus if things weren't going in her favor. Linda had been a victim of that behavior on a few occasions, resulting in the higher-ups coming down on her for every little thing. She tried to match Phylis's energy at times, but the woman was just too good at being a terrible person, and Linda couldn't keep up. Nor did she want to.

Over time, she had learned to stay out of Phylis's path and keep to herself. It wasn't fun, but it was better than sticking herself in the line of fire.

But the latest development was where Linda had to draw the line. At some point, it was bound to happen, having to eat shit day in and day out. But Phylis getting a promotion, a raise, and now being put in charge of Linda's hours and paycheck was far too much for her. The damn woman had been there less than a fifth of the time that Linda had put in.

So Linda was ready to let her have it. She would lose her job, sure. Hell, she might lose a lot more than that. But it was going to be so damn satisfying, she could just taste it.

Phylis would never see it coming, and if anyone tried to intervene or get in Linda's way, well, Linda wouldn't want to be in their shoes, because she wouldn't hold back. Even if it meant someone else got hurt in the process.

She'd just been pushed too much to care.

It was early, still before opening hours, and yet the parking lot had more cars than she'd expected. She didn't count them, but figured it was due to the print shop next door. They were having their asphalt resurfaced, so seeing an extra six or seven cars in the lot wasn't anything alarming to her. The odd thing was, that business wasn't open, either.

She didn't question it because she was too distracted by the white Pontiac in the parking lot, sitting in a spot far closer to the door than it should be. Phylis was here, and she clearly didn't care about the rule that stated employees should park further in the back. At least she was on time for what might possibly be a first in her entire career with the library. But it was too little, too late. Linda was dead set on letting her have it at this point.

Linda found her own parking spot—in the back of the lot, of course—and made her way to the front door, her keys in hand jingling a little tune with each step as she approached. The three metal keys clanging together was a reminder that she only had three things going for her at this point. Her home, which was a crumbling rental that was in desperate need of a landlord who would invest in something more than white paint to cover the cracks in the walls. Her car, which she was only confident in getting her three miles in a single drive— exactly what she needed to get to work and back home. And her job, which, at this point, was being more than just a little threatened now.

There was no way that Linda was going to let Phylis take the one place that had been a sanctuary for her when everything else seemed to be falling apart. Well, she wouldn't let her do it without making a scene about the whole thing.

Her reign had gone on long enough.

Linda selected the key to the library door on her ring, but before sliding it in, she cocked her head as she noticed the door. It wasn't flush with the wall. She sighed, knowing she was already angry enough. The last thing she needed was to be out of control and ranting. That would only make her seem crazy.

But Phylis hadn't locked the door. The library wasn't supposed to be open yet, so it was a major safety issue to leave the front door unlocked. On top of that, it was such a pain in the ass dealing with folks who came in early, wanting books when the computer system wasn't fully up yet. The system was old and outdated, so rushing it would only make things go slower.

But those things didn't matter to Phylis because she knew Linda would be there. She was going to leave Linda to deal with all the riffraff that came in. Not to mention getting impatient and angry with Linda, yelling in her face, and being downright nasty with her. Linda's blood boiled even more thinking about it.

But she reminded herself again that she needed to be calm. She wasn't going to let anyone take this job from her, trying to belittle her feelings by saying she was too emotional about it.

She pulled the handle and walked straight into the building. She turned and locked up behind her, smiling to herself that she was foiling Phylis's plans of throwing her under the bus.

But as soon as she walked inside, all her plans of controlling her anger went right out the window.

The place was trashed. The first thing she saw was the pile of books on the floor. It wasn't even a stack but a full cart that was supposed to have been put away last night. It had been tipped over and left in a pile, the pages folded and covers bent in ways that made her cringe. This was beyond unacceptable.

"Phylis!" Linda yelled out to the empty building.

There was no answer, of course. Why would there be? Phylis didn't normally answer to Linda, but today, she was going to.

Linda gripped her purse, unzipping it, ready to pull out her little surprise for Phylis as soon as she saw her. There was no way in hell she was going to lift a finger to fix any of this mess. Phylis would learn soon enough that she couldn't get away with treating others this way.

But Linda needed to find her first.

The library was a mess just about everywhere her eyes landed as she scanned the open room. It wasn't a large building, but the various bookcases were laid out to make it look like there was more room than there actually was. Books were strewn about, like they normally were at the end of the night. Most people did not put things back where they found them, instead opting to set them on random places, like the chairs that sat at the end of the bookcases, the rolling carts, and atop the tables placed throughout the room.

The desk for checking out books was just ahead, and much to her surprise, the computers were already on and clicking away. Their inside components always made a light hum and sound that most people actually enjoyed during the quiet hours they were there. And right now, it was the only sound in the building that Linda stopped to listen to, trying to detect where Phylis might be.

In the back of the building, at the end of the long room, were the private conference rooms that were available for reservations. Phylis was either there, or in one of the bathrooms that were next to the conference rooms. Either way, Linda would find her soon.

She reached into her purse, anticipating pulling it out and waving it in front of Phylis's face.

Phylis would never see it coming.

Linda made her way through the library, ignoring the piles of books and traipsing around the trash that had been left behind. That wasn't her concern right now. She could smell the familiar, welcoming scent from the pages and the glue that held them together. It was like a warm hug most days.

But as she approached the conference rooms, something else tickled her nose, mixing with the smell of the library. It was almost metallic, like copper or iron. Just a hint, but it was still noticeable.

Just in front of the door to the conference room was a muddy footprint on the carpet. Linda stopped to stare at it, shaking her head.

This mess was far worse than a regular night Linda had ever worked, or had ever walked in on the next day. What had happened?

Not that she was giving Phylis any credit, but maybe she was in the middle of cleaning whatever destruction had happened in the conference room. The solid door was ajar, but not enough that Linda could really see anything.

She reached her hand out and pushed the door open.

She immediately regretted it.

First, her eyes set on the blood streak on the floor just inside of the door. It led back to the footprint that she had seen earlier, which told her it wasn't mud at all that had made the shape of the shoe. The blood inside the door was much more than just the outline of a print. And as her eyes drifted upward, it led straight to a body.

It was a woman. Her hair was gray, and her eyes were wide open, staring straight ahead, her chin propping her head up so it looked as if she were trying to look under the door. Linda couldn't tell where the injuries were because she was soaked in blood all over, and she wasn't going to touch her to find out. But she did look familiar. And that's when she figured out that it was Amy Jefferson. She was a regular at the library.

Linda's eyes kept wandering upward, over the tables and the entire room. She couldn't focus on one thing, because there was too much going on.

Bullet holes in the walls.

So much blood.

So many bodies.

Linda took a much-needed breath, holding it ever since opening the door. She wanted to scream and cry. She had no idea where Phylis was right now, and even if she did, she needed to call someone else for help.

She spun on her heels and headed straight back the way she came.

Was whoever did this still here?

She didn't know, and she couldn't even think of an answer. All she could think was that she needed to call for help. She dipped behind the counter, reaching for the phone tucked next to the computer.

But before she put her hand on it, she saw what looked like a large streak of blood. It traveled down the handle, onto the counter, and then just over the lip, making it right to the edge.

Linda blinked a few times, then slowly turned.

Sitting only three feet from where Linda stood was Phylis. Her body was slumped over, and this time, Linda could tell what had happened. Her entire chest was riddled with bullet holes. The poor woman was soaked in blood. Her chest never rose, nor fell.

She was dead, and except for Linda, so was everyone else in the library.

CHAPTER TWO

HE WORE A HOODIE WRAPPED OVER HIS HEAD WITH A BALL CAP underneath, keeping most of his features out of sight from any cameras or people trying to get a glimpse of him. Aviator sunglasses, which looked almost comical on his small head, covered his eyes. A beard wrapped the lower half of his face.

Other than that, there was nothing much to go off of. The biggest description they could use was that he was white, but that described over ninety percent of the whole damn state. He was shorter, maybe about five foot six. And he was fast.

Tank knew that for a fact.

They had been trying to catch this guy for months. He'd been hitting all the gas stations, grocery stores, and feed shops in the area, stealing whatever he could get his hands on, it seemed. There was almost no rhyme or reason to it. Almost as if anything that fit in his arms was fair game.

But Tank did figure one thing out. It wasn't just *anything* that was being stolen; it was food, medical supplies, and other daily-use things. There were no big-ticket items like electronics or even cash. If it were found in a pantry or cabinet, that's what the thief was interested in.

And no amount of stuff seemed to slow him down, either.

Two weeks ago, Tank was on the guy's heels, arms stretched out, inches away from yanking that stupid hood right off his head and pulling him backward. But somehow, the thief had some sort of internal turbo boost and picked up speed. Tank lunged, but all he caught was a handful of air, and when the shift in his body weight caused his feet to lose balance, a face full of floor and a fat lip to boot.

This time, it was going to be different, though. This time, there was a plan.

Tank was an easy spot for the thief since he'd seen his face already. It wasn't like he could throw a disguise on, either—being the size of a barn, he stood out like a sore thumb. Intimidation, he could do, but undercover had to be left to someone else. That's why Tank found himself in the car, making sure to bring the only undercover vehicle they had in the department: the car they'd termed "The Sneaker," an old Crown Victoria that probably didn't help any bit to go unnoticed. But it was all they had.

It was a cold day out, closing in on winter soon. He kept the window down, letting the breeze drift over his exposed skin. He'd rather sit in the vehicle this way now versus doing it in the summer when he'd be sweating his ass off. Plus, there was the possibility of having to run, which he'd rather do in the cold as well.

He hoped he didn't have to run, though. Not after last time.

If they were correct in their theory, the new stock announcement at Jake's Feed and Speed would garner a lot of attention. And with all the people came cover for a thief. Jake couldn't keep an eye on everyone, and even *if* the thief thought the authorities were there, he would think there were far too many people to police.

That might be true. But in this case, they weren't trying to police *everyone*. They were there for one specific thief.

The one they kept getting calls about from every damn store in the county. It had become a running joke at this point. There had been whispers throughout the county that weren't so quiet anymore, saying that the sheriff's department couldn't even catch this one guy, so how did they think they would protect and serve in other ways?

The thing about it was, Tank was starting to believe it, too.

It had been months since Elven had been shot. Months since they'd arrested Hollis Starcher. Months since Madds had been found out to be related to him and, apparently, a double agent. And months since Elven had let his emotions get in the way, which had ended up with good people getting killed.

To say the investigation had been handled poorly would be putting it lightly. Sure, the bad guy had ended up being killed, and another one had ended up behind bars, but in Tank's opinion, the cost far outweighed the results.

Most people in the county didn't disagree.

So in Tank's mind, they really needed a win, and catching this thief could really be it. No, it wouldn't make up for all that had happened in the past, but it could be a step in the right direction to quiet the whispers at least. He just hoped that day was today.

He wished he had his own eyes inside the store, but while Jake's store had a camera, neither of them had the tech to get it connected to something in Tank's vehicle. And even if the thief didn't already recognize him, someone needed to be in the car in case anything went wrong and a chase ended up on the road.

Another lesson learned from experience.

The radio crackled, pulling Tank's attention. "Be ready," the voice on the other end said. It was laden with static, but Tank knew it was the new deputy on the other end. Tank had gotten to know the man over the past couple of months after being given the go-ahead to hire him. He had worked with Elven unofficially on a previous case in Monacan, which was why Tommy was looking for a new job. Apparently, Sheriff Reed Bando hadn't much cared for Tommy's helping Elven out, so once he was out of the hospital, Tommy was put on desk duty until he was finally let go completely.

Tank liked working with him, but the office definitely felt different these days. And it wasn't just because of Tommy.

"Shit, Tank! Go, go, go!" Tommy screeched through the radio.

Tank righted his spine and sat at attention. He had no idea what that message even meant. Did it mean he was supposed to go inside? Was he supposed to drive around to a different spot? He had a great view of the whole area from his unmarked car, but he didn't see anything out of the ordinary yet.

He picked up the radio. "Where the hell am I going? Be specific." Frustration filled his voice, though it wasn't fully intended for Tommy. It was mostly because he couldn't be inside to see it himself.

"The back," Tommy said, his voice coming out like he was bouncing on a trampoline. "Out the—back of—the store."

Shit. Tank shifted into drive and pulled the car through the parking lot as fast as he could while being as safe as possible. There were a load of cars and a good grip of people walking in and out of the store from the parking lot. The new stock sale was working too well, and he had to be careful not to hit an innocent civilian in the mix.

Tank managed to navigate the parking lot without clipping anyone and zipped around to the back of the store. The door was closed, and Tank wondered if somehow he had missed the man running out the back, but when he scanned the empty lot behind the store, the only thing he saw were a bunch of empty boxes, a pile of trash next to the dumpster, and a whole heap of pallets in a haphazard stack. Nobody was running away, or even in sight.

Tank picked up the radio and held it to his mouth, clicking the button. "Where is he?"

As if to answer him, the door of the back of the store flung open.

Tank quickly opened his door and stepped out, taking a firm stance with his arms wide open. He lunged at the man running through the door toward his car. He was covered in a white powdery substance that Tank hoped was flour and not a sack's worth of cocaine. The air surrounding him was thick with it as he came out of the building.

He was much bigger than the man, taking him down to the asphalt immediately. Tank put him on his face, but then the powder in the air subsided, and Tank saw the uniform. Then he saw the gun and handcuffs on his belt.

"Tank, it's me," Tommy said.

Shit. "Tommy, what the hell—"

"Where'd he go?" Tommy asked, lifting his chin up from the asphalt.

Tank was still wondering what had happened to Tommy, not ready to even attempt answering another question.

"What is that?" Tank asked, motioning to the flour everywhere.

"Long story. Now get off me," Tommy said.

Tank let up off of Tommy, but before he could help Tommy up or even get up on his own feet, something caught his eye just above them where the edge of the roof was.

It was movement.

Not only was it movement. It was something flying through the air.

A person.

Tank looked up and saw a man in a black hoodie, white powder on one sleeve, in mid-air. He had jumped straight off the roof, but where did he plan on landing?

That was quickly answered as soon as his feet hit the roof of The Sneaker. He tucked himself into a roll, tumbling down the back of the car and onto the ground, taking off into a run. He never once stopped. The whole thing was elegant, and if Tank hadn't been so caught off-guard or angry at the whole thing, he would have been damn impressed.

"Did he really just Peter Pan himself off the roof?" Tommy asked, trying to get to his feet.

Tank managed to get on his own feet, nodding. "Sure did," he said, grabbing Tommy by the arms and helping to hoist him up.

They wasted no time chasing down the man who had just launched himself off the roof. Tank had seen him turn around the corner to the side of the building, so he and Tommy took off as fast as they could. Tank had witnessed how fast and agile the thief was, but he was hoping that he couldn't make it to his car before they could grab him.

Tank ran as fast as he could, but Tommy was even faster. He overtook him; his gait was smaller than Tank's, but his legs moved much quicker. They pushed on past the side of the building and around to the front.

By the time Tank made it around the whole way, Tommy had stopped on the sidewalk just in front of the store. Tank met his eyes. Tommy shrugged and shook his head.

There were plenty of people rummaging about, going in and out of the store, loading their vehicles up with the items. There was also a handful of people by the gas pumps.

But there was no hooded man with a floured sleeve. There were a few beards and sunglasses, but as far as either of them could tell, the thief was nowhere in sight.

Tank shook his head, trying to retrace his steps, and that's when he saw it. Just behind him, at the corner of the building on the ground, a black hoodie with white powder on the sleeve.

Tank bent over and held it up in the air with one hand. He looked back around at all the different people, reminded that the garment could belong to any one of them.

Once again, they'd lost the thief, along with the opportunity for the sheriff's department to save face.

CHAPTER THREE

TANK FOLLOWED TOMMY INTO THE STATION. NOT A SINGLE word had been said in the car on the drive. They were both far too worked up to say anything pleasant, on top of the fact that the ride itself was cramped. That little stunt the thief pulled by leaping off the building and onto the roof of their car had put more than just a dent in the ceiling. The whole thing had crumpled inward right in the center, creating a V shape in the roof and a barrier between the driver and the passenger.

The car wasn't much to look at to begin with, already known for being the least inconspicuous undercover car, but it was what they had. Now the old, unmarked Crown Victoria needed more than just new shocks and struts. And if it didn't get the service it needed, it was going to be even easier to spot. But Tank knew there would be little money—and little interest—in getting the thing fixed. Their under-cover operations were few and far between.

Tommy was still covered in flour. Tank had learned from watching the video footage inside Jake's Feed and Speed that Tommy hadn't been paying attention as he chased the thief through the store, and when he was given the slip and tried coming back around, the thief had been ready with a bag of flour. Tommy made it to the end of the aisle, and *bam*, antiqued right then and there in front of everyone.

Even though Tank was pissed off, he couldn't help but let out a loud cackle as the tape rolled. Jake even had a good laugh as it went down, wiping tears from his eyes, not seeming too concerned about the loss in inventory. Tommy, however, did not find any of it funny.

Tank didn't blame him. It was embarrassing as hell, and the kid probably felt like he had something to prove. And this thief was making a fool of them both.

Tommy didn't even hold the door open for Tank, instead stomping his way straight through the lobby. Tank caught the door and followed the white footprints that trailed around Meredith's desk, where she sat bemused but smart enough not to say anything to Tommy.

Instead, she directed all questions to Tank. "What the hell happened to him?" she asked, her voice low as she leaned back in the computer chair. She quickly swiveled and watched as Tommy trudged to the hallway.

Tank didn't answer her right away, just stopped by her desk. "Hey, what the hell happened?" Tank asked Tommy, his anger still bubbling from losing the thief.

Tommy stopped but didn't turn around. "You saw the tape," he said. "I'm not sure what else there is to say about it."

"How about why did you say he'd be coming out the back door?" Tank asked.

Tommy finally turned around, a frown on his face. He was angry, but it seemed like he was also disappointed. Scared, even. "If you didn't notice, I was running through a cloud and had low visibility," he said. "The perp ran toward the back where the door was, I heard a door open, and I radioed it in. I didn't know that the riser room connected to the inside and that it was right next to the back door." He stood a moment, mulling the next words over in his head. "What I don't understand is why you tackled me to the ground and let the perp get away."

"You what?" Meredith asked Tank. He ignored her.

Tank furrowed his brow. "I was going off your instruction to be ready, and like you said, there was low visibility. I had no idea it was you running out through the door."

"Fine," Tommy said, turning back around, not escalating it but also not apologizing. That wasn't good enough for Tank. There was a lot on his plate right now, and with the thief getting away and the situation being a total embarrassment to the department, he wasn't ready to let Tommy off the hook quite yet.

"I don't know where you think you're going, but this isn't over," Tank said. "I have seniority, and you don't just walk away."

"Tank," Meredith said softly, but Tank didn't want to hear it. Meredith was like the office mother, and he wouldn't say a word against her, but he didn't have to acknowledge her right now.

"You really fucked this one up, you know that?" Tank said to Tommy. "This department is in shambles. You were brought in to help out, but it seems like ever since you came in, you haven't done much of anything."

"Oh, come on," Tommy groaned, throwing his head back and spinning back around. "You can't blame me for this one. *You* haven't even been able to catch this guy, either."

"And if you had been paying attention, then we'd know he was heading up to the roof. Hell, you're the one that made me drive around to the back, where I gave him the perfect landing spot. Now the car is barely drivable and isn't in any shape to bring to a sting operation again."

"Like it was doing any good in the first place," Tommy retorted.

Tank gritted his teeth. "Elven isn't gonna be happy about this."

That seemed to be just what Tommy needed to flip a switch. He threw his hands in the air, his eyes filled with fire. "If you hadn't noticed, Elven ain't here! Hell, it was a whole month from when I started to when I first saw him, and since then, I can count the times on one hand that I've said a word to him or even peeped him on the job. So if he's not gonna be happy about this, will anyone even know? Who gives a shit?"

Tank watched as Tommy's chest heaved up and down. He was worked up far more than Tank had expected, especially because this wasn't even about Elven. If anything, Tank figured being blamed for not catching the thief would set him off, not the fact that Elven wasn't around. But Tommy had a previous working relationship with Elven in Monacan, even though Elven wasn't technically supposed to be working that case.

And to be honest, Tank didn't blame Tommy. Tank had been picking up the slack for Elven for far too long. Everything that Tommy had just said was exactly how Tank had been feeling. But he felt like he'd be betraying his friend if he said it out loud.

At some point in Tommy's rant, Johnny had popped into the lobby from the hallway. He sheepishly made his way to the back table where some stale donuts from yesterday sat. He poked at them, not actually picking one up. Bernadette, his girlfriend, had been working with him on losing weight, and for the most part, he'd been good at limiting his sweets intake. For that reason, Tank thought it obvious he was eavesdropping instead of coming in for a snack.

Not that Tank minded. Johnny was still part of the team even if he no longer was a deputy. There was always a place for him in the office one way or another.

They were all just trying to make it work however they could right now, and that's what Tank needed to remember.

Tank softened his stance. It was frustrating how the morning had gone at Jake's Feed and Speed, but at this point, Tank was pretty sure that nobody was pissed they hadn't caught the thief. It was just that they were all flying blind with no direction. No leader. No Elven.

"You're right," Tank finally admitted. "Elven not being here sucks. And I don't have much of an answer for that."

Tommy nodded. "Look, I don't want to end up saying something out of line. And I'm definitely not trying to storm out of here and quit or anything like that. I need this job. Even if I could go back to

Monacan, there's no way in hell I want to do something like that. Bando is insufferable. And I like working here. I appreciate the job and just want to be part of the team. But right now, it feels like..."

"I know," Tank said after Tommy trailed off. "And you don't need to worry about any of that happening. There isn't much you can do that would be out of line."

Tank immediately thought of Madds after he said that. That had been a doozy.

"Tank," Meredith said, and he took a look at the woman who was lifting her eyebrows in the direction behind him.

Tank turned around to find Oliver Meeks standing there. The look on his face told him enough—he'd been standing there for a while. How long exactly, he wasn't sure. But it must have been a decent amount of time because he had a frown that bordered on a scowl. The man wasn't happy, which wasn't great considering he was the mayor of Dupray.

"I was going to ask to speak to Elven, but from what I just heard, sounds like he hasn't been in today," Oliver said. "Or yesterday. Or much at all this month, is that right?"

Tank held his breath for a moment, unsure what to say. He wasn't great with nuance, instead opting for being a straight shooter. But he also knew when to keep his mouth shut to keep those he cared about out of trouble.

How much trouble could Elven get in? Tank didn't know for sure. He wasn't into the politics, and that's where the line was between his job and Elven's.

Oliver, however, was nothing but politics. "Don't try to explain all at once, now," the mayor said.

Tank wanted to roll his eyes, but it wasn't his style. Oliver gave Tank a slimy vibe, but in Dupray, that wasn't uncommon. He supposed that in this county, Oliver was on the less slimy side of the spectrum.

Tank opted for deflecting. "What can I help you with today,

Mayor Meeks?" he asked, keeping things formal. The less chummy he could be, the better he felt about it.

Oliver took a deep breath and shook his head. "Not a whole lot, Deputy," he said, contempt dripping from his words. Tank didn't mind. He was used to dealing with assholes on a regular basis in this job, and as a marine. "Was coming by to speak directly with your boss," Oliver added.

"If you'd like, I can leave a message for him," Meredith said, trying to soften whatever mood was in the room. Tank could tell that Oliver was on some sort of mission. No matter what they did or said, nothing was going to make the man happy unless Elven himself was here in front of him.

"What I have to talk to him about needs to be said face to face," Oliver said. "He has been in, though, right? Since the injury, I mean."

"Of course," Meredith said. "He just does a lot of work from home."

"Home?" Oliver asked. "I figured it was all burned up." Everyone was well aware of what had happened to Elven's home before he had been shot.

"Well, where he's been staying, anyway," Meredith clarified.

Oliver nodded. "Don't tell me it's at Alvin and Victoria's," Oliver said, referring to Elven's parents. Of course, Oliver referring to them by their first names like old friends was a stretch. Elven's parents weren't friends with anyone unless they were useful to them. And the mayor of Dupray was a little below their level of shoulder-rubbing.

Meredith shook her head. "Here it is," she said, sliding a piece of paper across the desk. Tank noticed she didn't physically hand it to him, so Oliver had to grab it from the desk himself.

Oliver read it and sighed. "You're kidding."

Meredith wasn't, and she didn't give him an answer.

The mayor shook his head. He eyed each and every one of them, taking his time.

"Keep up the good work," he said, unable to hide his disappointment.

CHAPTER FOUR

IT WAS THE WET NOSE THAT ALWAYS WOKE HIM UP, THE FIRST shock that pulled him from whatever kind of slumber he was in. Usually, he couldn't remember how he'd slept exactly, but he knew it hadn't been restful. He rarely opened his eyes right away. He wasn't sure if waking up was better or worse than staying in bed.

That's when the rank breath came in, which caused him to pull his head away and open up one eye. The giant white floof of his Great Pyrenees dog, Yeti, was the first thing he always saw when he opened his eyes. It never failed, though it was never like clockwork. Yeti was anything but punctual or predictable, but he was always there. And that was all Elven could ask for. Not a whole lot of people were there for him these days, it seemed.

Or maybe that's just how Elven felt, as he'd been throwing himself a pity party every day since being shot. He hated it, yet he leaned heavily into it.

Maybe he was protecting himself. And maybe he just wanted to be left alone so he could figure things out.

Because he had a whole lot to figure out.

And it seemed that just about everyone was trying to get in his way of doing so.

Elven pulled the blanket off himself and over toward Yeti, who slumped over on the mattress. He was a big dog, and Elven wondered if Yeti waking him up every day was looking out for him or just wanting more of the bed to himself. He stood up, staring down at his furry companion and giving a half-smile. Maybe it was a little of column A and a little of column B.

That was fine with Elven. He had more work to do right now anyway.

He looked down to his abdomen like he did every morning, or was it the afternoon now? He didn't even have a clock in the room to tell him. He had to make some sacrifices when moving into the motel, but not the kind that most people had to make. There had been a clock in the room originally, but Elven had to remove it to fit in the king-sized bed he had special-ordered online. The bed took up far too much space to keep the nightstand.

Besides, the clock was hideous and had only made him anxious whenever he looked at it.

Marcus, the now-manager of the motel, had let Elven bring in the bed as long as he agreed to leave it there when he finally moved out. That was fine with Elven as long as Yeti could stay in the room with him. Marcus hadn't batted an eye at that proposal.

Not only that, but Elven had actually come to enjoy Marcus's company from time to time. The man could be a downright idiot, but he also knew how to not worry about tomorrow and just be in the moment. It was a breath of fresh air, since lately, Elven had been about nothing but the future.

Which led him back to his abdomen, where just on the side was a mangled red scar. It was healed, but still fresh enough to be noticeable. Eventually, it would fade, maybe go white or even blend into his skin, but the memories would always be there.

Elven remembered what had happened about as well as he could. Not like it was yesterday because he had lost consciousness, of course. But he remembered saving Hollis Starcher's life, of all people, by diving between the man and a bullet. Probably not the smartest thing, but Hollis was still alive.

Saving Hollis Starcher was something he felt he owed the man. They had a long history together, one that had both sides of the good and bad coin. Hollis had come through for Elven many times before, as much as Elven hated to admit it.

But it wasn't just Hollis he'd done it for. It was for who fired the gun.

Finding out who Madds really was had been a punch to the gut. And on paper, Elven knew things were simple. Cut and dry.

But life wasn't a piece of paper.

Even though he was angry with her, that she was a criminal, that she had betrayed him in ways he could have never imagined, he'd wanted to save Madds. To help her. To not let her make any more mistakes that she couldn't take back. And so he did what he thought he had to.

After that, things got blurry.

He remembered Hollis yelling at him. Madds was there... until she wasn't. And then, nothing. He woke up the next day in the hospital. The doctor had dug out the bullet from his gut, stitched him up, and said that he needed to take it easy so his body could heal.

That, he could do, but it didn't mean his mind had to follow.

Madds had fled, and instead of chasing her down, Tank decided to rush Elven to the hospital, more than likely saving his life.

Elven didn't know what to feel about the whole thing. So, instead of feeling anything, he got to work.

He turned to the wall, where all his photos were pinned. He wouldn't go so far as to say it was crazy, because to him, it all made sense. There were pictures of Hollis and all of his kids, dead or alive. Wade, Lyman, Corbin, and even Penny. There were Hollis's cousins and other distant relatives. And, of course, Madds herself.

Every case he'd worked with her was also up on the wall, all the way back to the very first one when Sophia Hawkins had been killed.

The very case that had caused Elven to hire Madds in the first place. And then there was Madds's ex-husband, Kurt, who had completely fallen off the face of the earth. Now that Elven knew who Madds's uncle really was, and how everything had shaken out in Monacan, he had an idea of what had actually happened to Kurt. Of course, there was no proof, and even though Hollis was behind bars, he wasn't going to incriminate himself on anything.

Elven wouldn't expect anything less from the man.

Yeti lifted his head, his ears perked at something outside of the room. Elven wondered if Marcus was stopping by or just wandering around. There weren't a ton of people in the motel right now, but sometimes Marcus liked to come by and chew the fat with him. The man didn't have a whole lot else going on, but he got really excited about watching HBO and giving Elven recommendations of shows to watch. On occasion, Elven even found time to give the shows a chance when he wanted to turn his brain off from thinking about Madds and where she had run off to.

But when the knock came on the door, it wasn't Marcus's usual "shave and a haircut" pattern. It wasn't overly aggressive, either. Elven figured if someone was coming for him, they wouldn't bother knocking, but he also didn't want to assume anything these days.

That's what got him in trouble in the first place.

He reached under his mattress, pulled out his revolver that was tucked underneath, and gave it a quick check, even though he knew it was fully loaded. He pressed himself against the side of the door and moved the curtain from the window next to it so he could take a quick peek. He saw the back of a man, but couldn't see his face. Instead, he could see him leaning and whispering to someone. Someone who was just out of view.

Elven wasn't going to wait for anything else to happen, so he grabbed the door, unlocked it, and flung it open, lifting his gun straight at the man standing there.

CHAPTER FIVE

Oliver Meeks's eyes widened as he turned to see the revolver inches away from his nose. His face went stark white. Elven could see that the man didn't even register what was happening at first. His expression had gone from being startled by the door opening while he was speaking to whoever was to his left, and, as his eyes had focused on the barrel, terror at the fact that there was a gun in his face.

Some men would have grabbed at the gun, or perhaps swatted it to the side. Others would have ducked, swayed, or flat-out run off. Both types, Elven could understand, even appreciate. But Oliver was the third type of man. The type that froze in his tracks, unable to move, unable to speak. If Elven hadn't pulled the gun away almost immediately, he was certain that Oliver Meeks's only reaction would be to release his bladder.

Lucky for both of them, Elven had a much quicker reaction. With a quick glance down, Elven could see that Oliver's trousers were as dry as his mouth.

"You can breathe now, Oliver," Elven said, walking away and

setting his revolver down on the bathroom counter as he passed by the room.

Oliver took a deep breath that sounded like it was being dragged through a narrow, ragged pathway. The mayor cleared his throat and patted down on his chest. Elven took a look at the man as the color started to fill back into his cheeks, flushing them bright red. From embarrassment or anger, Elven couldn't be sure, nor did he care much to figure it out.

Footsteps came up to the door from whoever Oliver had been talking to. Of course, it was Marcus, and he'd been scrambling to beat Oliver there. Panting heavily, he held up a hand before speaking.

"Elven, sorry, I wasn't aware of any visitor trying to see you," Marcus said, his outfit so wrinkled that he looked like he'd just fished it from a pile off his floor. "He didn't even stop by the office to find out which room you were in."

Marcus took a look at Elven, his cheeks reddening even more before he turned his head away. Elven looked down, suddenly remembering that he hadn't had the chance to put on pants before being ambushed—or what he'd thought was an ambush—by Oliver.

"It's alright, Marcus," Elven said. "I'm sure the mayor got the room number from the station."

Elven walked back to the side of his bed where his cell phone lay on the floor, plugged into his charger next to the jeans he wore yesterday. He picked up his phone and saw a text from Tank.

Mayor heading your way.

At least they'd tried to warn him.

"Well, if you need anything—" Marcus began.

"I know where you're at," Elven said. He wasn't trying to be dismissive to the man, but to move things along. Marcus could get chatty, and he was sure Oliver was in no mood to linger. That was something Elven could appreciate.

He would have appreciated it even more if Oliver had decided not to come at all.

Marcus gave a salute and wandered off back to his office. Oliver

Meeks didn't give him another glance. Instead, he walked straight into Elven's room without an invitation. Elven finished zipping up his jeans before facing him again.

"Do you always make it a point to shove a gun in a man's face for knocking on your door?" Oliver asked, his fear having quickly subsided and replaced by his arrogance.

"Only if I don't trust them," Elven said.

"Buck naked, I might add," Oliver said.

Elven smiled. "I suppose it's true what they say. Being the mayor comes with perks." He added a wink, then immediately dropped his smile. He was ready to be done with this conversation. "So, what brings you here?"

"Well, despite how you may or may not feel about me, I came by to check on you," Oliver said. "See how you've been, now that you've been out of the hospital a while and on the job."

Elven sighed. Maybe he had been a little too harsh on the man. His only crime so far, as far as Elven could see, was that he was a true politician. Elven was in an elected position himself, but it felt different. Elven used his status to work for the people. Oliver used his status, well, to be known by the people. And to reap whatever perks came with that position.

Still, here he was, checking in on him. Tank hadn't mentioned any other reason the mayor was coming to see him, so maybe he should give him the benefit of the doubt.

"Alright, I suppose," Elven answered. "Might have taken a little to get used to, what with being a few hands short, but it's like riding a bike."

Oliver meandered about the small room, his eyes wandering all over, lingering on each little mess they could find. Human curiosity, perhaps, but coming from Oliver, it was probably spying or, at the very least, judging.

Oliver smiled as he reached for Yeti. The dog didn't bother stirring as he ran a hand through his thick, white fur.

"From what I've heard, you haven't been into the office a whole lot," Oliver said.

Elven threw a shirt on and started buttoning it. He shrugged. "I still go in as needed. I work from here a lot. It's easier to use as my base to figure things out."

Oliver nodded, pulling his attention to the wall behind Elven. "I can see that," he said, motioning with his chin to the papers splayed out. "And how is that investigation going?"

Elven took a quick glance. "It's coming," he said. "Getting closer." He made sure to be as vague as possible, because the truth was, he had no idea where Madds had gone after she shot him. The last he saw of her was just before he blacked out. "Is that why you came by?"

"One of the reasons," Oliver said.

Elven sighed. "Go ahead and spit it out, then," he said, wishing the mayor's impatience was greater than his own.

"Straight to the point, then," Oliver remarked. Still, he fiddled with something near the window, taking his time to get it out. Finally, he stood straight, staring at Elven, and made his statement. "You need to get your act together."

Elven smirked. He would be in disbelief if Oliver hadn't crossed the line in telling Elven how to do his job in the past. This was nothing new, and all it did was make Elven curious about what sort of political gain the man had by saying this to him now.

"Not sure when it ever wasn't *together*," Elven said.

"Elven, you and I both know that you are capable and even good at a lot of things," Oliver said. "But lying has never been one of them."

Elven didn't drop his stare down at Oliver. He didn't need a lesson on what his weaknesses were; he was well-aware of them. "And you think—"

"Drop the act," Oliver said. "Your deputy, your girlfriend, was in it with Hollis, and you never knew it. I'd say that isn't really keeping it together. And ever since, you've been a damn near recluse when it comes to the job."

Elven couldn't help but let out a cackle.

"You might think this is funny, but I'm here as a friend," Oliver said.

"Oliver, no offense, but the only friends you have are ones that can help your status," Elven said. "And I ain't that guy."

Oliver took a deep breath. "Well, Elven, if I were anyone else, I'd say you intended a great deal of offense by saying that."

"You're the one who said I can't lie worth a lick," Elven pointed out with another smirk on his face. The back-and-forth might not be what Elven wanted this morning, but he had to admit it was a little fun.

Oliver smiled. "Alright, then," he said. "There's an election coming up."

"I'm well aware," Elven said. "But from my understanding, out of all the options, you're still the best one for the people."

Elven meant it. Oliver was a lot of things, but there were far more wild cards when it came to who was planning on running against him. And while Elven thought Dupray might deserve better than Oliver, he had to settle on the idea that they could also do a lot worse.

"So you've got my endorsement," Elven added.

"That's great to hear, but that's also why I came to visit," Oliver said. "Because you don't have mine."

CHAPTER SIX

"What are you talking about, Oliver?" Elven asked, trying to get a read on the man. "Last time, you were singing my praises to the people."

"Last time, you were a deputy coming off of a huge win after you and Beatrice's daughter caught L—" Oliver stopped himself a moment, knowing nobody wanted to say his name. "After you two caught the killer."

"And what would you call what I just came off of now? Only a couple of months ago, I put Hollis Starcher behind bars. Wouldn't that be considered a major win?" Elven asked.

Oliver gave a half-smile. "Half this town loves that man and his family. You taking down his eldest and then putting him behind bars didn't do you any favors with that side of town."

"And what side of the town are you on?" Elven asked, his tone more than just a little accusatory. "You're the one that went into business with the man, after all. How's the car lot and garage going these days? As much as I love Lyman, I'm sure he isn't holding things up quite as well as his daddy was, now is he?"

"Business is business," Oliver said. "It doesn't make me friends with the man. Besides, I wasn't the one traipsing around with him over in Monacan. Now that one is something I'd love to hear all about."

Elven rolled his eyes. He was over this little visit from Oliver. "Great, so while you decide not to back me in the election, I'll still get the vote just like last time because nobody else is trying to run for the position."

Oliver clenched his jaw. "God, Elven, you really have your own bubble going on here, don't you?" He motioned to the room they stood in. Yeti was still lounging about, uninterested in the conversation that was taking place right above him.

"What are you gettin' at?" Elven asked.

"You've got yourself an opponent this time around, Elven," Oliver said, his tone softening slightly.

That was something Elven wasn't expecting. Though he'd been caught a little off-guard, he wasn't rattled. "Since when? From my understanding, nobody filed by the time the cut-off date—"

"He's running as a write-in candidate," Oliver explained.

Elven chuckled. "So, what, he's gonna post on some Facebook group and have his friends and family vote him in?"

"He's not just some boner on the ballot," Oliver said. "It's Zane Rhodes."

"Zane Rhodes?" Elven asked. "The son of Emily Rhodes? Wasn't he—"

"The owner of Bottoms Up Coffee Cup," Oliver said.

Elven knew the name—it was hard to forget something so idiotic —but that wasn't his area of expertise. He also knew that the business wasn't based out of Dupray. "Zane hasn't lived here since—"

"He moved back last year. And as you know, his family is beloved in this area," Oliver said.

"So a businessman wants to play sheriff," Elven said. "And he's a write-in candidate. I'm not too concerned, and to be frank, you backing him is a risky play."

"No riskier than the man who is hated by half the county, ended his big win with far too many deaths, and on top of that, has some thief making him look like one big joke," Oliver said. "Not to mention the whole deputy thing. And the fact that not only did you not catch her, but you haven't given up on it. It's consuming you entirely." Oliver pointed to the wall behind Elven again.

"So which is it, then?" Elven spat. "Find her or not? Which choice is gonna instill confidence in the county? Or in the mayor to back me? You can't have it both ways, Oliver."

"And neither can you, Elven," he said. "Either you're the sheriff, or you're not. But if you are, then you need to get out there and be seen by the people doing the job they hired you to do. Not hole up in this bubble of yours. That's why I'm giving Zane my support."

Elven clenched his jaw. "I appreciate the face-to-face on this one, Oliver," he said, trying to hold the anger at bay.

"Look, Elven, it's just—"

"I don't need any more explanations. You made your decision. Now stand by it," Elven said. "I know I would."

Oliver nodded, then gave Yeti one more pet before turning around and heading for the door. He opened it and stood in the doorway for a moment.

"Look, Elven," he said, cocking his head to the side. "I am really sorry about everything that happened before. I'm sure it can't be easy, learning what you did and then being put in the position you were. But we need someone who will keep this county safe. You used to be that person, but now things have gotten too personal for you."

And with that, Oliver left the room. Which was good, because Elven had picked up the chair from the opposite corner of the room and flung it at the door just after it closed. It was immature and stupid, but the anger Elven felt was greater than his self-control at the moment.

Yeti lifted his head up from the bed, cocked his head at Elven, and gave a little whine. Elven looked at his furry friend and sighed. "I know, I know," he told the dog.

Elven could play like he wasn't concerned, but that was far from the truth. Write-in or not, Zane Rhodes running against him was the last thing he needed right now.

Of course, what he didn't know yet was that far worse things were soon to be added to that list.

CHAPTER SEVEN

Linda Kunneke sat in the passenger seat of Tank's truck, sobbing periodically while breathing into a paper bag. She was a mix of emotions from what Tank could see. Ready to pass out, scream, cry, and maybe even throw a punch if pushed to it. What she'd seen had been a lot, even for the strongest of people, to handle.

And it was even worse for her because these were people she'd worked with, people she knew, people she loved.

She had mentioned not liking some woman she worked with, but every time she brought her up, the floodgates opened again. Tank could tell she felt guilty for thinking whatever it was she had thought about this woman. Linda was clearly a good person, and good people didn't want anyone to die, even if they had beef with them.

This was not in Tank's wheelhouse, however. He had emotions, sure, but he made it a point to keep them contained. Not in the way of burying them down and not letting anyone see him cry, but, well, he just wasn't big on making a spectacle of himself.

Which also meant he was lost when it came to dealing with other people's emotions. Johnny was the best at that; he'd probably be crying right along with Linda and able to comfort her in a way Tank could never understand. And while Elven wasn't quite at Johnny's level, he was still much better at it than Tank. He could keep himself contained while being able to comfort Linda and move the job along.

But neither Johnny nor Elven was here right now, and Johnny was still at the station, no longer a deputy. Sure, Tank could have asked Johnny to come along, maybe put up some caution tape and keep any crowds from forming. Not that there was anyone other than the people who worked next door and two people who wanted to check out some books, but after everything that Johnny had been through—and how Bernadette would have Tank's ass if he brought Johnny to a crime scene—well, it just wasn't worth the headache.

And then there was Elven. Tank sighed just thinking about him. Something had snapped in him during the last case. Tank had never thought it could happen, but Elven had been cut deep. It wasn't just one thing, either, but a combination of things. The betrayal of Madds, the injuries, all the lives lost, specifically Penny's, and as much as Elven wouldn't admit it, taking down the man who had looked at him like a son, no matter how much Elven had wanted to arrest him, had probably taken a lot out of him.

In a way, Tank didn't blame him. But other times, he wanted to grab him by the collar and tell him to pull his shit together.

But as Tank knew, he wasn't great at dealing with other people and their emotions.

Tank looked on as Tommy did all the things that Tank had originally thought Johnny could do. He watched as the new deputy rolled out the tape, then made sure the two library patrons didn't try to enter. Tommy was kind and happy to help in whatever way was needed. Of course, Tank wished he could come over and handle Linda, but right now, he was the lead on this investigation whether he liked it or not.

"Why so many people?" Linda finally asked, looking up at Tank with swollen, bloodshot eyes.

Tank gave a single shake of his head. "We're going to try to figure that out. You said earlier that Phylis had made some enemies?" he asked, trying to take this opportunity to talk to Linda when she'd stopped crying for a moment.

Linda nodded, twisting her face so much that Tank thought she was going to launch into another fit, but she managed to hold it together. "Yeah, I mean, I wasn't her biggest fan. She pissed off a lot of people, and I was—well, I was going to tell her off today."

"Tell her off?" Tank asked. He knew what the term meant, but something he'd learned on the job was to repeat back to people the same things they told him to get more details. If he just made assumptions, then he might miss something.

"I was planning on quitting," she admitted, looking back at the building. She put her purse in her lap and dug inside, pulling out a letter. She handed it to Tank, and he saw it was a letter of resignation. "I love it here, but she made things miserable for everyone. But me, especially."

"How so?" Tank asked.

"The usual bad coworker stuff. I gave so much of myself at this job, and she came in acting like she knew better, that she should be running things. She had no respect for me, no respect for the job, and honestly, she just wanted the power."

Tank wasn't aware of what kind of power a librarian could have, but as much as he hated to admit it, he didn't spend a whole lot of time reading. "What kind of power do you mean?" he asked.

Linda shrugged. "Anything you can think of, she'd do it. Late on a library book by a day? That's a fee. Want to reserve a conference room but forgot to date the paper? Looks like the conference room is going to sit empty."

"Sounds like a bitch," Tank said, half under his breath. He didn't mean for it to come out; somehow, it just did.

"You aren't wrong," Linda said, then quickly wiped at her eyes and sobbed twice. She was able to stave off any more tears that tried to fight their way through. "So I was gonna make a big show of it. Leave her high and dry. It would have been a big deal, considering she didn't do shit around here and just leached off the work that everyone else did."

"I see," Tank said, not wanting to get involved in that mess. But it did have him wondering who else might have felt this way. Linda wasn't really high on his list of people who could have done this. The tears seemed genuine, especially considering how open she was about her dislike toward the woman. Still, it didn't help narrow down who might have done this if a lot of people felt this way about her.

"You think that Phylis pissed someone off so much that they did this?" Linda asked. "But why kill everyone else, too?"

Tank took a deep breath and let it out slowly as he surveyed the entrance to the library where Tommy stood with his hands on his hips. "I'm not sure right now," he said. "But it's what we're here to find out."

CHAPTER EIGHT

ELVEN CLEANED UP HIS ROOM ONCE HE CALMED DOWN. He hadn't made a huge mess, just broken a chair and caused enough ruckus that Marcus had to come down to check on him. Apparently, whoever was renting the room next door to him had called Marcus to complain about the loud banging.

Elven apologized to Marcus and told him not to worry. Not that Marcus was worried, not about the chair or the incident, anyway. But he did seem genuinely concerned for Elven in general. That was a surprise to Elven, considering that when they first met, Elven had zero patience for the man.

Now Elven might consider him the only one in his corner—besides Yeti, of course. Heaven knew that the mayor surely wasn't.

"Do I need to go next door and apologize to the neighbor for you?" Elven asked. "I don't mean to cause you any trouble."

Marcus smiled and gave a wave. "Georgie? Nah, fuck that guy. He likes to hassle me over every little thing that goes wrong. If it wasn't the noise, I'm sure it'd be the piss stain on his sheets. Mind you, he's the one that caused the stain. Not sure how many times a man can wet the bed, call me over to moan about it, and all the while have no shame about it. I think next time he does that, I'll drop off a pack of them adult diapers. Maybe he'll get the point."

Elven cackled. "That's one way to get the point across. If he becomes too much of a problem, I can always have a chat with him."

"Send the sheriff over to him? Hell, with his bladder, you'd scare the piss right out of him," Marcus said, chuckling.

"At least it wouldn't be on the bed."

"True enough. But Georgie's harmless. If him pissin' and bitchin' is the worst of it, I'll take it. Far easier than the other guests I deal with. Present company excluded, of course."

"Of course," Elven agreed.

"You sure you're alright, though?" Marcus asked again. "It ain't often I hear you riled up like that. Other than when your foot was still healing and you toppled over, that is."

Elven smirked. Marcus loved bringing up that little story whenever he had the chance. It was as if he liked to remind Elven that he had come in and "saved" him. Sure, Marcus had helped him, but it was far less of a big deal than Marcus made it out to be. But Elven let him have it. It was the least he could do.

He was grateful that his heel had healed up now. It had been a struggle between that and the bullet wound while living in this motel room. Now his foot was better, his wound only a scar, and all that was left to remedy was his current living situation. That one might be a while, though. It wasn't like they could rebuild his house on the side of the hill with any haste.

At this point, he wasn't even sure he cared enough to have it rebuilt.

"I appreciate the concern," Elven said to his friend. "Nothing crazy like that happening. Just got told something that I wasn't expecting is all."

"From Mayor Meeks?" Marcus asked, and Elven gave a single nod. "That man is a pompous ass. I wouldn't take to heart anything he says."

Elven chuckled. "You ain't wrong about that one, but this was more news than anything else." Though Oliver had shared a few opinions with Elven, he didn't feel the need to tell Marcus about that. Besides, Marcus's read on the mayor was already spot-on.

Marcus nodded. "Oh, I see. Is it about all that ruckus going on down by the library?"

Elven shook his head. "What's going on at the library?"

"Ain't really sure," Marcus said. "All's I know is some people can't get in right now 'cause it's all taped off. I got a friend at Paul's Print Shop. You know the place?"

Elven nodded, but Marcus explained anyway. "It's next door, and they sometimes share a parking lot when there's overflow or whatever."

"Marcus," Elven said, beyond impatient now, "the library." He remembered one of the first interactions with the man when he was looking for Madds after she'd been kidnapped. He'd liked to run off on tangents then, and today was no different. What was different, however, was that Elven had learned to tolerate him and actually found him a little endearing at times. Still annoying, but endearing.

"Oh, right, you know me, sometimes I just get—"

"Yes, and the library," Elven cut in, not waiting for him to go into another tangent just off the one he was already on.

Marcus nodded, finally picking up on it. "Right, like I was saying, not really sure. My buddy next door says one of the ladies that works there is upset. Says it must be real bad."

Elven nodded. He wasn't sure if he had any more information than before Marcus had started talking, but at the very least, he knew something was going on down at the library. The libraries in Dupray might be small, sometimes only slightly bigger than his motel room, but there were a handful sprinkled throughout the county.

"The one at Rhinehart and Crest?" Elven asked. It was the main library, and the biggest. There was only one Paul's Print Shop, so he already knew the answer.

"That's the one," someone said from the doorway.

Both Marcus and Elven turned to see Johnny standing at the

door. He looked like he had lost some weight. Nothing drastic, but enough to notice. He wore a long-sleeved Henley shirt tucked into a pair of khaki pants. It wasn't the deputy uniform he used to wear, but the small stitching on his breast pocket told anyone who looked that he still worked for the Dupray County Sheriff's Department.

Elven was glad that Johnny could still work for them in some capacity, but he knew there was a fine line the man had to walk. One that wasn't just because of Bernadette, but himself. Johnny had something to lose now, and someone to lose him. That made things a lot different.

Of course, it also made things even more complicated, considering how short-handed they were again. Elven was sure that his own pulling back from the job didn't help that in any way, but there were more important things he had to do.

"Johnny, what brings you down here?" Elven asked. "Everything okay at the station?"

Johnny nodded and lifted his eyebrows, as if asking permission to enter. Elven held a hand out, signaling him to come inside. Johnny's eyes drifted around the room, from the bed where Yeti lay to the dresser with the clothes piled on top and then to the wall.

Elven mused that everyone liked to focus on the wall. Except Marcus, though he'd seen it almost every day.

"Still working on finding her," Johnny said. It wasn't a question but a statement. One that Elven didn't feel the need to acknowledge.

Besides showing up unannounced, from the way Johnny was shifting his weight and fidgeting, Elven could tell there was something on his mind. He was beating around the bush about something.

Though Marcus didn't seem to pick up on that.

"Hey, Marcus, you mind giving me a minute alone with Johnny?" Elven said to the man.

Marcus lifted a finger and nodded, finally understanding. "You know where I'll be," he said, heading down the walkway outside.

"You seem chummy with Marcus these days," Johnny said.

"He's not so bad once you're around him a while," Elven said. "So, what's up?"

"There's a case down at the library, but it sounds like you've heard already," Johnny said.

"About all I know is that it's taped off and nobody can go in," Elven said. "What happened?"

"People are dead," Johnny said.

Elven sighed. That's how it always was, wasn't it? People dying all around. Elven felt like he'd had enough of that, but then again, this was still his job, wasn't it?

"I'm assuming natural causes is out of the question?" he asked.

"You'd be right about that," Johnny said. "Someone went wild with a gun or guns and killed a bunch of people. The librarian this morning found them and called it in. Tank and Tommy are there right now dealing with it."

"Well, that's good to hear," Elven said. "That Tank and Tommy are there, I mean. Not, well, you know."

"Sure," Johnny said.

The two of them stood in awkward silence for longer than they should have. Johnny didn't have a hat, but if he did, Elven was sure he'd be turning that brim between his fingers. Nervousness? Maybe. Whatever it was, Elven wasn't gonna dig for it.

"Well, thanks for letting me know, Johnny. Give Bernadette my best when you see her tonight," Elven said. "And next time, maybe just give me a phone call so you don't have to make the trip."

"That's the problem," Johnny blurted. "I did call you, but you didn't answer. Hell, I called a few times."

Elven fished his phone out and looked at it. There were five missed calls. Four from Johnny, one from Meredith.

He looked up from his phone and held his hands up. "Sorry, Johnny, must have had it on silent. I'll make sure that doesn't happen again." He fiddled with his phone, turning the notifications on, but he was well-aware it might happen the next time he woke up. He was so busy in his own little world of trying to find any trace of Madds that he was liable to forget to turn on his ringtone. "Thanks again, Johnny."

"That's it?" Johnny asked, his nervousness starting to slip away. Johnny had become a lot more confident since meeting Bernadette. Not to mention that taking out a world-class hitman wasn't on most people's resume.

"What else is there?" Elven asked.

"How about you come to the library and work the case," Johnny said, though he didn't phrase it as a question.

Elven narrowed his eyes. "You just said Tank and Tommy are there," he said. "I'm sure they've got a handle on it."

"They do, but that's not the point," Johnny said. "You're the sheriff."

"I'm well-aware of my job title," Elven shot back. This morning had been one huge distraction ever since waking up, and Elven was over it. "And as far as yours goes, you aren't even a deputy anymore."

Johnny grimaced, and Elven immediately regretted saying it. "Fine," Johnny said. "But the way that Tank called down to the station and told us what had happened, well, I just think he could use you being there is all."

Elven sighed.

"Look, Elven, we all get it," Johnny said. "You're busy. You're working on this other thing. But there's still stuff going on here. Tank is great at his job, but that's it—*his* job, not yours."

The two once again stood staring at each other for far too long.

Finally, Johnny went for the doorway and put his hand on the frame. "Alright, well, I'll leave you to it, then," he said.

"Hey, Johnny," Elven began, already not wanting to say it, but Johnny just had a way of making Elven feel like he was kicking a puppy if he didn't say yes. "How about giving me a lift there?"

Johnny turned, and his grin was all the answer Elven needed.

CHAPTER NINE

"Meredith said when that lady called, she was a mess," Tommy said, standing in the entryway of the library. "She thought there was still someone here attacking people, from the way she was screaming." Tommy swallowed as he looked across the wide-open room.

Tank did the same and couldn't help but notice that from here, it looked almost like nothing had gone wrong. There were no bodies in sight, no blood or bullet holes. There was a bit of a mess, with toppled over carts and books in piles and some chairs on their backs. But that could be explained away as a simple accident that hadn't been cleaned up yet.

But Tank and Tommy both knew better. The library was in far worse shape than a simple accident, and it was up to the two of them to figure it out. Tank hoped for everyone's sake that there were enough clues to lead them to whoever did this.

Because not being able to catch a thief was one thing. Not being able to catch a mass murderer was another.

They approached the desk, where the first sign of carnage was located. Linda had informed them that Phylis was dead on the floor behind the check-out counter. And there she was. Her body was slumped, her arms to her sides with her legs spread out. If she were still alive, it would not be the most comfortable way to sit, especially at her age.

Far more bullet holes than necessary to do the job filled her chest. Whatever color her blouse was before, Tank couldn't tell, because now it was blood red.

Before they started on Phylis, they needed to cover the rest of the library. Tommy and Tank had done a preliminary check to make sure nobody was still alive and had cleared it completely, finding that whoever had killed these people was no longer inside. But they hadn't taken the time to really look at the scene the way they were now.

It was far worse than Tank had thought.

Phylis's body was one thing, still terrible, still unnecessarily brutal for a woman whose biggest sin was being a stickler for the rules when it came to an overdue library book. But it was the conference room full of bodies in the back of the library that really churned his stomach.

Once Tank and Tommy entered the room, stepping over the dead woman in the doorway, Tank immediately realized how tight the space had become. There were no windows, other than the little one on the door that looked into the library, but nothing to the outside world. His immediate thought was *fish in a barrel*. It was far easier to shoot them that way.

And from the scene in front of him, Tank didn't think it took too much effort to do it.

"We're gonna need to ID these people first," Tommy said, and Tank nodded in agreement. "I've barely met anyone since moving here. You don't recognize anyone right off the bat, do you?"

Tank gave a quick scan of the bodies from where he was at. At first glance, he didn't think he knew anyone. Dupray might be a small place, but it was still large enough that even the most social of persons couldn't know everyone in town. And Tank was far from that type.

"Off the top of my head, I don't think so," he admitted. At the very least, there was nobody here he'd regularly conversed with.

Also, if he had met them briefly and passed them a few times before, that might be hard to tell with all the blood and brains everywhere.

"We're gonna have to get some wallets," Tank said. "Maybe even bring Linda to Doc Driscoll's place once he gets the bodies cleaned up enough."

Tommy snickered. "Not sure how that one'll go."

Tank didn't disagree. Linda was a mess of emotions right now, and having to face it all over again was probably going to be rough for her. "We'll deal with that if we have to. Right now, let's take pictures, gather evidence, and wait for Doc Driscoll to get here."

Tommy nodded. He pulled on gloves and squatted beside the first body by the door. "You have any idea of where to start on this?" Tommy asked.

Tank knew he didn't mean with the bodies, but where to look for who had committed the crime. Tank wasn't even sure how to answer that. Being in charge of a scene like this was way beyond his level, but he figured they'd start with the basics of what they knew.

"According to Linda, Phylis wasn't at the top of anyone's friend list," Tank said. "If that's how she was at work, maybe she was worse at home."

"I guess that's as good a place as any to start," Tommy acknowledged.

"It would be a lot easier if Elven were here, though," Tank remarked.

"From where I stand, it looks like you've got a good handle on it."

Tank spun around to see Elven standing there, dressed in his uniform, a half-smile on his face.

CHAPTER TEN

"WHAT THE HELL ARE YOU DOING HERE?" TANK ASKED.

Elven could tell his deputy was playing it cool, because his tone was nothing but relieved. His eyes were sunken in, like he was exhausted, but also, he looked older. Elven suddenly worried that he was placing too much responsibility on Tank and it was taking a toll on the man.

Elven reminded himself that Tank was a marine. He once called him an ex-marine, but Tank made it very clear that it was never *ex*. "Once a marine, always a marine," was what he'd said, though Elven still messed that up on occasion when speaking about Tank. But the fact was, Tank was tough, and he could handle just about anything that came his way.

So this was no different. And now Elven was here to help if Tank needed it.

"I heard that this case wasn't just a run-of-the-mill situation," Elven said.

"You did, did you?" Tank asked. "I know word travels fast, but unless whoever was responsible for this got in your ear, then I don't know how you know much 'cause I'm still in the weeds right now. Speaking of, I better check on Linda real quick before—"

"Johnny's out there with her," Elven cut in with a smile.

Tank smiled. "Oh, thank God."

Elven chuckled. "I think you might be more relieved that he's here instead of me being here."

"That woman out there is a mess," Tank said. "I feel awful for her, but you know how it is when it comes to grief and tears. I'm all thumbs."

"I hear you," Elven said. "I spoke with her briefly before leaving her in Johnny's very capable hands. He'll get anything else we might have missed."

"She give you anything about these people?" Tank asked, motioning to the room behind him.

"Said it was the book club meeting they have every month," Elven said, looking behind Tank, where the door was only open about a foot. He could see an arm on the floor as Tommy squatted next to it.

"What the hell would someone want to shoot up a book club for?" Tank asked.

"I take it you've got no leads?" Elven asked.

"I'm thinking that someone had a grudge against Phylis, the other librarian," Tank said, motioning to the dead woman behind the counter Elven had briefly noticed. "But to be honest, this is not my expertise. So if you have any ideas, I'm all ears."

Elven shook his head. "Sounds like a good place to start. Seems like you've got this under control."

Tank stared at Elven a moment before opening his mouth. "Look, Elven, I really could use you on this one."

"And I'm here," Elven replied.

"As in, you take the lead on this," Tank said. "This is a mass murder, and it feels like an all-hands-on-deck situation. And when it comes to that, the sheriff should be at the helm."

Elven chewed the side of his cheek while he thought it over. He wanted to tell Tank that he was so close to finding Madds, but that was a downright lie that Tank would easily see through. And to say he just wanted to focus on that case would be the wrong thing to do.

If Johnny was coming to his motel room and Tank was standing here on the verge of begging him to lead this case, well, then it really must be serious. He owed it to his friends, and to his county, to solve this thing.

"Alright, fill me in on everything," Elven said.

TANK HAD GONE over every last detail, starting with the mayor, who had absolutely nothing to do with the case, but he clearly felt the need to let Elven know they had been practically ambushed by the man. Elven gave Tank enough reassurance that he wasn't holding any grudge over the mayor discovering where Elven was living these days. With how people talked in Dupray, he was surprised the whole town hadn't figured it out already.

Once Tank was satisfied that his backside wasn't on the line, he launched into the phone call from Linda they received at the station, and then all the details leading to where they stood right now in the library. It was a lot, and at the same time, it wasn't much at all.

The most they had was that Phylis wasn't well received by her peers and the patrons of the library. The people here were part of some book club that met once a month, and last night was this month's meetup. Given that nobody had reported it, it was probable that the killings occurred just before closing. Linda had informed them that the last hour of the night usually didn't have too many people coming in or out, other than those leaving the book club.

"I got everyone's ID. There's seven total, other than Phylis," Tommy said, holding a piece of paper up with scribblings on it. "Wrote them all down here so the identification could stay with the body."

He exited the conference room, the door now open much wider.

Elven could see a little more of what had happened inside, but he was still going to have to see for himself soon enough.

Elven gave Tommy a once-over. He had a dusting of white all over him. "Were you dusting for prints?" he asked.

Tommy scrunched his face, looking down at himself, and sighed. "No. It's a long story," he said.

"You recognize anyone?" Elven asked, not interested in that story.

Tommy shook his head. "I haven't been here long enough, Elven. And none of the names ring a bell."

Elven nodded, then turned to Tank, eyebrows lifted. "You?"

Tank shook his head. "No one that I recognized," he said, taking the paper from Tommy. He quickly scanned the paper, then let out a little breath. "There's one name that is familiar. James Preston."

"That someone of note?" Tommy asked.

Tank shook his head. "Not really. The guy is quiet, keeps to himself. Only run-in I ever had with him was when he was in a fender-bender a year back. Everyone was fine, they just needed a report of it."

Elven grabbed the paper and skimmed it. "Sure is. A few of these I recognize," he said. "There's also Wendy Selle and Morgan Fisher."

"You know them well?" Tommy asked.

"Not really," Elven said. "Went to school with Wendy's son Geoff, and Morgan Fisher always volunteered at Dupray Methodist when I was younger. Haven't been in some time, but I imagine he still was. Not sure if it's necessary, but we can follow up with Pastor Magner if we can't find next of kin."

"None of these people seem like standouts for the cause of this," Tank said, motioning to the library. "They're mostly people that don't get out much."

Elven nodded. "Doesn't seem so, does it? Did Driscoll get a call already?"

Tank gave a nod. "Told him he'd need to make multiple trips, so he said he was going to clear some space back at his place first."

"That's a good idea," Elven agreed.

"You wanna take a look? Maybe see if there's anything we might have missed?" Tommy asked.

Elven looked to Tank, still not wanting to take over from him, but it was clear the deputy was in agreement when he gave an eager nod.

"Of course," Elven said, taking a deep breath. He'd seen plenty of murder scenes before, but this would be the first one since before catching Oswald and landing himself in the hospital. Trying to find Madds was like trying to scrounge up breadcrumbs for clues. This case was going to be completely different, because the murder scene was going to be like getting handed an entire loaf of clues.

Seeing Phylis's body was just an appetizer to the main course. He had seen the blood on the carpet, and even the body by the door when Tommy held it open for him. But Elven couldn't have been prepared for what greeted him on the other side.

He was surrounded by a massacre. Blood was everywhere. The carpet was soaked in it, leaving random spots of brown, which Elven realized were the true color of the carpet. Red had spread like the plague over the cheap fibers. The walls were streaked with it, too. Some spots were heavy splotches, some spatters of multiple dots, and others were streaks where the body had slid down the wall. Elven was sure that there was even a handprint, like someone had tried to stand, only to fall right back down as they succumbed to their injuries. Or maybe they had been shot another time.

Immediately, he felt like he was suffocating. The air was thick with death, and Elven could smell the iron in the air. It had only been one night, and the weather had been cold enough, but Elven swore it stank worse than any crime scene he had been to. Neither of the deputies seemed bothered by it, though, which made Elven feel even more isolated.

The walls were closing in on him, and he closed his eyes briefly. As soon as he did, he saw the bodies of Tina, Dylan, and Oswald. The faces of those he'd walked straight into that house, only to send them to their demise. If only he'd waited for Tank before. If only he wasn't so cocky, so arrogant, so stubborn, they'd all be alive.

He closed his eyes for a moment, but immediately, he saw Penny's face. He saw her limp body as he held her in his arms.

He immediately snapped his eyes open again, knowing he'd rather face seven dead bodies than see her that way again.

"From everything I can tell, she was the first one shot," Tommy said, pointing to a nearby body and snapping Elven out of his thoughts.

Elven took a deep breath, sucking in air greedily. He'd been holding his breath at some point after walking into the room, his lungs burning with the need for oxygen. He let out a long cough, holding back the vomit that tried to bubble up inside of him, as he could practically taste the death in the air.

Tommy stopped speaking, and Tank placed a hand on Elven's back. "You okay, Elven?" Tank asked.

Elven cleared his throat and licked the spittle from his lips, standing upright. "Yeah, yeah, just sucked something down the wrong pipe," Elven said. "Go on."

Tank nodded to Tommy, who continued to run through each and every body in the room. At some point, Elven stopped listening. It was all speculation as to who was killed in what order, and that was fine. Tommy seemed to be doing good work, but Elven was so focused on keeping it together that he didn't have the mental capacity for much else. Elven nodded along, pretending to listen, but all he could see was the scene in front of him. It was overwhelming.

"And that's it," Tommy said, finishing up. "Not really sure if it is very helpful, but that's all I've got."

"Good work," Elven said, hoping to leave the room soon.

"Where do you think we should start?" Tank asked.

Elven blinked a few times, his mind totally blank. He noticed a monitor on a TV cart pushed against the wall in a way that made it seem the chairs were angled toward it. That seemed a little out-of-place for a book club.

"Do we know anything about this?" Elven asked, pointing to the setup.

Tommy shrugged. "I think they offer it for presentations in all conference rooms," he said. "Not sure if they were even using it last night."

"Okay," Elven said.

"I can ask Linda about it if you want," Tommy said.

Elven bit his lip, hesitating to make a decision.

"Let's go ahead and ask her about it. I'm sure Johnny has her pulled together a bit more," Tank said, taking the pressure off of Elven.

"Great," Elven said, stepping aside so Tommy could leave.

Once he was gone, Tank turned to Elven with a look of concern. "You doing okay?"

Elven nodded. "Of course," he replied. "Just haven't been standing this long lately." He shook his leg like it was bothering him. "Still sometimes gives me some trouble, I guess."

"Gotcha," Tank said. "We'll wrap this up quick then. Once we get word from Linda about the monitor, what's next?"

Elven swallowed. "You said something about Phylis. Maybe we can start with who might have held a grudge?" he said, his statement coming off as asking permission more than anything else.

"Yeah, we can find out her home situation. Maybe even go through the records of anyone that had trouble with her fining overdue books. Might be a long shot, but seems like somewhere to start," Tank said.

"That sounds great," Elven said, but honestly, he wasn't sure. It was a stretch, and his gut was telling him something was off with the room. The monitor, the chairs, how nobody was further out in the library when they'd been killed. Something didn't add up.

"I'm gonna go sit a minute," Elven said.

"Of course," Tank said, letting Elven push past him.

Elven couldn't get out of the library fast enough. His heart was pounding, his forehead wet with sweat even though it wasn't hot at all, and his mouth had run dry. He gave a quick smile to Johnny, Tommy, and Linda.

He also noticed a tall, older man standing nearby, looking at the library like he was confused. He held a few books in his hands, like he needed to return them. Elven was too focused on not losing it to pay the man any real attention. Johnny or Tommy could help the guy with his books. Elven headed around the back of the library, just out of sight.

He bent over and took a ton of shallow breaths, trying to hold it together. His vision was blurry, the edges turning black, and he knew he was close to passing out. But he managed to hold it together, pushing his back against the wall and sliding until he sat down on the ground, trying to catch his breath.

CHAPTER ELEVEN

THE STATION. ELVEN HAD BEEN INSIDE A HANDFUL OF TIMES since being discharged from the hospital, but every time, it felt so foreign to him. It used to be a second home to him, or his first home, even. It was where he'd taken a job because he thought it would be fun, with the added benefit that it would defy his parents. When he was younger, that was always something worth exploring for him.

But then it became more than that. It was where Lester sat him down and told him he needed to make a choice—be in or out. That man meant everything to him, teaching him a lot about the job, but even more, a lot about himself. And the office he now called his own had once been Lester's.

The transition from Lester to himself wasn't the easiest, considering how Lester had left the job. But he'd made it work. He'd made it his own, and nobody could have taken that away from him.

Well, that's what he thought, anyway.

They may not have taken it away from him, but they'd changed it for him.

Tainted it.

Stepping out of Johnny's car, Elven looked across the street, where he spotted a yard sign dug into the dirt on a metal frame next to the sidewalk. It wasn't overly large, but big enough that Elven could read it.

TAKE THE HIGH RHODE
VOTE ZANE RHODES FOR SHERIFF

Elven stared at it, thinking how Oliver Meeks had told him he was backing Zane instead of him. It was one thing to pull support, another to give it to someone else. What he thought he was a shoo-in for had now become a real race. One that he was questioning if he could truly win.

Of course, it was just a sign and the word of—what was it Marcus called him? Oh, right, a pompous ass. Not his words, but he didn't disagree.

"What's up with that, anyway?" Johnny asked, staring at the sign.

Elven turned to his friend. "Zane? Guess he thinks he can do better."

Johnny shook his head. "No, I mean the election. Feels like you just took the job, like, a little over a year ago. Thought you didn't have to run again for four years."

Elven nodded. "Because Lester retired before his term was up, they had a special election. I was elected for only until his original term was up, and now it is up."

"Zane Rhodes, though," Johnny said, wording the name like it was a tall order to compete with.

Elven wasn't in a rush to get inside, but he also didn't want to keep talking about the election. Far too much was being put on his plate all at once, and with that *hiccup* in the alley—there was no way he'd admit even to himself it was a panic attack—he wanted to compartmentalize everything he could. So for now, he needed to stick to the case and not think about the election.

"Thanks for the ride," Elven said, trying to pull the conversation back to something neutral.

"Anytime," Johnny said. "Maybe, uh, don't tell Bernadette that I went to the crime scene, though?"

"Johnny, I'll do whatever you want," Elven answered. "But I will tell you that it's best not to keep anything from Bernadette if you truly care for her. The last thing you need are secrets. I know she ain't my biggest fan, but feel free to tell her that it's because of me you were there. That'll probably take the heat off you a bit, and it's the truth. Better me than you."

Johnny smiled sheepishly. "Thanks, Elven."

Elven nodded and headed for the door. He took a deep breath before heading inside.

CHAPTER TWELVE

A WAVE OF WARM AIR BLEW ACROSS HIS FACE AS HE ENTERED the building. It smelled so familiar, so comforting. Every memory of that place filled his head, from when he was first hired by Lester, to when he took over as sheriff, to when he solved so many crimes, and then, finally, to how things fell apart just a few months ago.

The feeling of comfort quickly dissipated, and his stomach turned to knots as he remembered what had happened. He let out a long sigh, trying to hold back any emotion, any sudden urge to turn around and leave, anything that might cause him to crack and break down right where he stood.

Johnny waited a moment with Elven, studying his face, expecting him to make a move or say something. The man quickly placed a hand on Elven's shoulder and gave it a pat.

Elven turned to him and offered a smile. He wasn't sure if Johnny was reading the situation or just being friendly. The former deputy's face showed concern, but Elven didn't think he could pick up on how deep his worry actually went. Johnny was worried enough to make an effort, and Elven appreciated it, but at the same time, he didn't want any of it. The last thing he needed was for everyone to think he wasn't capable of handling the job. If everyone treated him with kid gloves, they'd never solve the case. Never catch the murderer. Have more bodies pile up on his watch.

And then word would get out in Dupray, which meant that he would soon find himself without a job. Especially now that Zane Rhodes was more than happy to fill the position.

Elven sucked in a deep breath and cleared his throat. "Hopefully with me being so busy, you guys haven't missed all the donuts and coffee in the office," he said, forcing a smile.

Johnny chuckled. "I try to bring them in when I can, but I'm trying to cut back." He patted his stomach.

"And we've still been working through the last batch of coffee you ordered," Meredith said, coming into the lobby from the hallway. She always made sure she was put together whenever anyone saw her. She was the type that took pride in her appearance, and she was a stunner for her age. Elven hadn't known her in her younger years, but figured she was a jaw-dropper in her day. Not that she'd ever hint at that now. She'd been with Chester, her husband, for as long as Elven could remember—until he'd passed, of course.

"But we are getting low," Meredith added, "so if you're here to do an inventory check, put it on the order. The fancy stuff you order always takes so long to get here."

Elven smiled. Meredith liked to make a fuss about the fancy coffee Elven had delivered, but he knew she secretly loved it. She liked to act like she wasn't bougie, but just looking at her, it was obvious to anyone that she liked to enjoy the nicer things in life. Working for Elven allowed her those small luxuries, and at the same time, she could play it off like they were his idea.

He let her have it, of course. She was entitled to enjoy what she did. And she meant a lot to Elven, having picked him up far more times than he could count. She might give him a hard time about a lot of things, but everyone in that office knew that she would be there for any one of them if needed. She was like the office mother, if there were such a thing at the station.

"So are you here just to take a coffee order, or do you plan on actually working?" Meredith asked, sliding into her chair behind the desk at the front of the lobby. Her eyes never drifted away from him as she waited for an answer.

"My original answer might change, now that I see how well everyone's been doing without me here," Elven said with a smirk. "I'm not even sure anyone is missing me around here."

Meredith cocked her head and gave it a small shake. "Not even I can play it off like we don't need you here, Elven," she said. "The four of us are holding it together as best we can, but this thing at the library happening, and right now? There ain't enough glue in the world that's gonna keep it holding any longer."

That was a lot, coming from Meredith. And as much as he should have felt flattered, maybe honored, it only deepened the pit in his stomach. He swallowed and gave a nod.

"We'll get to the bottom of this and figure out who's responsible," Elven said.

"Good. Tank is already in the back, putting files together. Tommy's still at Driscoll's with the bodies," Meredith said.

"Great," Elven said, heading past her desk. He paused a moment when he approached the entrance to the hallway. Just in front of him was the spot where he'd felt his biggest loss. Where he'd lost Penny. When he had dived away from the line of fire, not realizing that she was just behind him.

If he'd known she was right there, he would have stood his ground, taking the bullet himself.

Or maybe he was lying to himself. The reaction had kicked in, and he did what he did. He killed Jeb, diving to the side and drawing on him.

And then Elven lay on the carpet while Penny bled out in his arms. He held her for what seemed like an eternity, but it would never be long enough.

The bloodstains were long gone. Whoever Johnny hired to clean had done an excellent job. But not even they were good enough to scrub the image out of his mind.

"Elven?" Tank asked from the hallway. "That you?"

Elven snapped out of it and looked up into the hallway. He walked right over the carpet, shoving away any pain or guilt as he did, and blinking away anything that might have tried to escape from his eyes. "Just got in," Elven said.

"You find anything else while you hung back? Anything in the alley?" Tank asked, popping out from his office to the right of the long hallway. Madds's office, now Tommy's office, was to the left. The holding cell was farther down, still to the left, and at the very end was Elven's own office.

Elven turned to Tank and shook his head. "Nothing of note," he said. "But figured it was worth a shot."

Elven had told Tank to head to the station, and he'd meet him there after he got a better look at the area surrounding the scene. But in reality, Elven was just trying to hold it together. He gave a cursory look just to say he had, knowing that Tank had already given it a thorough check, but nothing had popped up.

He'd let Tommy handle helping Phil Driscoll take the bodies to the funeral home, which doubled as the morgue in Dupray. Elven didn't think there would be much of anything for him to do there, and he didn't feel like spending any more time with the dead bodies. But now that he was at the station, he wasn't sure he would have felt any worse than he currently did.

The dead didn't talk as loud as the memories in this place.

"I did end up talking to Linda a little bit more before letting her go," Tank said. "Asked her what the monitor was you were curious about."

"Anything useful?" Elven asked.

Tank shrugged. "She said with their book club, they sometimes have a video call with the author whose book they just read."

"Not many authors I know in Dupray," Elven said.

"Right," Tank said. "So they get them to join in and discuss the book from wherever they are."

Elven nodded, trying to piece something together. "Think there's anything there? It feels like a lead, doesn't it?"

Tank shrugged but stared at Elven for a moment. It was like he was sizing him up, trying to figure out why Elven was asking instead of telling. Elven wasn't so sure himself, if he were being honest.

"We can find out," Tank finally said. "But at this point, I'm leaning heavy at looking into Phylis. Seems personal, doesn't it?"

Elven nodded. It was a decent theory, and one he couldn't really argue with. But something still didn't feel right about the whole idea. It was worth checking into, but his gut was telling him it didn't add up.

"Let's go to Phylis's place," Elven finally said. "See if we can find out something. Maybe her neighbors or next of kin will be around to fill us in."

CHAPTER THIRTEEN

"Your truck not working?" Tank asked. He sat in the driver's seat of his own truck as Elven sat beside him in the passenger seat.

Elven was staring out the window, enjoying his reverie of nothingness as the world passed by. Sometimes it was better that way. The alternative could be soul-crushing.

But Tank's question pulled him back into the thick of it all. Of course, it was just a question. Innocuous, even. But to Elven, it felt heavy for some reason.

"Yeah," Elven said, though it wasn't true. He didn't want to outright lie to his friend, so he pulled back. "I mean, just a little trouble, nothing major. Figured it was easier if Johnny gave me a lift just in case. And now you get to be my chauffeur. We can take the HOV lane and bypass all the traffic." He forced a smile.

Tank chortled. "Wouldn't that be the day. Dupray getting an HOV lane."

Elven smiled. Most of the roads in town weren't big enough for two lanes, let alone an entire lane dedicated to people carpooling.

The most traffic they ever got was when two trucks decided to take their sweet time trying to pass each other on the highway.

Tank shifted quickly back to his solemn demeanor as they pulled up to the address they'd found listed for Phylis's residence. It was a small community, almost like an outdoor apartment complex, but in reality, it was a group of townhomes. About six or seven residences connected in a line, with maybe ten or so rows on the right and the same on the left. A road split right between them all. Parking spots sat in front of the homes. Some spots were covered, and others weren't.

It was a cute little area, albeit a tad faded and rundown like most things in Dupray. Elven wasn't sure if the entire place was owned by a single company or if each of the homes were owned by individuals. From the outside, it looked like each building was somewhere around a thousand square feet inside. Small and quaint, and probably more than enough space for someone Phylis's age.

There had been no next of kin listed on the file they'd gathered from the library. The only emergency contact listed was a woman by the name of Gail Pine. Her address was the same as Phylis's.

Tank pulled into a free parking spot about four doors down from Phylis's unit number. They got out and approached the door.

"How do you think she's gonna take the news?" Elven asked. "Assuming she's home."

"I had Johnny give her a call when we left," Tank said.

Elven clenched his jaw, not liking when someone was given news of a death over the phone unless absolutely necessary.

But Tank quickly reassured him. "Don't worry, just wanted to make sure she was home. She was a little worried that Phylis hadn't come home last night, so Johnny let her know we were headed over."

"She wasn't suspicious or demanding any answers as to why we were coming?" Elven asked.

Tank shrugged. "Guess not," he said, knocking on the door.

The door immediately swung open, and a woman with shoulder-length gray hair stood in the doorway. She wore thick-framed glasses and had an apron tied around her waist, dusted with flour.

She let out a sigh. Her eyes softened, and she frowned. "She's gone, isn't she?" she asked.

"Are you Gail Pine?" Elven asked.

"You got it," she said. "Come on in." She stepped aside and let the two men enter her home.

Tank headed in first, and Elven followed. The house was much warmer than outside, which was welcome. The scent of something earthy and meaty clung to the air. It made Elven's stomach rumble, reminding him of the breakfast and now lunch he'd skipped today. He wouldn't make that same mistake when it came to dinner.

As if reading his mind, Gail said, "I've got a stew in the Crock-Pot if you guys are wanting a bowl. I like to leave it a little longer to be fork-tender, but it should be fine now. Lord knows I ain't gonna be able to eat it all myself."

Elven and Tank exchanged a glance, unsure who should speak first. Elven decided to decline. "We appreciate it, but we can't stay long. Just have a few questions."

His stomach growled in response, throwing a fit at not being fed. Elven felt betrayed by his own body in that moment, reminding himself that the stew might smell great, but he was willing to bet dollars to donuts that the meat in that Crock-Pot was beef. And he wasn't about to break his long-running streak of abstaining from meat.

Gail gave a shrug and threw up her hands. "Fine by me, I'll have leftovers all week. Don't think I'll be up for much cooking, anyway," she said, leading the men deeper into the small living room.

There was no entryway where they'd entered, only a small space between the door and the couch that mimicked a mudroom or foyer. A small shoe rack sat to the left of the door, but only one pair of shoes actually sat on it. Two more pairs were strewn about in a small pile next to the rack.

The living room was cozy. Not much furniture filled the room, keeping it as open as it could be. Had Gail and Phylis decided to have more than just a sectional and a coffee table, it might have felt like the walls were closing in. Overall, there wasn't much of a mess, only a few items out of place like the shoes, a throw blanket that had slid off the back of the couch onto the hardwood floor, and a bowl of soggy cereal on the dark wooden coffee table.

Elven wondered what the dynamic between the two women had been while living together. Was one more of a clean freak than the other? Did they get on each other's nerves? Were they rarely in the building together, other than to sleep?

They were all mundane questions, but it might give some insight into who Phylis was outside of what her coworker had said about her. Many times, a person's version of themselves at work was highly different than who they were in their private life.

And much to his surprise, or maybe his disappointment, it turned out that Phylis was very different than how Linda had described her.

Gail went into all the details she could about Phylis. How they first met through an ad in the paper, which led to them being roommates for ten years now. They became friends over that time, but nothing that would have suggested they were close ones. More than acquaintances, but nowhere near inseparable. "We were overall friendly, and we got along," was all Gail had to say. It was odd to Elven, considering they'd lived together so long.

"Did she rant about work? Coworkers, customers? Maybe anything about a neighbor?" Tank asked.

Elven stood, letting him do most of the questioning. If there was anything that Tank didn't cover, Elven would speak up, but so far, Tank had a handle on it. He was great at the procedural part of the job.

Gail shook her head. "No, she rarely talked about work, to be honest," she said, though Elven figured she had nothing to lie about. "Her having enemies would be a shock to me."

"How so?" Elven cut in, thinking Tank might have just left it.

"Anytime there might be some sort of conflict, like a neighbor needing her to move her car because she parked over the line, she'd do it with no hesitation. Or even this one time, someone was blocking the mailbox like a jackass. Absolutely in the way and gave no shits—sorry, no *care* about anyone else. Phylis had to get the mail, but she just hovered until they were gone. Wouldn't even say a word to them about it," Gail said. "I wouldn't say she was a pushover, but I'd say she avoided conflict at any chance she was given."

Tank frowned, and Elven could read his reaction on his face. This wasn't the woman he thought he would be hearing about. She had some sort of authority at work, and maybe she liked the power, but when off the clock, she was nobody of note.

Unless someone lost it about an overdue library book fee, or a coworker with a chip on their shoulder, Elven was sure Phylis had no enemies. And as far as he could tell, Linda had the most beef with her. And that wasn't enough to shoot up her entire place of work.

They lingered a while longer, asking more questions, but being met with similar milquetoast answers about Phylis. Gail was pleasant and more than willing to spend as much time as needed with them, but at a certain point, it became clear to both Tank and Elven that this was going nowhere.

"I wish she was here so I could tell her she was a good friend. A good roommate," Gail finally admitted. "I feel bad that we spent so much time together but never developed a deeper friendship, you know? All that time together, and I feel like, I don't know, I barely knew the woman."

"I'm sure she knew," Tank offered, but Elven wasn't confident. He wouldn't say that, of course.

"I'm sorry for your loss," Elven said before they left.

Gail shut the door behind them when they left. Before they got to Tank's truck, Elven let out a long sigh.

"You okay?" Tank asked.

Elven nodded and opened the truck door. The truth was, this felt like one big dead end. He didn't believe Phylis was in any way related to the murders. There was something else that they were missing. But Elven didn't know what that was, and he wasn't going to express his thoughts out loud either.

Right now, leaning on Tank was the safest bet.

CHAPTER FOURTEEN

GAIL AND PHYLIS'S TOWNHOME WAS OFF THE HIGHWAY THAT eventually curved around the downtown area. Tank took the exit to make a straight shot back to the station.

About a mile down, there was a large crowd gathered in the parking lot where a few shops shared space. A small farmers' market usually occupied the spot on weekends, bringing in people from around town selling whatever it was they grew in their backyard, who would then exchange something with other people who grew something else.

But today was no weekend, and there was no market happening. This was something else, and as they grew closer, Elven's interest was piqued.

"Slow it down here," he told Tank. "Pull in where you find a place."

Tank gave a grunt and a nod, pulling into the parking lot. Elven could see the crowd better. It wasn't too large, but big enough. Everyone was facing the same direction, as if they were watching a show. They all appeared captivated by one figure.

Tank didn't find an empty parking spot, so he just pulled to the side of the building, leaving the engine running. Maybe not techni-cally legal, but for a late afternoon, the shops themselves weren't the draw. It was whatever was happening on the asphalt.

As soon as Elven stepped out of the vehicle, though, he saw what was going on. He hadn't noticed the signs on the drive since they were facing away, but now he saw them all in big, bold letters surrounding the commotion like a fence holding in cattle.

He frowned when he read the name.

Zane Rhodes.

Not a single person even glanced his way when they pulled in. And now that both he and Tank were standing behind them, they didn't seem to care. He supposed they didn't need to, but he was concerned by how engaged they were by whatever Zane was up to.

There was no stage, but there didn't need to be. Zane was tall, and even if the crowd was larger, Elven was sure that anyone who might have been height-challenged would still have been able to see the man. On top of that, his voice carried all the way across the crowd, right to where Elven stood. No microphone or speakers necessary.

"Right now, they have no answers," Zane stated, pacing back and forth like an animated preacher in front of his congregation. "And I just wonder if they will ever find any. From what I hear, it's the deputies doing most of the work as it is. We deserve better in Dupray. *You* deserve better from your elected officials."

His words were followed by claps and even a whistle and a cheer from the crowd.

Elven let out a long sigh that turned into a grumble.

"We can get out of here," Tank suggested.

Elven shook his head slowly as he watched Zane continue to tell the crowd the things that they wanted to hear while offering up no real solutions. Except, of course, that *he* could do better. Elven knew different, though. Playing a Monday morning quarterback was always easier.

"Like a bag of hot air on a summer day," Elven commented. "Useless."

Tank gave a chuckle and a smirk. "Glad to hear you still have that confidence in you," Tank said.

That's when Elven realized that Tank didn't necessarily find his remark funny, but he'd been scared Elven had lost his nerve.

Was he that obvious?

Elven spun toward Tank and stuck a leg inside the truck. "Alright, we should get—"

"And would you look at that," Zane called, cutting his speech short. "The man of the hour himself."

Elven hung his head briefly like he'd been caught in the act, unsure of what *act* that might actually be. Whatever the case, he didn't even need to look at the crowd to know that all eyes were trained on him.

Only a moment ago, they didn't give two licks about him being there. But one word from Zane, and suddenly Elven was in the spotlight.

Maybe this election wasn't going to be as straightforward as he thought. But it was still just a small sample size. Everyone had their haters, and being a Hallie, he knew it happened more to him than most. He just thought by now he might have garnered a little more grace from those who started off as naysayers when he was elected.

"We can just give a wave and head out. You're already half in," Tank muttered through gritted teeth, held in a forced smile.

Elven lifted the corner of his lip, grateful for his friend. But it was too late, and he wasn't about to hightail it out of there after being called out. He might have been knocked down a few pegs recently, but he wasn't sure his cockiness could ever be fully snuffed out. Besides, Elven had a long track record of wins on his side. Zane had a bunch of promises and nothing to back them up.

"Sheriff Hallie, come on over here," Zane said, waving his hand in a beckoning motion. "I'm sure the people would love for us to have a friendly chat. Assuming you have the time, that is."

Elven grinned and waved his hand while heading toward Zane through the crowd. "How is everyone doing today?" Elven asked, his voice bordering on a shout.

There was no answer, but at least he wasn't met with a booing crowd, either. He'd take it for now.

"Let's give him some room, shall we?" Zane asked. And like Moses, Zane raised his hands and waved them, parting the sea of people so that Elven could make his way to meet Zane. Though, to Elven, it was more like a puddle—maybe at best a pond—of people. Elven had seen bigger crowds gathered when meat was on markdown at the grocery store.

"Hi, Zane," Elven said with a smile. He held his hand out, and Zane grabbed it with a firm grip, shaking it far more eagerly than Elven shook his.

Zane stood almost a half-foot taller than Elven, though Elven was no slouch when it came to height. He thought that Zane's height could rival Tank's, but that's where any similarities stopped. Tank was far wider in the shoulders than Zane. Not that Zane was a string bean by any means, he just had nowhere near the muscle as Elven's deputy.

Zane was a little soft in the midsection, but from the way his blazer was fitted, Elven had no idea until he came right up to him. He had brown eyes and brown hair, save for the sides above his ears that streaked gray. Overall, he was a decent-looking man, though Elven made note that Zane could not rival him in that department.

But looks alone weren't going to win him this election, and Elven knew it. He was going to have to compete on merit. And even though he might have fumbled some things recently, Elven still felt like he had a good standing here.

"I was unaware you were gonna be out here today," Elven said. Then he brought his voice down and spoke to Zane through his smile so nobody could hear. "Or that you'd be running at all." He lifted his eyebrows, hoping for an explanation.

Zane chuckled but didn't respond directly to Elven. Instead, he spoke loudly, making sure that the rest of the people could hear. "You know, we put up flyers and announcements about it. Hell, I even tried contacting your office myself," Zane said, still gripping Elven's hand. "Kind of hard to get a hold of you. Was beginning to wonder if you still were sheriff. Not many people have seen you these days."

Elven pulled his hand back before the continued hand-shaking looked too awkward, like some lame arm-wrestling match. Zane did the same, but neither of them broke each other's eye line.

"Funny," Elven said. "Haven't seen you in Dupray much at all the past decade or so. A bit of a surprise to me that you announced you were running. Where've you been all that time?"

Elven took a quick moment as if allowing Zane to speak, but before the man could get a word out, Elven cut him off. "Oh, that's right, you were off opening stores and making money outside of Dupray instead of putting it back into the county you're looking to serve."

Elven generally didn't think of himself as the snarky type, but he felt pretty darn good about that one. He didn't mind that Zane was running for his office; that was his right to do. But what he did mind was Zane's attitude about the whole thing.

It didn't have to be a one-up competition, either, but Zane had brought it to him. And if that was the case, he was going to stand up for himself.

He watched Zane's face, expecting a frown, but much to Elven's disappointment, he didn't falter.

"Actually, I am opening a location right here in Dupray," Zane said, this time breaking eye contact with Elven so he could scan the crowd to let them all know. "It's going to bring a lot to this small county of ours. But I'm not really here to talk about that. I'm here to talk about my campaign. The one I'm running against you." He turned back to Elven, a sly smile on his face.

That was completely unexpected. And if anything, all Elven's comment had done was set it up for Zane so he could spike it right back down to him.

Elven wasn't quite sure how to respond. Anything he might come up with now seemed desperate, like grasping at straws, and he found he didn't have much else to say off the top of his head. He immediately realized that he didn't know anything about the man. All he'd done was severely underestimate him.

He felt like a deer caught in the headlights, with all eyes on him, waiting for a response. He swallowed, his mouth feeling drier than normal, his face warm even on such a cool day. He opened his mouth, hoping some string of words would come out.

But they didn't have to.

The siren on Tank's truck sounded, followed by a quick honk. Everyone turned their attention to Tank, who was pulling away from the window of his vehicle. "Sorry, Elven, we gotta get back to the station! Something's come up in the case!" Tank shouted toward them.

Elven gave a nod and turned to Zane. "Well, good luck with all this," Elven said, putting his charm and confidence back on. "I've got a crime to solve." He offered his hand one last time.

Zane took it, shaking it briefly this time. "From my understanding, you've got a lot of crimes piling up. Would be nice to get a few of those caught up before more start happening." This time, no grin accompanied Zane's words.

Elven made his way through the crowd, not wanting to say another word to the man so as not to give him any more opportunities to land another zinger against him. Because right now, he sure seemed full of them.

If Elven were a lesser man, he might come up with a few things to call someone like Zane. But lucky for Zane, Elven was not that guy.

CHAPTER FIFTEEN

"Did they give you any inkling what this new development is in the case?" Elven asked Tank when they were a block away from the station.

Tank gave him a quick glance, then put his eyes back on the road. He let out a long sigh, his lips flapping as he did. "Elven, hate to break it to you, but I was throwing you a life preserver," he finally admitted.

"A what?"

"You looked like you were drowning out there, so I made up the thing about the case so I could pull you out of the deep end," Tank said. "Zane wasn't leaving any scraps."

Elven sighed and leaned his head against the window, watching the buildings go by. "It was that obvious, wasn't it?"

Tank lifted an eyebrow. "The good news is, the crowd wasn't all *that* big. I mean, it wasn't small by any means, but I think—"

"Thanks, Tank," Elven said, cutting him off. "Next time, just lie. Tell me it wasn't that bad."

Tank gave a single nod. "You got it," he said.

Tank was a straight shooter, something that Elven absolutely respected in the man, but it also meant he was blunt at times. And right now, Elven didn't really appreciate the tough-love treatment. Still, he didn't want Tank to change.

"Sorry, just, I don't know. Don't lie. I just didn't want to hear it right now."

"Fair enough," Tank said. "Just because I didn't hear from anyone at the station doesn't mean they haven't found anything out, though. Tommy should hopefully be back. Maybe he got something from Driscoll already."

Doubtful, Elven thought. There were a lot of bodies Phil had to deal with, but Tank was trying to offer something a little more positive, so he didn't want to naysay him. "Let's hope," Elven said instead.

Tank turned down the road and approached the station. He pulled into one of the empty spots right in front and then let out a low growl.

Elven turned to his deputy and saw his gaze. He followed it, and then he gave the same growl.

Lyman Starcher was there, more than likely waiting for them from the way he had his eyes locked on Elven. There was no other reason Elven could think of for his being there, unless of course he had an actual report he needed to file with the station. But even then, he could already be inside doing that with Johnny or Meredith.

"Want me to drive around back or something?" Tank asked.

Elven chuckled. "I don't need you to save me at every minor inconvenience, but I appreciate it. It's just Lyman. I can handle this one."

Tank cut the engine and stepped out. "Fair enough," he said, giving a single wave to Lyman before heading for the station.

"Hey, Tank," Elven called out after slamming the vehicle door.

Tank turned, the front door handle in his hand.

"Thanks. For back there, I mean."

Tank nodded and left him to deal with Lyman.

"Elven," Lyman said. "How are you?"

Elven stared him down a moment. He had been Elven's best friend for as long as Elven could remember. They had come from two major families in Dupray, the Starchers and the Hallies. They were similar in some ways, and vastly different in others.

But they had never let any of that get in the way of their friendship.

Everyone in town knew Lyman's father, Hollis, was a criminal. And not just a run-of-the-mill one. No, Hollis had his hands in just about anything and everything one could think of. He was Dupray's own crime boss, the local Tony Soprano. Of course, it was a little different than that. Dupray was a much smaller and tighter-knit community.

Hollis liked to think he controlled it all.

Elven, however, put a stop to all that when he finally arrested Hollis.

But that wasn't why Elven was reluctant to see Lyman. No, it was because Lyman had betrayed him.

"What do you want, Lyman?" Elven asked.

Lyman's expression had started off hopeful, but it quickly slipped away once he heard Elven's tone. "I just came to see you. You never pick up the phone, and when I leave messages... well, I'm sure you're busy," he said. "I see you're back in one piece."

Lyman motioned to where Elven had been shot, then down to his foot where his heel had broken after jumping out of the top story of his own home. The home that Lyman's cousin had lit on fire with Elven and Yeti asleep inside.

"I am," Elven said. He was keeping it short and, well, not so sweet. But he was in no mood to talk to Lyman these days. He didn't think he'd be in a mood to ever talk to him again.

Not after what he had done.

"Look, Elven, you know that what our families do, or did, was never what you or I were about," Lyman said, his tone somber now.

What he said was true, but Elven wasn't going to admit it.

"You know damn well that I couldn't just be your mole for what my daddy was up to. Hell, you know what it took for me to stay out of all his businesses? You know how he looked at me because of it? So now you're—"

"Shut it," Elven said, no longer wanting to listen to Lyman's whining, his excuses, his denial of what he'd partaken in. "You know darn well what you did and did not do. Sure, you might have stayed out of Hollis's businesses, but that didn't mean you didn't know what was going on. Or did you forget who your cousin was?"

Lyman averted his eyes, which told Elven what he already knew. Lyman knew he was in the wrong.

"What in heaven's name did you think she was doing working as a deputy?" Elven demanded. "All the while still checking in with Hollis, too?" He shook his head and stepped toward Lyman, only inches away from his face. "I expected this from Hollis. I expected it from both of your brothers. I can even expect it from Maddison because I never really knew her before she walked into my life. But you? I never expected it from you."

Elven turned away and headed to the station.

"And what about Penny?" Lyman shouted. "Is she forgiven in all of this just because she's dead?"

Elven stopped, gritting his teeth so hard, he thought his molars would crack.

"I know it was fucked up, what happened to you," Lyman continued. "With Madds, with my daddy. And maybe I messed it up by staying out of it and letting you continue on. But she did, too."

Elven pushed on, trying to ignore it all.

"I lost my whole family because of you!" Lyman shouted. "My brother's dead because of you. My sister. Both Hollis and Wade are locked up. Here I am, trying to be your friend still! I got nobody because of you! My cousin is off who knows where—"

Elven spun around, stomping straight toward Lyman until he was back in his face. "Do you know?"

"What?"

"Do you know where she is?" Elven demanded.

Lyman shook his head, his chin quivering out of fright. "N-no, I swear it. I got no idea."

Elven turned and went to the station. "Then you're no use to me," he said.

He could have sworn Lyman started saying something else, but Elven wasn't giving him any more of his time. He went straight for the station and didn't stop, leaving Lyman as alone as he claimed Elven had already made him.

CHAPTER SIXTEEN

Elven walked into the station, trying his best not to let Lyman's words bother him. Easier said than done, but he was somehow managing. If he wasn't, then he'd either be a bumbling mess on the floor, rocking back and forth, or he'd be locked up in a cell with a broken hand from punching Lyman until someone stopped him.

He gritted his teeth again as he set eyes on Meredith. But Tank must have prepped her, or she'd put it together herself from all the shouting happening right outside the door, because she quickly darted her eyes to her monitor as if she was deep in work. Elven knew it was a lie. Meredith was never too busy to stick her nose in other people's business.

Tank stood at the back desk, putzing around like he was trying to keep busy until Elven came in. Nobody was good at covering up the awkward silence, however.

"Meredith," Elven said as he passed her desk.

"Oh, hi, Elven," she said as if she had just seen him.

Elven shook his head, deciding not to comment.

Tank turned around and gave Elven a small lift of his chin while raising his eyebrows. "Everything okay out there?" Tank asked. "What'd Lyman want?"

A more direct approach, one that Elven was surprised to see from Tank. He wasn't one to get nosy. But he was also a good friend.

"Fine," Elven said. "Just the usual Lyman stuff." Elven didn't feel the need to elaborate, and in true Tank fashion, he didn't feel the need to push the issue.

"Good," Tank said, lifting a mug of something to his lips and taking a sip. It was far too late in the afternoon for coffee, but then again, it had been a rough day.

"Where are we at now?" Elven asked.

"Tommy is back from Driscoll's," Tank said.

"Good, anything there?"

Tank sighed. "Doesn't sound like it. You know how Driscoll is, though."

That Elven did. Driscoll liked to get a look at everything without someone hovering over his shoulder. He would either make them wait outside the office or tell them he'd be in touch.

"Hey, Elven," Tommy said, coming from the hallway. His uniform was disheveled, most likely from all the help he gave Phil Driscoll. Elven knew that the old doctor couldn't hoist the weight of a single body alone, and this case was even worse, considering how many bodies were involved. "Other than verifying all of the victims' identities, which we knew already, no news," Tommy said. "He hadn't done a full report yet. Said he'd call if something showed up."

Elven nodded. It wasn't the news he was hoping for, but it was what he'd expected. "Thanks, Tommy," Elven said. "I know it was a lot of work you had on your hands while we were off looking into Phylis."

"How'd that go, anyway? Did her roommate have anything to say?" Tommy asked.

"No," Elven answered. "Sounds like Phylis didn't have any enemies outside of work, and the worst someone was going to do was quit on her with no notice." Elven thought of Linda. "Nothing but a dead end there."

He looked to Tank, who nodded in agreement. Elven felt better with his deputy's confirmation.

Johnny walked out of the hallway, squeezing just past Tommy. "Where've you been?" Tank asked.

"I ended up taking Linda home. Poor lady was still in shock, so I didn't think it was safe for her to be driving. Told her whenever she was ready, I'd take her back to her car, or even somehow get it to her," Johnny said.

Elven smiled, appreciating how nothing had changed for Johnny. He might have been hurt by someone purely evil, might have seen the horrible side of people, but in the end, he never gave up on helping. He had a kind heart. One that Dupray might not even deserve. But they were lucky enough to get it.

"Thank you, Johnny," Elven said.

"But that's not all," Johnny said. "You remember that monitor that was in the room?"

Elven nodded. "Sure, Tank said it was for video calls."

"That's right," Johnny said, sounding a little disappointed that Elven already knew.

"Did they have an author drop in yesterday?" Elven asked.

Johnny nodded. "Linda was able to look up their calendar for me from her phone. They had it all connected through the cloud so that the library could entice people to come to the book club. She said it didn't seem to matter much and that the usual people showed, author or not. They didn't always get an author to show, but yesterday on the calendar, one was supposed to."

Elven stared at Johnny, who had a big smile on his face like he'd cracked the case. When he didn't continue, Elven pushed. "You didn't happen to catch this author's name by chance?" Elven asked.

How quickly he'd gone from appreciating Johnny to being irritated with him. Johnny just had a way of doing it, like it was an art.

"Oh, right," Johnny mumbled. He pulled out a small notebook

from his back pocket. "I wrote it down just in case I forgot." He began to read from the paper, which he seemed to struggle with, though it was his own handwriting. "The author was some guy named Mike Lindsay, and they were discussing his book *Downward*."

Elven didn't really need to know the book they were discussing, but he wasn't going to lay into Johnny for that one. At least he had some information for him. "Great. Do we know if he actually showed up for the talk?"

"No," Johnny said. "Linda said they just schedule it, and the authors show up. Anyone who would know is…"

Elven nodded, knowing Johnny meant those who would know were all dead. "Get this author on the phone, and let's ask him," Elven said. "If we can find out if he got stood up or not, then we'll know if it was before or after his scheduled chat. And since he's not reaching out to us, I think it's safe to assume that the attack didn't happen during his video call."

"Already on it," Johnny said.

Now Elven was actually impressed. "Great work, Johnny. What did he have to say?"

"Oh, nothing," Johnny said. "I didn't get a hold of him. Didn't have his number."

"So, how are you on it?" Elven asked.

"Linda sent me the information they had, which was his agent's number," Johnny said. "Someone named Scott Landry."

"Okay, and what did Scott Landry have to say?"

"I didn't get a hold of him either," Johnny said. "But I did get through to his assistant."

Elven sighed. Once again, Johnny just had a way, didn't he? "Johnny, tell me the whole string of calls, messages, whatever else you did to get wherever you ended up, and then tell me where we're at now. Okay?"

Johnny nodded quickly. "Right. Sure thing, Elven. Sorry about that."

Elven nodded and held up his hands to urge Johnny to just get on with it.

"Anyway, I didn't get a hold of his assistant," Johnny said. "Just got the assistant's voicemail, but it said they'd be with me at the latest by the end of the day."

"Great," Elven said, though he wasn't confident that would happen. "Even if that does happen, we need to jump through hoops to get to the author, and all just to see if he even made it to the call or if he was stood up because they were already dead."

"Maybe once we do, he can tell us whether something seemed off in the room if he did make the meeting," Tank said, trying to soften the blow.

"Sure," Elven agreed.

The phone rang at Meredith's desk, which she promptly answered with her standard greeting—background noise in the office at this point.

"And even then, we've still got nothing," Elven continued. "All we've done is eliminate a suspect and have nothing to go off of while we wait for some random writer to tell us if the room was tense or not." He didn't mean to sound so sour, but he was frustrated. He sighed. "Guess in the meantime, we've got seven people to talk to. Tommy, you have the list of the victims? It's gonna be a long rest of the day notifying next of kin."

"Elven," Meredith said, hanging up the phone, "that was Phil Driscoll. He wants you to come down to the funeral home. He said he's got something to show you."

CHAPTER SEVENTEEN

ELVEN HADN'T BEEN TO THE FUNERAL HOME SINCE BEFORE HE had been shot, which was months ago. When he was healing from both the gunshot and his broken heel after getting out of the hospital, Elven was required to have frequent checkups. Other than a few times he had to travel to the hospital to see a specialist, Phil Driscoll had been the one he saw to make sure there were no issues, like an infection.

While he was healing, Elven had requested Driscoll come to his motel room instead of him driving to the funeral home. That made it much easier since he wouldn't have to drive, but there was another reason Elven wanted to avoid the funeral home, though Elven could barely admit that reason to himself. It probably had something to do with all the people who ended up at Driscoll's due to Elven's inability to protect them.

But now, Elven didn't really have a choice. He was back on the job whether he liked it or not, and Driscoll was requesting his presence because of something related to the case he was working.

He would have to suck it up and deal with it.

Tank grabbed the door and held it open for Elven, allowing him to enter the building first. The top floor was quiet, almost cozy. It was an old and very big house that had been converted into a funeral home. The entrance was warm and homey, helping loved ones who needed Driscoll's services feel as comfortable as possible.

Elven walked through the entryway into the lobby, which was really just a large living room. A couch sat in the center of the room on the carpeted floor. Driscoll was nowhere in sight.

"Elven, that you?" Driscoll called out from somewhere in the house.

"Sure is," Elven called back. "Tank's here with me. Where are you?"

"Oh, good," Driscoll said. "Come on downstairs, I'm still gloved up."

Elven sighed. He was hoping Driscoll was going to just show him something on the main floor. Downstairs was where he did all the work with the bodies. Elven had seen far too many people on the doctor's table, including a few people whom he'd loved dearly. After his little *moment* at the library—he still wasn't about to call it a panic attack—he didn't want to put himself in another situation that could trigger that reaction.

"Come on," Tank said, patting Elven's arm before heading down the steps on the other side of the wall. Elven took a deep breath and followed him down to the morgue.

Unlike the main floor, the downstairs was cold and sterile, hardly inviting at all. Not only was it where the bodies were stored, but it also doubled as Driscoll's pseudo-autopsy room. It was really more of an examination room where Driscoll could go over any inconsistencies and find things that could potentially help Elven with his cases.

As soon as Elven entered the room, he was relieved to see that only one body lay on a table instead of all seven of them from the library. Doc must have tucked them all away in his storage wall. He didn't go too far inside to identify who was on the table, instead hanging by the entrance.

Phil Driscoll wore a lab coat, his thick glasses, and, true to his word, latex gloves on his hands. He smiled and gave Elven a single wave when he spotted him. "Glad to see you out and about," Driscoll said.

"Phil," Elven said with a nod. "What have you got for us?"

"Straight to business," Driscoll remarked. "Alright, then." He walked around to a small silver tray on a rolling platform. He motioned to it, gesturing for Elven to join him.

Elven sighed and reluctantly walked around the body, keeping his eyes locked on the tray. He knew if he looked at the table with the body, he would see Penny Starcher lying there instead, though he never saw her on Phil's table when she died. Yet, he'd had plenty of nightmares about it while he was in the hospital.

He managed to avoid any visions and stood next to Phil, looking down at what the doctor wanted to show him. On the tray were seven pieces of paper. They were small, and most of the edges weren't straight, telling him they'd been torn out of a notebook. They were all crumpled, and some were speckled with blood. But each of them had something different written on them.

"What is it?" Elven asked.

"I found these in each of the victim's mouths," Driscoll said. "One per person."

"What do you think it means?"

Phil shrugged. "Nothing, medically speaking. If I were to take a guess, I'd be trying to do your job."

Driscoll picked up a metal instrument that looked like pliers or small tongs and handed it to Elven. Elven used them to pick up the pieces of paper, noting that the handwriting was the same and reading each one.

REPULSIVE PERSON
IMMATURE AND POINTLESS
DEEPLY INSECURE
NO IDEA HOW LIFE WORKS
NOT GOING TO AMOUNT TO ANYTHING
WILL NEVER EXPERIENCE REAL LOVE

DO THE WORLD A FAVOR AND DISAPPEAR

Elven frowned as he read them all. He didn't know what any of them meant, but clearly, this wasn't just a single person who was targeted and others got in the way. He'd figured as much already, but this was even worse than he'd thought.

"Think it's personal?" Elven asked, partly thinking out loud. The idea of each person being targeted had really tugged at him from the start. And now there was proof that might give his hunch a foothold.

Tank sighed. "Pretty nasty stuff. Other than the library, I don't see the victims being all that close. What would they have done to cause someone to hate them so much? And all together?" He shook his head. "I'm starting to wonder if it's just someone that isn't right in the head, taking out their own frustrations on some poor people who found themselves in the wrong place at the wrong time."

Elven nodded, unable to argue with that. They were all just theories, and they were taking shots in the dark right now. "I guess we'll find out," Elven said. "We'll fill Tommy in and start interviewing next of kin. Ask them if they know what these notes might mean." He turned to Phil. "You remember which note is from which victim?"

"I've got a list," Driscoll said.

As if it wasn't already a long enough day, this detour was going to make it even longer. But at least they had somewhere to start. Elven didn't have high hopes that anyone would know what it all meant, but it didn't mean he wasn't still going to try.

CHAPTER EIGHTEEN

Robin Sullivan walked along the sidewalk on the right side of the street where the majority of the shops were. Dupray wasn't known for its shopping or boutiques, mostly because there wasn't much in the way of stores, but the town still had a handful that somehow stayed in business. Robin frequented them, mostly just wasting her time chatting with the owners and clerks while she dreamt of being able to afford everything.

It wasn't that the clothes in the shops were expensive; she just liked everything she saw. Most of the shops were secondhand thrift and consignment shops, lending them to being much more affordable for her. She was even able to sell some of her own items from time to time. Mostly, however, she liked to buy and repurpose. Her sewing skills weren't the best, but she liked to learn and improve whenever she could. And since she was between jobs, she had a lot more time to do that.

Even if the items she wanted were affordable, not having work made it more difficult to purchase things. But she had a plan for that, too. She hoped that if she could hone her skills a little bit more, she could start selling her items at the local market, or even on consignment at the shops.

Plus, there was always online. She hadn't dabbled with that much, but finding people who made more than the average person in Dupray could be a game changer for her.

Was she there yet? She wasn't quite sure. She liked to think so, but she had always been the type to second-guess herself. She was so critical of anything she did, which probably made her critical of everything others did, too, that she had a hard time getting anywhere in life, much less enjoying anything in life.

It was a vicious cycle sometimes.

But she was working on it, and thought maybe she could break the cycle if she could just get some stability. The only stable thing in her life right now was her rent every month. And without work, even that cost was starting to feel like it wouldn't last much longer.

But she had a plan for that as well.

Her car was down the block, in the parking lot on the side of the building. She'd hit every single store today, seeing a lot of the same items from the last time she'd stopped by.

She saw a few new items she wanted, but waited on pulling the trigger. If they were still there by the end of the month, she knew they'd be marked down to almost nothing so the shops could get rid of them and recoup a little bit of money. That's when she would pounce on it.

Sometimes the clerks even gave her a discount on top of that if she bought a few items together. If that happened, she would be riding high all day. She couldn't wait until then.

As she got closer, a cold breeze came at her from behind, making her shiver. Her hair blew forward, and she grabbed her hat to keep it from blowing off her head. She turned around to glance behind her as if she could give the breeze itself a dirty look. That's when she saw a man a few stores behind her on the sidewalk.

He wore a peacoat that reached down to his knees and a beanie tight on his head, but he had longer hair coming out from the edges, covering his ears. He had his hands in his pockets, and he was staring her down. It gave her an uneasy feeling almost immediately. She swallowed and turned, trying to brush it off, but the feeling wouldn't go away.

She suddenly felt extremely alone and exposed on the sidewalk. Not another soul was in sight, just her and the man behind her. The world felt so dark now, when only a moment ago not much seemed to bother her. It didn't help that every other streetlight seemed to be burned out.

She tried to pick up the pace, working her legs harder, but she was short, and the man was taller. She had to take at least two steps for every single one he did just to keep an equal distance. But as soon as she picked up the pace, so did he. She could tell by the way his voice carried in the air.

He was saying something that she didn't understand. He wasn't shouting or trying to get her attention, but he spoke as if he were talking to someone, as if she could hear him. Maybe he wasn't right in the head. If that were the case, she definitely didn't want to let him catch up to her.

Why was he following her? Why was he so intent on picking up the pace whenever she did?

She stole a quick glance over her shoulder and saw that he had closed the gap significantly. His hands were still buried in his pockets, and she could just imagine what he was holding in them.

Was he going to rob her? If that was his plan, then he'd be pretty upset to find that she had hardly any money on her. And then what would he do?

And if he wasn't there to rob her, then what?

Something far worse that her imagination could easily get carried away with thinking about.

Just up ahead, she saw her favorite thrift store. Inside, she knew that Lenny would be working because she had just gone in not long ago. She prayed it was still open so she could duck inside. Lenny wasn't anyone she'd think of as threatening, but his presence alone might be enough to scare off this guy.

Now she could hear the man behind her clearly, his words louder as he came within inches of her.

"I don't care," he said. "It's going to happen, and then I will have to deal with it like I always do. I don't care. I'd hoped the last time was going to be it, but here I am."

He sounded completely unhinged. Ranting and raving to himself, and about what? Something going to happen? Whatever it was, she didn't plan on being a part of it.

Robin took off into a run, throwing all caution out the window. She didn't want to ignore what her gut was screaming at her. That someone was watching her, someone was coming for her, and if she didn't act, then trying to be polite and not make a scene was going to end up getting her hurt, or killed.

"Stay back!" she yelled as her soles pounded the pavement. She reached for the door and saw Lenny two feet away, jostling his keys and whistling to himself. She pulled the door open and slid inside, pulling it shut as she did.

"Oh, hey, Robin, back so soon?" Lenny said, referring to the fact that she had just been inside less than an hour ago. She didn't look at him, though. She pressed her face against the glass door, eyeing the man as he approached the building.

He wasn't as close to her as she originally thought, but still close enough. He furrowed his brow, but not out of anger. He looked confused more than anything.

"Lenny, come lock the door, please," Robin said, not letting her eyes off the man as he grew closer. His eyes were on the door where she stood.

"Robin, what is going—"

"Lenny, just do it, please," she begged. She gave him a quick look, her eyes pleading with him.

Lenny seemed to understand and he trotted up to her, sliding the key in and locking it from the inside. "There, is everything okay?" he asked, his tone concerned.

The man came up to the door, looking confused. He stood for a second, directly in line with the door, but about five feet away. He took one step toward it, brought his hands out of his jacket pockets, and lifted his beanie off his head.

"Hey, just one second," the man said.

Now it was Robin's turn to look confused. She watched him bring his hand to his ear, just under the hair that covered it, and pull out a little piece of plastic. It was a Bluetooth device, the kind that was both a speaker and microphone.

"Are you closed now?" the man asked. It wasn't directed toward her, but to Lenny. "Sign says you're still open."

Lenny shook his head. "No, actually," Lenny said. "Was just checking something out." Lenny slid the key back in the lock and pulled the door open. Robin took a few steps back and stood in disbelief as she watched the man.

"Thanks," he said. "I got worried I was going to miss it. I tried picking up the pace to get in before you closed. I was just telling my friend on the phone that I wasn't going to be able to buy a gift for my girlfriend and she'd be pissed at me again. I know it's my fault for waiting so long, but man, I was booking it." The man seemed out of breath, but looked grateful for being let in.

"Of course," Lenny said. "Come in and take a look. I'm open for another fifteen minutes."

"Great, I shouldn't be that long," the man said. He turned to Robin, who stood staring at him. "Hi," he said to her. "Everything okay?"

He smiled at her, no longer looking like a threat. Hell, he no longer felt like a threat. He was just some guy trying to buy his girlfriend a present. What the hell had come over her?

"Yeah," she said, shaking her head. "I'm so sorry."

"For what?" he asked.

"Nothing, never mind," she said. "Good luck on your gift. Lenny has great stuff here." Robin sheepishly walked around the door and went back outside.

Lenny watched her and shrugged. "Bye, Robin. See you later," he said, giving a little wave.

At least Lenny hadn't put her on the spot and ridiculed her by letting that man know she was afraid of him. And for what? Talking on the phone?

She couldn't wait to get home, pour a glass of wine, and pretend like this little scene never even happened. She was so embarrassed.

Of course, now she had to stop at the liquor store and buy a bottle of wine, which was definitely out of her budget. But right now, she didn't care. She wasn't picky, and she was willing to swing four dollars to put this day to an end.

She walked to the end of the sidewalk, one building further, and turned the corner into the parking lot. It was a paved surface, but it hadn't been retouched in at least a decade. The asphalt was so cracked that at this point, it was borderline gravel. The lane lines had long been weathered away.

Her car sat against the wall, just on the other side of the dumpster. She could just see the bumper sticking out behind it. There were a handful of other vehicles dotted about, more than likely belonging to the employees or shop owners. And quite possibly the man she'd just run from, who was now picking out a gift and not mugging her.

She unlocked her car with her key fob and pulled open the door. It creaked as she did, then popped out at an awkward angle that she had become used to. The dent in the door reminded her of the car accident she'd been in two years ago. Instead of using the money to fix the car, she'd used it for groceries and rent, opting to live with the noise and awkward way the door opened.

She plopped her butt down in the seat and bounced once, laughing as she did. The adrenaline had finally caught up with her, and she could reflect on how stupid she had been. It was comical. At least she hadn't told anyone that she was being stalked. Now *that* would have been extra-embarrassing, accusing someone of something they weren't doing.

She shook her head and reached for the car door. Just as her hand grasped the inner handle, someone stepped in front of the door.

She looked up, confused, and her eyes widened.

"What are you—"

That's when she saw the knife come out. She couldn't even react because it was so quick. In one swoop of the person's arm, the blade was there, then it wasn't, then it was again. But now it was red.

They slammed their hand against her face, catching her mouth open, and quickly pulled back. A paper drifted in the air, out of her car, and onto the asphalt.

Robin was still more confused than anything else. She looked up at the face again, but they were quickly gone. It was the weirdest thing. It was almost like she'd made the whole thing up with how fast they'd left.

That's when Robin felt a sharp pain in her throat. She swallowed. It was on fire.

She tasted iron. And suddenly, she was wet down the front of her blouse. She tried to take a deep breath, but she couldn't really fill her lungs.

She looked down and saw all the blood down her front. She reached her hand up to her neck and felt the warm wetness of it. Then her fingers found where the knife had entered and exited. Straight across her throat, and deep, too.

She coughed, and blood shot out from her mouth and her neck. It dotted the dashboard, and that's when she realized she was in real trouble.

She tried to scream for help, but it came out a garbled mess. She took a deep breath, but it was like someone had poked holes in a straw while she tried to take a sip of a drink. Only little bits of air reached her lungs as they sucked in more blood.

She tried to stand, but when she slid out of her car, she stumbled onto the cracked asphalt. Her purse fell out of her lap, the contents spilling when it hit the ground. She couldn't lift herself up. She looked around frantically, seeing the person who had done this run off somewhere deeper into the parking lot. Their footsteps grew further away until they were no longer in sight.

Robin turned her head toward the direction she had come from. Just around the corner was Lenny's shop, where he would be closing up soon. She tried to crawl toward it, but now she felt weak and light-headed. Her hands had gone numb. Her feet were no longer there. The numbness slowly closed into her center. She felt like she was in a dream.

Her face lay on the asphalt as she watched the sidewalk in the distance.

Then the man from earlier came into view. He held a bag from Lenny's shop and wore a smile on his face. He was happy with whatever he had bought for his girlfriend. His beanie was back on his head, his hair covering his ears.

She tried to call out for help again, but it came out in a raspy whisper.

He continued walking right past the parking lot, never entering. He hadn't driven there, so he walked past the end of the sidewalk and then waited for a brief moment before finally crossing the street and disappearing from view.

Robin tried to take one last breath, inhaling mostly blood now, and let out one final exhale.

CHAPTER NINETEEN

"Elven, don't you close your eyes, you hear me? Elven! Stay with me, Elven!" Hollis shouted. Everything grew dark around him. Madds had been there one moment. He remembered hearing her voice. Feeling her presence.

And then she was gone.

Hollis was the only one who remained. He yelled until his voice was hoarse. But he pressed and pressed. Until Elven couldn't hear him anymore.

Elven opened his eyes, staring straight up at the ceiling. He hated those nights when he dreamt of what little he remembered of the night he'd been shot. At least it was just when he had been shot. Not right before when he had gotten people killed.

He let out a long groan, not wanting to move his body. That's when Yeti rolled over, his face pointed right at Elven, his rank breath blowing straight at him. Elven turned his head. That was his wake-up call.

"I love you, Yeti, but we gotta do something about that breath," Elven said, his voice groggy and dragging over the words.

Elven shifted himself upward so that he was propped up on his pillows. He wasn't ready to move. He wasn't ready to get out of bed. He closed his eyes for a moment, slowly letting himself drift away again.

But then his eyes shot open. He couldn't let himself sleep all day. Yesterday was the most work he'd done in months. Well, the most work he'd done on a case that didn't involve finding Madds.

And it had been a brutal one.

When Elven had thought about working on cases again around Dupray, he kind of hoped there would be something that could ease him back into the day-to-day. But he would be lying to himself if he'd actually expected that. If it was something so simple, he would have handed it off to Tank and Tommy, like he'd been doing all this time.

No, it had to be something truly terrible to pull him back into it, taking him from the constant dead ends of trying to locate Madds.

And a truly terrible case, this was.

Between the three men, they'd spent the entire evening and night notifying those close to the victims about their untimely demise. And the people who Elven visited were nothing like Gail. Gail hadn't been overly close to Phylis, so she was able to compartmentalize. Maybe she broke down after they left, but Elven wasn't sure.

No, everyone else who Elven had to visit was broken. Torn apart by the news. They had so many questions, and Elven had almost no answers to give them. It was grueling, stumbling over his own words, trying to give them the news while also telling them they were going to find who did it.

The only saving grace about the whole ordeal was that he was able to split up the responsibility of telling next of kin between Tank, Tommy, and Johnny. Even though Johnny wasn't technically a deputy anymore, he still took on some of the duties that required a personal touch. And he was still one of the best at it.

Elven heard that it hadn't been a walk in the park for them, either, breaking the news. Some people sobbed, some screamed questions, others sat in silence, shocked or perhaps coming to terms with it. Sometimes those cases were worse than those who had emotional outbursts. At least for those people, Elven and the others could be there for some sort of comfort. For the silent ones, the news might sink in when they were all alone with nobody to lean on.

But Elven had no control over any of it. How someone reacted was up to chance. It didn't matter how he and the others approached, they could never predict anyone's reactions to the news because they usually didn't know the person well enough. And even when they did, sometimes a person's reaction could surprise even those closest to them.

The worst part about the whole thing, other than not being able to give the family and friends any sort of comfort or news on the killer, was that they couldn't offer them any reasons for why the massacre might have happened, either.

Most of the people were just your average Joe. Living their life in Dupray as one would, making money as they could with various jobs around town. Some people were even retired. Elderly folks who just enjoyed their time at the library, never stepping on anyone's toes.

Sure, a few victims might have an attitude problem. One person said they had gotten into a spat in a parking lot over someone taking the first spot near the store, but after a few words exchanged, it ended there. In fact, it wasn't even a stranger they had gotten into it with; it was someone they met every few months at a recurring family event because they were second cousins.

Elven made sure to jot that note down to question it further at some point, but he already knew it would be a dead end. This was a person who got into spats every so often, but made up at every family function. Besides that, there would be no reason for a second cousin to shoot up an entire library full of people if that person knew exactly where the victim lived.

And of course, just like he'd expected, nobody had any idea what the notes meant, the notes Driscoll had found in the victims' mouths. Tank might be right about his theory after all. Whatever the case, he felt like they hadn't gotten anywhere yet.

Elven sat up fully now. He wasn't quite ready to step out of bed, but now that his mind was turning, even on memories of last night, he was wide awake.

He looked over to the wall, the one that taunted him. The one with so many different faces he had studied for so long that he now knew every single wrinkle, every nook and cranny, every pockmark on their face. Some were alive, walking about in town. Others were locked up in county. And some were long dead. A few of them by Elven's own hand.

But none of it mattered. None of it got him any closer to finding where she was. He wanted nothing more than to find her, but she was long gone. There was an entire country, or even an entire world, for her to have disappeared into.

The FBI was no help. It wasn't that they couldn't help, but they didn't seem to care. There wasn't much Elven could offer them to make them care, either. Just a bunch of words, a few instances that didn't add up, a genealogy connection to criminals that didn't make her guilty of anything, and the fact that Elven was shot because of her. Though, of course, he had jumped in the way.

He just couldn't let it go.

And it was clearly affecting his work.

Actually, it was affecting his entire life.

He knew he wasn't the same man he was a few months ago.

And maybe that man could solve this case.

But the one who sat in bed right now didn't seem like he could.

Maybe he wasn't the right person to do this anymore.

He threw his hands over his face, trying to rub the sleep away, and that's when the knock came on his door.

CHAPTER TWENTY

Elven wasn't keen on these surprise visits he was getting of late. However, this time he decided not to go for his gun first, opting for just his pants instead. Pulling a gun on the mayor yesterday might have given him the slightest amount of amusement, but he didn't need to make a habit out of it.

Except when he went to open the door this time, he saw a far more familiar face than Oliver Meeks.

It was his mother, Victoria.

If there ever was a time he felt like he'd made the right choice, it was in this very moment. Pulling a gun on his own mother while wearing the very "suit" she'd brought him into this world in would have made for a terrible morning.

As if this morning was good to begin with. In reality, the remnants of yesterday were still lingering. Elven already knew it was going to be trying.

His mother's presence alone was going to kick it off. He loved his mother, but it wasn't easy to get along with her. She had a way of being difficult. Maybe most mothers did.

But in some ways, he was glad she was here. It had been quite a while since he was a child, but sometimes it was nice to be reminded that there was someone who cared about him. Someone who had taken care of him, albeit in that strange, detached way of hers. Being about status and how people perceived you wasn't quite the unconditional love one would have expected from a parent. But he could have had a mother far worse than Victoria.

"Hi, Mom," Elven said, his voice still groggy. A little part of him might have been happy to see her, but knowing her, there was a reason outside of just checking in.

"Elven," she said, her voice bordering on disappointment. She looked around the room, and he realized she probably wasn't disappointed in him, but where he found himself lodging right now.

Elven stepped aside to let her in, though he was sure she wouldn't want to set foot inside the room. If she wanted to talk to him from the doorway, that was her choice. He needed to get dressed and start the day, though what exactly he was starting was the real question. After last night, they hadn't gotten any new leads. At best, they might have heard back from the author, or his agent, or the agent's assistant. Elven wasn't even sure what kind of rabbit hole that was and was actually happy that Johnny was handling it.

"I'm surprised you're here," Elven said. He threw a shirt on and buttoned it up before tucking it into his pants. "Can't imagine you make it down this way much." He smiled at Victoria, trying to make a joke, but also a jab.

His mother's outfit probably cost more than the entire building alone. She wore oversized sunglasses on her face that she removed when she stepped inside. Her dress was appropriately tailored, but not in a revealing way. She swiped a strand of hair out of her face as she continued to look around, her eyes settling on the bed where Yeti lay.

"I wouldn't have thought you'd ever be staying in a place like this," she said, unable to hide her disgust. She stared at the bed and gently reached out a hand, stroking the sheets. "Though, I have to admit, while a bit big for the room, whoever picked the furniture and linens did a phenomenal job. Never would have guessed they had that kind of taste in a roadside motel."

Elven smirked. "I wouldn't expect to see that in every room."

Victoria looked up at the wall where Elven had pinned all the pictures. "This can't be good for you," she said with a frown. "Waking up to this every single day? Not to mention, this place, other than the bedding, probably breeds diseases. I'm itchy just thinking about it."

"Well, the good news is you don't even need to be here," he said, slipping his shoes on.

"Oh, come on," she said. "I come to see you—clearly out of my way, as you deemed it necessary to point out—and this is how you treat me?"

Elven sighed. "Okay, Mom," he said. "You're right. How've you been? You look good. I can see that your trainer is keeping you honest. That, or your surgeon?" He chuckled.

She put her hands on her hips and stared him down. "You know I prefer to age gracefully. I don't need a plastic surgeon for that."

"That's because any physician can inject Botox now," Elven quipped.

"That doesn't count," Victoria said. "Besides, looks like you might be needing some of that yourself sooner than later. You don't look like you've been sleeping well. And not sleeping well makes for deep wrinkles over time."

"Stress of the job, I suppose."

"Anything to do with Zane Rhodes?"

"Didn't realize you could see what was happening from atop your high perch."

Victoria frowned. "Is that really what you think? That I don't pay attention to what's going on in your life?"

Elven shrugged. "I don't know what I think," he admitted.

She didn't seem to hear him. "You ready?" she asked, heading to the door.

"For what?" he asked.

"I came to do this here, but I'm not staying in this place for one second longer. No matter. There's far more space to work at the house," she said. "Come on, Chase is in the car. He can give you a ride back when we're done."

She started walking down the sidewalk toward the black sedan parked in the lot, taking up three parking spots. Elven knew Chase was her driver, though that didn't explain much of anything else.

"What is it that you think we're doing?" Elven asked.

She stopped and looked back at Elven. "Working on your campaign, of course," she said, like it was the most obvious thing in the world.

CHAPTER TWENTY-ONE

ELVEN BRUSHED HIS TEETH WHILE HIS MOTHER RAMBLED ON about how he should present himself, how the county needed to perceive him, how he couldn't be doing things the same way as before, and, of course, how much better Zane was at doing this than he was. He tried to follow, but most of her talking became background noise while he finished up.

He hadn't planned on actually coming with his mother. But it was a reason to get him out of the motel, and he figured if there was any new development on the case, he'd have received a call about it. There were no missed calls on his phone, last he checked. Spending the morning with his mother, talking about a campaign that before yesterday he wasn't even aware he was running, wasn't high on his list of priorities. But sometimes, he knew, it was best to go along with what his mother wanted.

Persistence was one of Victoria's top qualities, and in the end, she usually got what she wanted. He would have wasted far more time arguing with her, all just to give in. So if this made it easier for both of them, he would just get straight to it and try to power through as fast as he could so he could be about his day.

He washed his face and stared in the mirror of the fancy bathroom his mother redecorated recently. To say it was a step up from the bathroom at his motel room would be quite the understatement. Not only was it newly renovated with quality—and expensive—faucets, recycled glass countertops, and the most plush hand towels he had ever felt, which were neatly rolled inside of a basket that somehow kept them warm, but Victoria kept it stocked with individually wrapped hygiene items as if it were a business class airline bathroom. Elven wasn't sure who exactly she thought was coming over to enjoy such luxuries on a regular basis, but he certainly wouldn't scoff at taking advantage of it himself.

A little part of him began to rethink the idea of staying at the motel.

"I swear, was it necessary to bring this—what exactly is he again?" Victoria asked.

Elven poked his head out of the bathroom and into the large room that had been set up as Victoria's makeshift office for Elven's campaign. He saw his mother with her palms sticking out, as if she were trying to stop a vehicle in the road. But they were aimed at Yeti, who was now sniffing at them.

Elven was immediately reminded why he'd opted for the rundown motel versus his parents' home. His parents' home was great, but it came with one thing that was nonnegotiable to him.

His parents.

"A dog?" Elven asked with a grin.

Victoria rolled her eyes. "Yes, I am well aware of what a dog is, Elven, thank you very much. But what breed is he?" she asked.

Yeti licked her palm. She pulled it back, twisting her face in disgust.

"Great Pyrenees," Elven said. "And it looks like he likes you."

"Yes, of course he does. What's not to like?" Victoria said. "But he is so large. Did he really have to come?"

"Where else was I going to put him, Mom?" Elven asked. "You were in such a rush to have me come with you. I wasn't gonna just leave him in the room all day. If you'd have given me a moment, Marcus would have taken him in the office. But it's good for him to get out of that place. Spend some time with his grandma."

Victoria put her hands down and stared at Elven. "Oh, please don't call me that," she said. "If you want me to have that name, then you better give me some actual grandchildren."

Elven sighed. "Not sure I want to subject anyone to that," he muttered while looking around the room.

Victoria let out a yelp. At first, Elven thought she might have heard him, but then he saw Yeti had jumped up on Victoria's lap where she sat on the couch. The dog was already large, but he looked massive compared to his mother. She pushed at his fur, but Yeti didn't seem to get the memo that Victoria wasn't interested.

Finally, she stopped pushing and gave him a couple of pats on the head. "Okay, okay," she said, talking to Yeti. "A little of this, and then can we have some space?"

Elven smiled, thinking they might just be the perfect pair.

Yeti got off her lap, but then he plopped right down next to her, putting his head in her lap. She sighed, continuing to pet him. Elven knew his mother was uppity, but she still had a good heart. And good people couldn't not love dogs. Especially not one like Yeti.

"I suppose he's not so bad," Victoria said. "A little rough around the edges, but maybe some time with a trainer would do him some good. You're lucky your father is out of town right now, or he'd have a thing or two to say, I'm sure."

Now it was Elven's turn to roll his eyes. "He's a good boy who is living his best life. I don't think he needs a trainer," Elven said, now a bit happy to hear his father wouldn't be adding his two cents. "So before we start vetting the best celebrity dog trainers, did you say you had some ideas for my campaign? I still have to do my job at some point today, you know."

"It's not my fault you brought him, but yes," Victoria relented. "Here." She managed to get Yeti to roll off her so she could get up from the couch. She grabbed a thick binder and handed it to Elven.

He opened it up, flipping through the pages. There was a lot more information here than he'd assumed. He thought his mother might put together some flyers, provide a room full of road signs, and at most, try to get him to have some sort of local commercial to promote himself.

Just thinking that made him laugh to himself. Even in his mind, he thought she would go all out, but this? This was far more than just putting his name out there.

She had gone through his entire tenure as sheriff and put together so many different points about how he had helped the community. How he had made it better. How, even though some people might not like the Hallie name, he had tried to turn it around.

"Mom," he said, completely floored by all the work she had put in. "This is... I don't even know what to say. Thank you. This had to be a lot of work."

Victoria smiled and waved her hand. "I won't say it wasn't," she said.

He looked at her again. "You did it all yourself?"

"I had help putting the physical file together," she said. "There wasn't much time to hire someone to do any outside research. Not yet, anyway."

Elven was actually impressed. And touched. "This is more than I expected," he admitted.

"I can't have my only son lose to some outsider businessman without a fight," she said, her chin lifted high. "You're a Hallie. And while I may not like the political office you've found yourself in, it is what you chose. I'm proud of you. And I meant every single word in there. You're good for this county. Better than they deserve."

Elven might not have agreed completely with all of it, but it was still nice to hear. He continued to flip through the folder page after page, reading the talking points, slogans, and various other tidbits she wanted him to use to win the race.

If he had ever considered himself polished when it came to

speaking to people, his mother made him look like he used steel wool to do it. She was on another level.

He neared the back of the folder, and that's when things shifted. It no longer was about himself, but rather, Zane Rhodes.

At first, it started off with the things Zane had done that he would more than likely use for his benefit. All the coffee shops he had opened, the charities he donated to. Apparently, he'd worked with the various communities and law enforcement of those towns to clean up the sites of his buildings, which then created small safe havens for people in higher crime areas. At least higher crime areas on paper, as some of the notes pointed out.

Most of it wasn't necessarily specific to how he would be a good sheriff, but how he was good for the community itself. He might not have a lot of law enforcement experience, but in a lot of communities outside of Dupray, the position of sheriff wasn't even heavily involved in law enforcement. He could hire good cops, or keep the ones who were already there. He just had to be a good leader. And that, he definitely seemed to be.

Honestly, from the way this dossier read, Elven thought he might have an even harder time running against him. The biggest thing that Elven figured he had going for him at this point was that Zane was relying on people having to actually write his name in versus checking a box next to Elven's. In Dupray, that might be enough to win, but it was a huge risk.

As he kept flipping the pages, the text drifted away from what Zane would use to promote himself and more into what Zane was trying to keep hidden. There were the stores he had closed, which had left deficits in the job markets of the small towns he was in, and then also created higher crime rates in those pockets. Those were things that Elven could use, but it wasn't his favorite thing to point out where others didn't excel or succeed.

But then, the contents switched to something completely different. Something borderline dark.

"Mom," Elven said, squinting down as he tried to make sense of it. "What is all this in the back?"

"It's what you can use to win," she said.

"I don't understand," he said.

"Elven, you're the sheriff of Dupray County. By now, I figured you would know that people make deals with those who are, hmm, less than scrupulous."

Elven flipped through it some more. "This is a lot to go through," he said. "But it looks like a lot of speculation."

Victoria nodded. "Sometimes it isn't about the hard evidence you have, but how you can spin it. How once it is out, people can put it together themselves and decide."

"So you're saying a smear campaign?" Elven asked.

"I'm saying that you can use whatever you need to win," she said. "And that you're a good detective. So, maybe you can find the evidence you need to feel comfortable using it. Because even with all the digging I did, Zane Rhodes sure is going out of his way to keep some secrets. Whatever they are."

CHAPTER TWENTY-TWO

Halfway back to the motel, Elven's phone had pinged. That's when he saw a few texts and even a voicemail. He found a pocket on the road that still had service, told Chase to pull over, and read through and listened to everything. He kicked himself for not connecting to the WiFi at his mother's house, but he had completely forgotten. Service was spotty all over Dupray, and now here he was, scrambling to figure out what he had missed.

And from the sounds of it, there was a lot.

Elven quickly called up Johnny, figuring that Tank had his hands full. "Elven, we've been trying to reach you," Johnny said.

"I know, I was out of range," he said. "What's up?"

"Not exactly sure, other than someone called in a homicide," Johnny said.

Elven pursed his lips. It wasn't that he didn't think that someone getting murdered was a big deal, but it was one more thing. They still hadn't gotten anywhere with the library murders.

"Okay, is Tank there?" Elven asked.

"Yeah, but Elven, if you hadn't noticed, we're scrambling here. Drowning, even," Johnny admitted.

Elven sighed. He could hear the desperation in Johnny's voice. He didn't blame him, but to Elven, they weren't the only ones who felt that way. "Alright, Johnny," Elven said. "Where am I headed?"

After Johnny described the stretch of shops and parking lot, he told Chase to take him straight to the crime scene instead of driving back to the motel. Yeti gave him a concerned look once he figured out that he wasn't headed back to the motel to hang out with Marcus.

"Don't worry, I've got a plan," Elven said to his dog.

Chase was more than willing to head to the strip of shops near downtown Dupray. It was closer to Victoria's house than the motel, so the ride back would be much shorter. Not that it mattered much to Chase. His job was to drive around and wait all day, plus with Victoria knowing how far the motel was, he wasn't expected back right away. Elven made sure to slip him some cash and tell him to stop for some food on the way home.

On top of that, he told Chase to take Yeti with him, get him his own meal wherever he stopped, and then take Yeti back to his mother's. Whether she liked it or not, she was going to be on dog-sitting duty. But with how Elven saw her take to Yeti so quickly, not even batting an eye as he hopped up on the couch, he figured she would love the company.

Elven had to admit, his mother had surprised him with the effort she had made with his campaign. Between that and Yeti snuggling up with her, he knew Victoria was a good person deep down. Maybe he could see more of that soon.

But for now, he had a brand new case to work.

Another murder.

CHAPTER TWENTY-THREE

THE CRIME SCENE LOOKED LIKE ALL HANDS ON DECK ONCE Elven got there, which really meant Tommy, Tank, and now himself. Johnny hung back at the station, not being a deputy anymore, though the job was his if he ever decided he wanted to step back into it. He didn't need to be at crime scenes, not unless they were desperate for help—which, it seemed, was most of the time these last few months. But Elven figured the three of them could manage this one.

"What are we looking at?" Elven asked Tank as he crossed under the police tape that had been stretched across the cracked parking lot. There wasn't a crowd gathering yet, but there was one man standing off to the side. He looked to be in his forties, with salt-and-pepper hair.

Tank stood next to a dumpster, blocking the view between it and the car that was parked next to it. He turned his head to see Elven, then stepped aside, motioning toward the ground. That's where Elven saw the woman, her cheek rested on the broken asphalt, staring out toward the street. A puddle of blood had formed around her neck, but most of it had found small avenues in the blacktop to travel through and down so that it didn't pool so much. But it was clear she had bled out from the wound in her neck.

"Her name is Robin Sullivan," Tank said. He motioned with his chin toward the man who stood off to the side, his arms crossed and shifting his weight back and forth on each foot. He was nervous, maybe distraught. "He found her here this morning when he came to open up. He owns the shop two doors over."

Elven gave a look. "The thrift store?" he asked.

Tank nodded. "Clothing, specifically."

"Did we get pictures already, or do—"

"Already got them," Tommy said, lifting the camera with both hands. His demeanor was way too eager for a dead body in the morning, which he seemed to pick up on when studying Elven's face. "Sorry, just glad you're here," he said quickly.

Elven nodded. He was glad Tommy was able to come on. After everything that happened in Monacan, there wasn't much love from Bando toward Elven anymore. Not to mention that Elven owed Tommy when he was sliced through the stomach with a meat cleaver because he'd decided to help Elven out. After Madds left, Elven was happy to bring him on.

"Appreciate the sentiment," Elven said with a smile. "Now, if only everyone felt that way." He gave Tank a side-eye.

Tank frowned. "Happy you're here, but I don't get excited about anything."

Elven chuckled. That was the truth, and he wouldn't have it any other way. He hated to admit it, considering there was a dead body right in front of them, but it was starting to feel good being back at it. He didn't want to give her too much credit, but Victoria believing in him and backing him up had really reignited him.

Of course, having a new murder on his hands was just one more case in the long line of unsolved cases he had on his plate, which Zane Rhodes was sure to point out again when he got the chance. Elven decided he wasn't going to give it to him.

Elven picked up the red purse on the ground now that he knew the pictures had been taken. Some of the contents had spilled out but remained close by. He dug through the purse, pulling out each item and lining it up on the hood of the car. He studied the lip balm, a small pack of tissues, a paperback book, and a wallet that held her identification, credit cards, and fifteen dollars in cash.

"Her cards and money are still here," Elven said. "And I'm assuming this is her vehicle?" Elven pointed to the nearby car. The driver's door was open.

"Yup," Tank said. "Keys are right on the seat. Looks like she had just gotten in from the way the blood is sprayed over the dashboard."

"So this wasn't a robbery. Not unless she had something valuable on her or in the car," Elven said. He gave her lifeless body a long look. He hated to make assumptions about people, but it was part of the job. "It doesn't look like she's the type to have anything more worth taking."

Tank nodded in agreement. "Lenny, the shop owner, says she comes in often, sometimes buying stuff off the clearance rack. Other times, buying nothing at all."

"What else did Lenny say?" Elven asked.

"He said the last time he saw her was a little before closing yesterday. She got scared about something and came into his store, but then it turned out to be nothing," Tank said.

Elven nodded, then took a look at Lenny before heading his way. "Lenny?" Elven asked.

Lenny nodded. "Leonard Balmer, but everyone calls me Lenny," he said. "Did you find anything?"

Elven shook his head. "Still working the scene. But I was hoping you could tell me more about what she might have said to you. My deputy says you mentioned she was scared?"

"Yeah. I mean, I think it was just a misunderstanding," Lenny said. "This other customer came in after she did, but he had his headphones in and got too close. Freaked her out, I guess."

"And he wasn't following her?" Elven asked.

"Nope. Came in and bought something for his girlfriend."

Elven sighed. "Did you get his information by chance?"

Lenny nodded. "Yeah, he paid with a card. I can find that for you. Not like we were all that busy, so it shouldn't be a problem." He paused. "You think he could have done this? I actually watched him leave. Went down that way and crossed the street over there." He pointed in the opposite direction of where they stood.

"I don't know yet." Elven figured he could put Tommy on that one. He didn't expect this customer to be their guy, but it was still part of the process. "We'll follow up with him. Did Robin say anything else to you when she was here?"

Lenny shrugged. "She came in before that, took a look around like she normally did. She didn't find much that she wanted, but really, she didn't have a lot of money to spend. She wasn't working, and she bought and resold clothes, sometimes modifying them. Occasionally, I did her a favor and bought something of hers, but they never sold. She mentioned some deal that she was involved in, too. Something that might help her out. Seemed to be on the fence about it?"

"What kind of deal?" Elven asked.

Lenny shook his head. "She said something about an offer someone made her," he said. "She didn't go in to a ton of detail." He let out a long sigh. "I mean, maybe she did, but to be honest, I wasn't paying all that much attention."

Lenny seemed pensive at the moment. Elven could tell something was on his mind. He lifted an eyebrow.

"Look, she came in all the time," Lenny continued. "She seemed a little lonely. I helped her out with some items here and there, and she liked to chat. Sometimes I just brushed off the things she said. I liked her fine, but sometimes it was a bit much. I can't always be *on* with my customer service, you know?"

Elven nodded. "Sure."

"Now I wish I had," Lenny said. "I feel terrible. I don't even know how I didn't notice her here last night. I saw her car still sitting here in my rearview mirror, but I just didn't see her. I wasn't paying all that much attention, I guess, and..."

Lenny's eyes drifted to where Tank and Tommy stood, mostly blocking Robin's body. Even if they weren't, it would have been tough to notice her on the ground with the dumpster there.

"You're not responsible," Elven said.

"I know, but—"

"Lenny, I can stand here and tell you that you have nothing to feel bad about. It's the truth. Sure, you may not have paid her enough attention, and that's also true. But that just makes you human," Elven said. He watched Lenny wrestle with it, and now it was up to him how he handled it.

"Now if you'll excuse me," Elven said. "I have to go catch whoever is responsible. And you have to go open your store."

Elven felt for the man, but he meant what he said. He wasn't there to make him feel better about his decisions. He didn't blame him for being busy. But he had his own regrets to battle with. It seemed like they all did.

CHAPTER TWENTY-FOUR

"You think Tommy's alright doing all the cleanup?" Elven asked as Tank drove them to the complex where Robin's address was listed. A little part of him wished he had gone back to the motel first to get his own truck, but Tank was happy to give him a lift, and Elven was happy to accept it. This gave him the excuse to need someone to go with him.

After all of the next of kin notifications they'd done the previous night, Elven wasn't in the mood to do any of this alone again quite yet.

Tank shrugged. "I mean, would he like to be more involved? Sure. But I think he's just happy to be part of the team," he said. "Besides, he's the newbie, so he gets the less fun stuff."

Elven chuckled. "Fair enough," he said. "He just was doing more of the hitting-pavement kind of tasks with you, wasn't he? And now that I'm working this case, he sort of gets shoved to the back."

Tank nodded. "That does seem to be the case. But I will tell you, I'm like ninety-nine-point-nine percent positive that he would rather you be working these jobs and pushing him to the back, as you say, than you not being on these jobs. He has a lot of good things to say about you from whatever happened in Monacan."

"Maybe that's all it is," Elven said. "Any sort of work in Dupray is far better than having to work for Bando."

Tank laughed. "I don't doubt it," he said. He lifted his eyes as he pulled into the parking lot in front of the apartment building. "Looks like we're here."

"Think she lives with anyone?" Elven asked.

"Doubtful," Tank said. "With how lonely Lenny made her sound, I'd be surprised if we find anyone. Maybe a couple of cats at most."

"If that's the case, we'll have to check with the neighbors," Elven said.

"Neighbors are fine. I just hope it's not the landlord," Tank said.

Tank parked the truck, and both men stepped out. It wasn't a huge complex, but it held somewhere around thirty apartments from what Elven could remember. It wasn't the first time he'd had to come here before, and he knew it wouldn't be the last.

Elven gave Tank a side glance, knowing full well who the landlord of the complex was. "Not a fan? Dennis hasn't given me much trouble when I've come around," Elven said.

Tank shook his head. "Sure, no issues. It's just something is off with that guy. I can't really put my finger on it," he said. "To be honest, I wouldn't be surprised if at some point we found he had a secret tunnel in the walls with a bunch of peepholes in them so he could spy on the women." Tank shrugged. "Or men. I don't know what he's into."

Elven snickered. "Let's hope that doesn't happen," he said. "Do you know the unit number?"

Tank nodded. "Twelve, right over here."

There were no second-level units in this complex, keeping them from having to climb any stairs. The entire place was painted white with yellow trim. The doors were all a deep blue. The only difference between the doors was the unit numbers just above the small doorbells.

Unit twelve had a small bench to the left of the door, a potted plant just in front of it. The pot was a nice purple color, but the plant inside was long dead, the leaves crunched off of the single dry stick that jutted straight up. The cold weather might have had something to do with it, but Elven figured Robin had whatever the opposite of a green thumb was. Not that he had any room to criticize.

Elven knocked on the door, taking a step back in case she had a roommate or family member she lived with. They waited a while, but there was no answer. He walked to the little bench, cupping his hands over his eyes and peering through the window just behind it.

"Can I help you two with anything?" a voice said behind them.

Elven turned, still half-kneeling on the bench. Just behind Tank was Dennis Conroy, the owner and manager of the building. Elven couldn't help but let out a small chuckle when he saw Tank's face. For such a tall, intimidating man, seeing Tank roll his eyes was funny. Elven stifled the rest of his laugh, trying to cover it as if he were coughing.

"Oh, Elven, how the hell are you?" Dennis asked when he saw the sheriff. He quickly stepped right past Tank and held a hand out to him. Elven got off the bench and shook it.

"Been a whole lot worse, that's for sure," Elven said, trying to keep it friendly.

"Oh, yeah, I heard 'bout what happened to ya. Hadn't heard you were up and at it again," Dennis said, running a hand through his long, stringy hair. It floated just above his shoulders, a few uneven strands barely grazing them. Elven could tell his hair was greasy and in desperate need of a wash. Flakes of dandruff scraped through the strands and fell onto his shoulders, looking much more pronounced against the black sweater he wore.

Elven immediately wiped his hand on his pants, wishing he hadn't shaken Dennis's in the first place.

"Been at it for a few months now," Elven said, but he knew what Dennis was getting at. Technically, Elven was back on the clock, but he hadn't really been back on the job until now.

"Oh," Dennis said, scratching at the back of his head. Elven could see Tank over Dennis's shoulder, his lip lifting in disgust. "So what is it I can help you with?"

"Robin Sullivan lives here," Elven said. A statement, not a question. "Does she live alone?"

"Yes and yes," Dennis said. "Though I'm not sure why you're here to see her. She's a bit of a quiet one. Can't imagine she'd be in trouble with the law."

"She's not," Elven said. "She was found dead this morning."

"Dead?" Dennis asked. "How'd that happen?"

"Homicide," Elven said.

"Homicide? Who the hell would have wanted to kill Robin? You sure it wasn't some accident?" Dennis asked, his bewilderment coming off as genuine.

"Not unless she accidentally cut open her own throat," Tank said, finally breaking into the conversation.

Dennis spun around as if he forgot Tank was even there. He quickly turned back to Elven, and the look on Dennis's face told Elven he didn't have a whole lot of love for Tank, either. He didn't know how their mutual dislike had come about, but there had to be some sort of story.

"Well, I don't know nothing about that," Dennis said.

"Hopefully you know something about how to let us into the unit, then," Elven said.

CHAPTER TWENTY-FIVE

THE APARTMENT WAS SMALL BUT PLENTY SPACIOUS FOR ONLY one person, with its single bedroom, bathroom, quaint kitchen, and a small living room right off the entry. With someone like Robin, it might even be too much space to live in. She didn't even have a cat to share it with.

It made Elven a bit sad. The motel room he stayed in was smaller than this, having no kitchen or living room, but he shared it with Yeti.

Dennis stayed outside the apartment, staring as Elven and Tank moved around the place. Most people might come in and look around, now knowing that Robin wasn't coming back to protest, but Dennis was respectful enough to stay out of it while they worked. What he did later was out of Elven's control, though Dennis was probably within his legal right to start clearing stuff out.

According to Dennis, the only person on his emergency contact list for Robin was Gerald Sullivan, Robin's ex-husband.

Most of the living room was taken over by clothing and other fabrics. A sewing machine sat against the wall, where a couch would normally be. There were various piles, and as Elven studied them, he could make some sense of each of them. The first was random bits of fabric, the second was fully completed clothes, and the third was clothing that had something missing, like sleeves, or the side wasn't stitched up. They were works in progress.

A television sat across from the wall with the sewing machine and table, and then the wall that ran perpendicular to it was where the single recliner sat. Books were behind the recliner, stacks and stacks of them at various heights. The tallest pile leveled off just under the window so the sunlight could still spill inside.

"Reading, sewing, and TV," Tank commented.

"Seems like you summed it up there," Elven said, again feeling sad that one's life could be summed up with just three words. He wondered what someone might say of his own if they were to walk into his motel room right now. It might be even more pathetic to hear.

Elven looked at all the stacks of books, examining each stack more closely. He grabbed a book off the top of one pile in the center. He wondered if there was a method to each stack, or if Robin had just done it randomly.

The cover of the book in his hand looked a bit amateurish to him. He was no designer, but the people on the cover looked as if someone had literally cut them out of a magazine and pasted them down. Except, it was all one singular image.

The title was *Hollow Hearts*, and going by the pink color and the loving way the two people looked at each other, it was clearly a romance book. He went to set the book back on the stack, but when he turned it upright again, a small paper slipped out from between the pages.

Elven bent over to pick it up and saw it was just scribblings on a page torn from a small notebook. He did a quick skim over the writing, picking up a few words that stood out.

Trite. Cliché. Doesn't make sense. Stupid. Boring. Bad pacing.

There was a lot more than that, too, with Robin's notes getting even nastier toward the author. Eventually, Elven stopped reading.

"Tough critic," Elven muttered, sliding the page back in the book and setting it down. He picked up another book from a different pile and fanned through the pages. Another paper stuck out when he got to the back of the book. This paper was filled with notes, albeit a lot kinder this time. Apparently, this book had been more to Robin's liking.

"Anything of use?" Tank asked.

Elven shrugged. "Not really," he said, tossing the book back on its pile. He turned to see a small notebook on the chair against the wall. It looked about the same size as the pages. He picked it up, thumbing through it quickly. He found nothing but more notes about whichever book she was in the middle of reading.

"Same here," Tank said. They'd checked everywhere else, but saw nothing that told them much of anything.

Elven and Tank exited the unit, letting Dennis lock it up. "Anything else I can help with?" Dennis asked. Tank stood off to the side while Elven faced Dennis straight on.

"Did she have anyone around that might have had an issue with her?" Elven asked.

Dennis shook his head. "She didn't have no problems with anyone. Hell, even her ex-husband still liked her. The only problem I ever saw was that she was starting to have trouble paying rent. She was between jobs, from what she told me." Dennis's eyes went wide, as if he had just fingered himself as a suspect. "But I worked with her on payments," he added quickly. "I ain't a slumlord or whatever."

Elven didn't think Dennis was that. From what he could see, he was actually fairly decent when it came to landlords in Dupray. Normally, people in Dupray didn't have the kind of money to own an entire apartment complex, but the property had been passed down a number of times through family until it had landed in Dennis's lap. His family had gotten in while there was still a bit of money to go around in the town, and they were smart enough to never let it go.

Though, some might also say that was stupid of them. Because the population was dropping in Dupray, which meant fewer renters to go around.

"Think she might have had issues paying anyone else?" Tank asked. "Someone that needed to collect debts?"

Dennis didn't even bother looking at Tank over his dandruff-flaked shoulder, acting as if Elven had asked the question. "Nah, not Robin," Dennis said. "If she had issues, her ex helped her out. She said she was trying to buy a trailer. Something about her owning a piece of land on the highway. Least, that's the story she told me. I kind of figure she was just trying to get me to reduce the rate. People are hard to come by around here, plus she was having trouble, like I says, so, you know, I let her have it."

Elven watched Dennis for a second or two without saying anything.

Dennis started to shift his weight, then scratch at his neck, his eyes going wider. "Oh, when I say I let her have it, I meant I gave her a break on rent. Not like... *let her have it* some other way, you know?"

Elven watched Dennis squirm. Tank was right about him, he did seem a little shifty. Like maybe he had something to hide. Elven just didn't think it had anything to do with this murder case.

Or maybe he was just the nervous type. Dennis hadn't been very social most of the times Elven had run into him outside of his complex.

"Dennis, I got it," Elven said, holding a hand up. He didn't want to keep going around in circles with the flustered man. They could be there for a whole week if he let that happen. "So you don't think she had any property, then?"

Dennis shrugged. "If she did, I wouldn't know where specifically."

"How about her ex?" Elven asked.

"Gerald?" Dennis said. "Oh, yeah. I'm sure he would."

"And they got along?"

"Yeah, he seems like a decent guy," Dennis said, but his eyes went down and to the right.

"You sure about that?" Elven pressed, stepping forward.

"He was every time that I saw him," Dennis said. "But there were a few times that Robin didn't seem so happy to see him. Like, I don't know how to describe it exactly, 'cause she liked him around, but something also put her off from him. Rumor has it he isn't completely on the up-and-up."

"How do you mean?" Elven asked.

Dennis gave another shrug, and his shoulders swept the flakes off his shoulders like a broom. "That one, I don't know. Just has his hands in some things. I saw him get real shy when your deputy," he pointed to Tank behind him, "came by to arrest John Ballentine in unit twenty for jackin' off down by the river."

Elven looked over Dennis's shoulder and cocked his head at Tank in question. Tank held up a hand and shook his head. "Long story," he said.

"Between you and me, that's the least offensive of the things that John Ballentine was doin'," Dennis said.

Elven wasn't going to tell Dennis that there wasn't a whole lot of *between* Elven and anyone. He was the sheriff, and his job was to keep law and order. But he also didn't want to get another long-winded tangent about anything else.

"Where can we find Gerald?" Elven asked.

CHAPTER TWENTY-SIX

Dᴇɴɴɪs ʜᴀᴅ ʟᴏᴏᴋᴇᴅ ᴜᴘ ᴛʜᴇ ғɪʟᴇ ʜᴇ ʜᴀᴅ ғᴏʀ Rᴏʙɪɴ, ᴡʜɪᴄʜ included the emergency contact information for Gerald Sullivan. It had a phone number and an address. His house wasn't too far away, so Elven and Tank figured they would pop by instead of call. With how close Robin had been with her ex-husband, according to Dennis, Elven would rather inform him of Robin's passing in person.

And this way, he could also get a read on the man. Elven couldn't get that kind of thing by voice only. Reading someone's body language was a big part of it.

Tank drove to the address, which led them to a single-story trailer. It had stairs leading up to a large wooden deck that sat just above the vinyl skirting. The deck looked like it needed some sanding and staining but was otherwise in sturdy shape. A grill stood in the corner, and some chairs were stacked up against the wall.

A Ford truck was pulled up along the left side of the building, facing toward the road. From where they parked right in front of the trailer, they could see a few other homes dotted around the land with seemingly no rhyme or reason. It was as if someone just picked a spot and put a home wherever they pleased instead of trying to maximize the amount of space in the neighborhood.

Tank and Elven both headed up the stairs, but Elven stood back a few steps so he wasn't all the way up to the deck. Tank opened the screen and knocked on the door behind it. They waited a bit, but there was no answer. Tank put his head close to the door and shook his head.

"Doesn't sound like anyone is inside," he said. "No TV, no rustling."

Elven frowned. He really didn't want to call Gerald. Even if Gerald didn't tell him anything about Robin in person, he would be tipped off if something wasn't right. If her ex-husband had anything to do with her murder, he would get scared off. According to Dennis, he wasn't a fan of law enforcement, anyway.

Tank gave another knock and stood with his hands on his hips. "Gerald Sullivan," Tank called loudly.

Elven heard a light *thud* from the side of the trailer. It was so quiet, Tank didn't even seem to hear it. But it piqued his interest, and he took a few steps toward the deck, headed past the chairs, and made it to the railing at the other end.

He heard more sounds—a *click*, like a door was engaged, then two quick footsteps.

Elven leaned over the railing and peered around the building. That's when he saw a man standing next to the Ford. The door was open, and he was climbing inside. It was clear that he was trying to sneak away.

"Hey!" Elven called out. "Gerald!"

The man looked up from the driver's seat, eyes wide as they locked on Elven. Elven could tell this was who he was looking for, and that for some reason, Gerald didn't want to be found.

He was halfway into the truck, reaching for the ignition while still climbing inside. Elven quickly hoisted himself up the railing and jumped off the deck, landing on the soft dirt below. He sprinted right toward the truck that was now just in front of him.

Gerald fired up the engine and spun to the door, trying to shut it before Elven could reach him. But he was too slow. Elven grabbed the edge of the door, pulling back with all the force he had so his fingers didn't get slammed against the metal body. He ripped the door right out of Gerald's grasp and leaned toward him.

Gerald lifted his foot and kicked Elven in the chest, sending him sprawling backward. Elven's back hit the side of the trailer, and he watched Gerald shift the truck into gear. The truck inched forward. Gerald was seconds away from taking off, but Elven wasn't down yet.

Elven lunged forward and grabbed at the man's shirt. Lucky for him, Gerald hadn't buckled his seatbelt, and Elven yanked him toward himself as hard as he could, throwing his own weight backward.

Gerald came tumbling out of the truck. Both he and Elven hit the ground hard, rolling on top of each other.

Gerald scrambled to get up, away from Elven. Elven scrambled to keep him down. Gerald won out, raising himself and taking three steps away toward the nearby trees. But Elven lunged again, grabbing his pant leg at the ankle. Gerald fell face-forward on the ground. He let out a loud groan and grabbed his face. Elven saw him pull his hand away. It was covered in blood.

That's when Elven saw the Ford truck Gerald had fired up and shifted into gear. It was no longer right next to them. It was headed down the slope of the drive toward the main road, completely driverless.

"You gotta be kidding me," Elven grumbled. He gave one more glance to Gerald, still trying to get to his feet. "Stay here," he told him.

Elven rose to his feet and took off running toward the truck, leaving Gerald where he lay. The truck was gaining speed from going downhill.

"Elven, I got it!" Tank shouted, heading toward the truck. He was taking much longer strides than Elven, but Tank wasn't as fast as

Elven. But if Tank was telling him he had it, then Elven was willing to let him do it. "Go get Gerald!" Tank yelled.

Elven saw Tank was now closer than he was to the truck, so he spun around to see Gerald running away. Groaning, he started sprinting straight for Gerald.

Gerald looked behind him, his face covered in blood from where his nose had exploded against the ground when he fell. His eyes widened, seeing Elven on his heels again.

And Gerald was no match for Elven's speed.

After his broken heel, Elven worried that it would give him issues. That maybe it hadn't healed properly. That chasing down people wasn't going to be so easy anymore. He'd been the running back in high school, skills that had transferred very well to the sheriff job.

Luckily, it didn't seem that any of his worries were warranted. Either that, or Gerald was just that slow.

Elven reached him with hardly breaking a sweat, his adrenaline already ramped up from the earlier struggle, and he tackled Gerald to the ground. "I told you to stay put," Elven growled, driving his knee into Gerald's back while grabbing his hands and pulling them behind him. Gerald let out a yelp, but Elven knew he wasn't applying too much force. Besides, Gerald had put himself in this situation.

Tank had stopped the truck just in time from drifting onto the main road. Not that there was any traffic at this time, but the last thing they needed was for some car to come by at just the right time when the truck flew into the road.

Tank jogged up to Elven and helped him hoist Gerald to his feet.

"Look at that," Tank said, looking at Elven.

"What?" Elven asked.

"You look pretty damn happy right now," he said.

Elven shrugged. "Guess all it took was tackling someone on the job," he said. But he had to admit, even though there were a lot of murders unsolved right now, it was starting to feel good being back on the job.

CHAPTER TWENTY-SEVEN

GERALD SAT IN ELVEN'S OFFICE, HOLDING HIS NOSE. THE SKIN there was pink from the blood staining, but for the most part, he'd cleaned himself up. Gerald had tight, curly hair and wore a long-sleeved flannel shirt. It looked too light for the weather, but that was probably the least of Gerald's worries since being caught sneaking out of the window.

"I think it might be broken," Gerald said, his tone nasally as he squeezed his nose.

"Not my fault you decided to high-five the ground with your face," Elven said. "Maybe you should have just talked to me instead."

"Sure. Let me just get arrested willingly," Gerald retorted.

Elven sat on his desk in front of Gerald. He'd opted not to have the injured man in a cell so he could try to clean himself up. Besides, this way, it might make the man feel a little more at ease. Elven could play the role of a disappointed principal, and Gerald would be the troubled student.

"So you assaulted me instead," Elven said.

"Assault? That?" Gerald said. "More like just trying to keep you out of harm's way of a moving vehicle."

Elven smiled. "That's clever. The thing is, I never intended on arresting you in the first place."

Gerald scoffed. "Bullshit."

Elven leaned backward and stretched his shoulders. The office held a lot of good memories for him from when he had worked for Lester. Elven had once sat in the very chair that Gerald found himself in now, Lester in Elven's spot. Elven smiled, thinking about the old guy.

"No lie," Elven said. "Was coming to ask you a few questions, but now, you trying to run, shoving me, resisting arrest, it sure does make you look guilty."

Gerald shook his head and slumped back in his chair. "Fine, whatever. Just write me a citation or whatever it was you were gonna do and be done with it."

Elven frowned as he studied him. "You don't seem to be too upset."

Gerald shrugged. "Didn't realize selling a bunch of knock-off purses was something to be worried about. What does that come with, community service? Not like I was making a ton as it was, if I'm supposed to pay some company restitution or whatever it is."

Elven leaned forward and let out a laugh. "That's why you were running? For Pete's sake, resisting arrest is worse than that. You ain't the sharpest, are you?"

Gerald rolled his eyes. "Then what the hell were you coming to me about?"

"You would know if you had just answered the door, Gerald," Elven said. He let out a long sigh. He hadn't expected that Gerald was responsible for Robin's murder, but it was a thread to pull at least. And when Gerald had taken off running, well, Elven thought he might have had something.

But now?

Now he was positive that he was going to be breaking some hard news to Gerald. There was a lot more of that than Elven preferred happening these days. Of course, zero was his usual preference, but it was a part of the job he still needed to do.

"How close are you to your ex-wife?" Elven asked.

"Robin?" Gerald asked. "We get along alright. Why? That's what you came to ask me?"

"Gerald, I hate to have to tell you, especially like this now," Elven said, "but Robin was found dead this morning."

Gerald leaned back in the chair, looking around the room. Whatever answers he was searching for there didn't come. Instead, he opened his mouth wide and let out the slightest squeak. He closed his mouth, shaking his head.

Elven let him have some time to figure out his words. Eventually, Gerald cleared his throat and sat up in the chair. He'd long forgotten about his nose and the supposed breaking of it. Elven knew he'd been exaggerating, anyway.

"I'm guessing it wasn't an accident since you were saying I look guilty for running," Gerald said. His eyes were soft and moist. It was clear that he was on the verge of tears but was doing his best to keep them at bay.

Elven gave a nod.

"Well, I didn't have anything to do with it."

"I've come to that conclusion," Elven agreed. "I spoke to Dennis—"

"That guy is skeevy as fuck," Gerald said in disgust. "But to be honest, I'd be surprised if you said he had something to do with it. Doesn't seem the type."

"He said the same about you, more or less. Minus the skeevy part," Elven said, deciding to keep out what Dennis had said about Robin not liking Gerald's company.

Gerald lifted his eyebrows as if in agreement. "So what did you want to know? You came to ask some questions." His tone was no longer combative. He was like a beaten-down dog now.

"You were divorced but stayed in contact with her?" Elven asked.

He nodded. "Yes. We are friends—or, were friends. Just because we weren't compatible for marriage doesn't mean we weren't still good in other ways."

"And you helped her out? I heard she was having trouble paying rent."

"Yeah, but she had a plan," Gerald said. "I was going to find her a trailer to put on some land she owned. I would have gotten her a way better deal than what Dennis could match."

"So, she did have the land?"

"Dennis didn't believe her, I'm sure. But she did."

"This is the same land that she was thinking about selling?"

Gerald looked up, confused. "How did you hear about that?"

"Someone said she had mentioned it," Elven said. "So, was it true?"

Gerald nodded. "Yeah, but she didn't say who the buyer was. Honestly, I didn't pay much attention to the idea. Selling the land meant she would have some money, sure, but not a ton. She was better off getting the trailer and living on it, eventually being free from any payments. That way, it wouldn't matter when her clothing didn't sell much. She told me she realized that and was going to turn down the offer."

"You have no idea who the buyer was?" Elven asked. "How did they take it when she shot it down?"

Gerald gave a little shrug. "Like I said, she didn't say," he said, letting his words hang in the air for a moment. "But she did give me the little handshake offer he had given her. He scribbled some notes down on a scrap of paper, and she wanted to run it by me."

"Do you still have it?"

"Depends on where we're at for the counterfeit handbags and resisting arrest," Gerald said.

How quickly he'd gone from morose at the news of his ex-wife to trying to save his own skin. But it was Dupray, so Elven couldn't expect anything less.

CHAPTER TWENTY-EIGHT

Elven held the piece of scrap paper that Gerald had given him. Just like Gerald had said, there were a few words scribbled on the paper along with an offer. One thing Elven noticed was that there weren't a ton of zeros following the number for the offer, so again, like Gerald had said, it wouldn't have been much. Though, in Dupray, a little could go a long way sometimes.

It looked like there were a couple of different payment ideas, but Elven couldn't make a ton of sense out of it. The handwriting alone was difficult to read.

He had no clue who it might belong to. If the offer was bigger, he'd have a better chance of narrowing it down to a handful of people. But since the figure was so low, it could be anyone.

Well, this was still Dupray, so not really *anyone*.

But the one thing that Gerald hadn't mentioned was the scrap paper it had been written on. It wasn't just a piece of paper. It was a receipt.

And the branding on the paper was something Elven was far too familiar with.

It belonged to Martin's Bar.

The back of it was entirely blank, aside from the notes that had been jotted down, of course. But the front had the little logo at the top printed on it. It wasn't a logo like an image, just the title of the business set in a pyramid shape. MARTIN'S was stretched across the word BAR, but BAR was much bigger, so both words were the same size across. Beneath that was a little squiggle that separated where the name ended and the rest of the receipt began.

There wasn't much else to the receipt, other than two drinks. One was a wine spritzer, the other a glass of cognac. If Elven had to guess, he'd have put money on Robin ordering the spritzer and whoever had made these notes ordering the cognac. But he would rather be safe than sorry, and in the end, what they ordered wasn't in question here.

Whoever made the offer was. Because if Robin had turned it down, then maybe they weren't too happy with that answer.

So now Elven just had to hope that Martin remembered who was with Robin that night. It wasn't too long ago, but it was long enough. Martin was a lot of things, but he saw a lot of people come and go through the bar. Unless something went awry, Martin remembering this much was going to be a stretch.

But it's all he had to go off of.

Later, when Martin saw Elven sitting at the bar, Elven could tell that Martin knew immediately he wasn't just there to drink and shoot the breeze. Not that he still wouldn't have himself a glass of scotch. He had cut back quite a bit on drinking recently, what with him going a little off the deep end after finding out whom Madds was related to, but that didn't mean he wasn't still drinking on occasion.

And Martin always kept a bottle of scotch just for Elven.

It wasn't anything too fancy, but most people who came to Martin's didn't order something like scotch. They were more the typical whiskey and moonshine types.

Martin had pulled his long hair back into a ponytail, wrapping it with a hair tie, and dug out a glass from under the counter. He poured a couple fingers' worth into the glass and slid it right in front of Elven without having to be asked.

"Alright," Martin said, scanning the room before settling his eyes back on Elven. "I'm hoping whoever it is you're trying to arrest here isn't going to create a huge mess of my bar."

The bar wasn't very busy today. A few people sat at various tables, keeping to themselves. One other man sat at the other end of the bar. Elven was sure in a few hours, it would be much more lively.

Elven smiled and took a sip of the liquor. It warmed his throat and then his chest as it went down. "Highly doubt it'll come to that," Elven said. "I'm just here for some information. Hoping it'll lead to an arrest, but not in here."

Martin grinned. "That I can get behind," he said. "What is it?"

"Robin Sullivan," Elven said. "Looks like she was here fairly recently. Maybe with someone else?" Elven slid the receipt toward Martin.

Martin picked it up and studied it carefully. Then he shrugged. "No clue," he said.

"You don't know her?"

"I mean, sure, but couldn't give you any details. Other than the date on receipt, that's all I got," Martin said.

Elven groaned. Martin was generally helpful, but right now, Elven wished he could shake him and make him remember. "That—"

"Hold on," Martin said, holding a hand up. Elven's hope perked up. "I ain't saying it's because I don't remember. I mean it's because I didn't help her."

"Who else would have helped her?" Elven asked. "Is Charlene still working here?"

Martin shook his head. "Sometimes, but Paige is the one who would have been here."

Elven shook his head, confused. "Paige?"

Martin smiled. "Holy shit, Elven. You really haven't been here in a while, have you?"

Elven bit his lip. "Sorry," Elven said. "Been busy." *Busy sitting in a motel room keeping to myself,* Elven thought, but he kept that part to himself. Since being released from the hospital, he'd holed himself up in that room quite a bit. When doing any drinking, he'd just bought whatever he wanted at the store and brought it back with him.

With the mayor and his deputies telling him he'd been missing lately, he tried to brush it off. But now Martin said he hadn't been patronizing his establishment much, either. Maybe it was time for him to venture out a little more.

"Understandable, Elven," Martin said.

"So, Paige?" Elven asked.

"She needed some work, came in basically begging me. I felt bad, 'cause you know, single mom, doing what she can. I don't have a lot of need, but she's good with the customers. I toss her a day or two here and there when it makes sense," Martin said.

That was more information than Elven was looking for. "I meant, where is she?"

Martin knocked on the bar and pointed at Elven. "That would have made a lot more sense," he admitted. Martin looked over to the clock on the wall across the room. "Considering it is about twenty minutes past her shift, I'd say she should be in here any—"

The door swung open, and a tornado of a woman flew through the entryway. Her jacket was barely over her shoulders, her purse was dangling by a broken strap in her hand, and her hair was frizzy.

"I'm so sorry, Martin," the woman said. "I couldn't find my keys, then I hit some traffic, and of course I ran out of gas on the way, so I needed to stop. Needless to say, it's been a day, but I'm here, I'm here. I'm ready to work, I swear it. Please just let me stay." She was practically shouting across the entire room, drawing all the patrons' attention.

Martin held both hands up. "Paige, no need to stress right now. You're fine."

She sighed and smiled. "Thank you so much, Martin." She bit her lip and strained her neck.

"What is it?" he asked.

"I also couldn't get a sitter, so I was kind of hoping..."

A boy, somewhere under ten years old, walked in behind Paige. He held a tablet and swiped his finger across the screen, looking up at his mother.

Martin relented. "He can sit at the end of the bar for a while, but if it gets busy, you send him to my office, alright?"

Paige threw her head back in relief. "You're a lifesaver," she said.

Elven wasn't sure he had ever seen a more frantic, less put-together woman in his life. Well, that wasn't quite true. There was one brunette he could think of, and he doubted that Paige was living in a stinky van like she was.

"Come on," Martin said, patting the bar. "Someone is here to ask you a few questions."

Paige grabbed her son's hand and walked him around to a seat, then gave Elven a once-over, not even trying to be discreet. She gave her son a quick kiss on the head, then covered his ears.

"Who the fuck are you?" she asked.

Elven couldn't help but smile.

CHAPTER TWENTY-NINE

His conversation with Paige went completely off the rails right away. With how she'd barreled through the door, Elven considered himself lucky they were able to have any conversation at all. Her focus wasn't quite all there, but Elven figured that by just casually chatting, she might be able to settle into her job. Which also meant she'd be at ease when he wanted her to remember Robin.

They only had to get to that point first. Because right now, she was far chattier than expected. And she seemed like an open book.

That was good, but also bad for him. Because there hadn't been any pause in the conversation for him to even attempt to pose a question.

She'd been rambling on for a while, and Elven was listening intently. He might have been impatient to get to his point, but he wasn't going to be rude. And he actually found himself enjoying someone just rattling on about their life. It was nice not to be so focused on what was going on in his own and take a break to listen to someone else's life troubles that he had zero obligation to fix or even be a part of.

Paige took a deep breath, sneaking a glance at her son, Sterling, who continued to sit on the barstool, playing on his tablet and staying out of the way of any patrons. Nobody in the bar seemed to mind, and if they did, Elven might have had a word or two with them because he was extremely well-behaved.

"This one keeps me on my toes," Paige said. "You ever talk to someone so young, they tell you something, and you have to Google it thinking they're wrong? But then it turns out they were right, and you start not questioning the information they give you because of it?" She gave a little laugh. "I mean, it's kind of an odd feeling sometimes."

Elven smiled, looking at Sterling as he worked the tablet. He was short for his age, which Elven had come to learn was eight years old. "I'm sure," he said.

"No, really, he can show you anything on a map. He loves that stuff," she said. "Sterling, baby, what's the capital of Nigeria?"

Sterling didn't look up from his tablet. "I'm not a baby," he said.

She rolled her eyes. "I know, it's just a loving word I call you," she said. She turned to Elven. "He's so literal sometimes." She knocked on the counter in front of Sterling. "What's the capital of Nigeria?"

He looked up from his tablet at his mother and smiled. "Abuja," he said, then turned to Elven. "But it's not the most populated city. Lagos has the most people in Nigeria."

Elven smiled at the kid, who quickly went back to his tablet. Elven would have been hard-pressed to come up with that answer on the fly.

"Smart kid," he said.

"You tell him a city, he'll point it out on a map, zooming in on the country with his little fingers. It's wild," Paige said. "He even tested and was accepted into Dupray Traditional Academy out by the country club."

"The private school?" Elven asked. It was a little uppity, but he was impressed. "That's a pricey one."

"You're telling me," she said. "But I'm working on it."

"How's that work?"

She groaned. "Trying everything I can think of. Odd jobs, side hustles. Socking it away as I collect. Hopefully, I'll have enough for tuition before the start of the next school year. It's tough, but he's worth it."

Elven smiled. "I don't doubt it."

"Harold was smart, but Sterling is another level. No idea where that came from," she said.

"Harold?" Elven asked.

"His father," she clarified, then sighed. "That's a story. Everything that went down with him. If I really stand here and think about it, I could probably say that's when everything fell apart and caused this whole mess of a life we've got going."

Elven watched Paige for a moment. She had given him an opening, but instead of asking about Robin, he was curious.

His eyes drifted down to the simple engagement ring on her finger. It was a single diamond ring, accompanied by a silver wedding band.

"What happened?" Elven asked. "Things not work out so well? Martin mentioned you were single." He realized then that he might have come off as hitting on her, though that was the farthest thing from his mind. "Sorry, didn't mean to pry," he added.

She smiled. "I've been practically telling you every little bit of my life story." She motioned again with her head toward her child. "I brought him up." She wiped down a spot on the bar, then pointed to Elven's glass. "Refill?"

He nodded, and she poured another glass. He let it sit instead of sipping right away.

"It's hard to work things out with a dead man," Paige said.

"I'm sorry," he said. He wasn't sure what he'd expected, but Paige being a widow wasn't at the top of the list.

She shrugged. "Life happens," she said. "He was a good father, a good husband, but he's been gone a long time now." She smiled fondly at Sterling.

Elven was going to ask more about it, forgetting that he was actually there to find out about Robin, but Paige turned the conversation for him.

"I've been rambling on and on, probably nervous that the sheriff wants to ask me things, you know, like I do. But I never even found out what it is you wanted to ask," she said.

"Right," he said, sliding the receipt over to Paige. She took it and gave it a quick scan. "Martin says you were here the other night helping Robin Sullivan."

"Sure was," she said. "She's a nice enough lady. I think she's a little lonely. And who better to talk to than someone that won't shut up? What about her?"

Elven looked around, making sure nobody was in earshot. Sterling was so deep in his tablet that Elven didn't think he could hear him. "Unfortunately, she was murdered," he said, trying to keep his voice down.

"Murdered?" Paige said, genuinely shocked. "Holy hell, who did it?"

"That's what I'm here to find out," he said.

She took a step back. "You think I know who did it?" she asked, putting her hand on her chest.

"Not specifically," Elven said. "But she was here with someone." He flipped the receipt over to show the scribblings. "Someone made an offer on some property she owned near the highway."

Paige nodded. "Sure, I remember. She was on the fence about the whole thing, opened up to me about it and everything. People just tend to do that with me, I guess."

"I bet," Elven said, able to see it from their conversation. Elven had to admit he was engaged.

"She was kind of torn up about the idea for some reason," Paige said. "Said she was trying to live on it, something about her ex getting her a trailer to live in. Sounded like a good gig, if you ask me, so I don't know if I'd be in a rush to sell it, either. Doubt it was worth all that much since she said it was so far out of town."

"Did you happen to see who she was with? The guy that wrote this down?" he asked.

"I mean, I didn't see him specifically write it, but he was with her," Paige said. "He seemed nice enough. Polite when ordering, which is more than I can say for a few of the other customers who come here. But I could tell he was pretty intent on getting an answer from Robin. Didn't seem all that happy when she didn't give him the answer he was looking for."

"Can you describe him?" Elven asked, pulling his own little notepad out.

"I could," she said. "Or I could just tell you who he was."

"That would be even better," he said.

"It's that guy running against you," she said. "Zane Rhodes."

CHAPTER THIRTY

It had been a slow day, and that was just fine with Lenny. Finding Robin's body, covered in blood, completely still, had been a traumatic experience. He'd never seen a dead body before. And definitely not someone he had actually known.

He wasn't even sure he knew anyone who had died, other than his grammy, who'd passed of natural causes in her sleep two years back. But that was a lot different. He was certain that he didn't know anyone who had been murdered.

Until now, that is.

The sheriff and deputies had left hours ago, leaving Lenny to himself. He wasn't even sure how he was supposed to operate his shop after finding Robin, but closing up and taking the day off to sit at home with the image of her in the street burned into his mind sounded awful. So he stayed, and he worked. Well, *worked* might not be the right word. He sat behind the counter, dicking around on his phone, first texting everyone he knew about what had happened, but then trying to play whatever game he could find in the free app section to take his mind off things and burn the time away.

It had worked, for the most part, but now it was time to close up and go home.

A couple of the neighbors had popped in during the day to see what all the commotion was, which he filled them in on. They were all gasps and feigned looks of shock. Justin made some tasteless joke that Lenny put up with. He didn't have it in him to argue or tell him he was being a massive jackass.

But now, it felt like there was no life along the small strip of stores. It was incredibly dark out, and the streetlights seemed far dimmer than normal. Across the street, the shops all looked like they weren't even open. And he couldn't see any of them on his side of the road from his own shop window, but he knew he stayed open at least thirty minutes longer than most.

That was only if they hadn't already called it quits for the day early, too. If they had the same amount of customers come in as him, they would have been stupid to stay open. He was kicking himself now for not going home sooner.

Something about going outside in the dark seemed eerie to him. He felt like there were eyes on him right at this moment. Someone lurking in the darkness, waiting for him to step out onto the street.

And then what?

He couldn't ignore the dread he felt inside himself. He was being stupid, though, wasn't he? Robin had been killed just a stone's throw away from his shop, and sure, that was scary. But that was only assuming the killer hadn't been targeting Robin and it was just a random attack. What were the odds that they would come back to the same place to do it again? Lenny was no criminal, nor was he a detective, but to him, it seemed like hitting the same place twice was the best way to get caught.

He sighed, looking down at the bag of trash he held in his hand. Another thing he was kicking himself about. He wished he had taken it out earlier. It's not like he'd accumulated much of it in the last few hours, but he had already let it sit for too long this week. And now it was overflowing, so it had to be done today.

He pushed the door open and stepped out, spinning around to lock the door up with his free hand. He normally would toss the trash, then head back in the store to make sure everything was ready for closing, but he wanted to be outside for as little as possible tonight. His heart was already racing.

He tried to keep his steps going at a seemingly normal pace. It was like he was telling himself that if he ran, all bets were off, and this eerie feeling inside him would come true. That if he picked up speed, there would be a killer right on his heels, chasing him with a knife, ready to plunge it into his own throat like they had with Robin.

He kept his cool, but he could feel his feet working quicker and quicker. But there was always one foot on the ground, so he wasn't technically running.

He looked around at the dark street, deciding to steal a glance behind him. There was nobody there, but that feeling, the one that was screaming that there was someone just outside of his vision, didn't go away.

He turned back around, and just when he did, he heard something slam behind him.

Lenny couldn't help it; he took off running. It was only a few steps until he reached the parking lot, then the dumpster where he would throw in the trash and take off toward his car. He held the keys in his free hand, knowing he could slide right into the car without trouble.

The only thing he hoped for was that the lid on the dumpster was already open. If not, he might just drop it next to the metal bin and worry about it tomorrow. The landlord might fine him if he found out, but at this point, Lenny was ready to tell him to shove it up his ass and close up altogether just to get out of this thing alive.

Part of him thought this whole thing was stupid. But he'd rather be safe than sorry. The primal instincts screaming inside him were there for a reason, weren't they?

He reached the corner and turned it, fighting the urge to take another look the way he came. He felt like it would cost him too much time, and, in turn, his life as well. He saw the dumpster just ahead, the lid propped open.

"Thank God," he said, tossing the bag over the lip. The bag landed inside against the metal bottom with a crash.

Lenny took another step, but there was no traction there, and suddenly, he was staring at the night sky. For the split second that he was in the air, he thought about what the scene looked like. Was it a cartoon image, like he'd slid on a banana peel, and whoopsie-doodle, there he went?

And then the asphalt hit hard against his back, and his muscles locked up. Lenny let out a loud groan and rolled to the side, facing the dumpster.

"Oh my God," he said. That was going to cost him in the morning. That is, if there was to be a morning for him.

He could hear footsteps coming toward him just as fast as he had been running to get away from them. But now he was no longer quick and nimble. He had aged at least twenty years from that fall, and there was no longer any competition in the race.

The footsteps were louder until he saw the legs in his peripheral vision. "Oh, shit, are you okay?" a familiar voice asked.

Lenny blinked a few times and rolled his head, seeing the owner of the tea shop that sat at the end of the block. For owning a tea shop, Matt had never quite looked the part. He had a long beard and wore a leather jacket. If Lenny had been asked what he'd thought of him at first glance, he would have put his money on Matt being a biker.

"Matt?" Lenny asked. "Aw, hell."

"What happened?" Matt asked, coming to Lenny's side.

Lenny shook his head. "I was—I don't know. I just got spooked and slipped. What are you doing here? Didn't you close like an hour ago?"

"I had some inventory to deal with, so I hung around," Matt said. "Figured I would catch up on that, then see if you were around for a beer. I tried waving when you looked back, but I guess you didn't see me."

Lenny chuckled to himself for being so stupid. "I think I need a beer now more than ever," Lenny said.

"You need some help up?" Matt asked, holding his hand out.

Lenny took it, ready to be hoisted to a seated position, but stopped as he looked at the dumpster. There was something just under it that caught his eye. He pulled his hand back and dug his cell phone from his pocket, swiping the flashlight on.

He shined it onto the small piece under the dumpster.

"What the hell is that?"

CHAPTER THIRTY-ONE

ELVEN SAT IN THE PASSENGER SEAT OF TANK'S TRUCK THE NEXT morning. He didn't really know why he wasn't driving on his own, but since everyone was offering up rides, he decided to take them up on it. Driving to Martin's Bar the night before had been about all the driving he'd done since working the library murders and now Robin's murder.

After asking around, and remembering what Zane had told him about putting money back into the community by opening a new location in Dupray, it was pretty easy to find the man. There was some buzz about him announcing where the new coffee shop would be and breaking ground that very day.

So Elven and Tank found themselves at the side of the highway with a bunch of other cars who came to see the show. But Elven wasn't there for that. He was there to make an announcement of his own.

He looked through the windshield at all the people who were gathered. There were a few people he recognized, like Oliver Meeks, who was now backing Zane in the election. Elven wondered what Oliver was going to think when he walked into this little ceremony.

Would he take back his support for Zane? Would he scramble and try to make excuses?

Honestly, Elven didn't really care what he did. He wasn't there to gloat, nor was he there because of the election. He was there because it was where the evidence had led him. There was a crime that had been committed. This was nothing personal for Elven.

But he would be lying if he denied he didn't feel just a little bit of smug satisfaction to prove that Oliver was wrong. That Elven was the best bet for the job. And that the mayor had made one of the worst decisions of his career by not backing Elven.

He turned to Tank, who was looking at the small crowd. "You think this is the right thing, don't you?" Elven asked, wanting to check that it wasn't his own hubris taking over.

Tank looked at Elven and nodded. "You getting cold feet?" Tank asked.

Elven thought for a moment, looking at the crowd. Did he really think Zane killed this woman for the land? He'd looked up the property records himself and found that the parcel Robin owned was right next to Zane's soon-to-be development. He didn't know how expansive it would be, but a residential trailer sitting right next to his brand-new business would throw a wrench into his plans. Plus, Elven was willing to bet that Zane could use the extra space for a parking lot, or some other type of add-on for his business.

"I don't know," Elven admitted. "I feel like it might be a little thin, I guess. On the surface, it makes sense, right? But ultimately, do I think Zane Rhodes is a murderer?" Elven asked, more rhetorically than anything else. And that was the real question, wasn't it?

Tank answered, anyway. "Elven, you're the boss," he said. "So don't take this the wrong way. But as a cop, you gotta follow the leads and evidence. Going with your gut can help sometimes, but you still need to follow up on these things. And with what happened last time, well, maybe it's best to stick to following through with the steps."

Elven nodded along, deciding to agree with Tank instead of arguing that he'd been going off his gut for most of his career. But then again, his gut had never told him that Madds was a plant until it was too late.

"If you're asking me," Tank continued, "going up there and bringing him in right now is exactly what I would do."

Elven looked at his friend and saw the strong determination in his eyes that he had come to always expect. "Alright, then. Let's go do it," Elven said.

CHAPTER THIRTY-TWO

ZANE STOOD IN FRONT OF THE CROWD LIKE IT WAS SOME BIG TO-do. There was some sort of reporter there doing an interview with him. Times must have changed in the couple of months that Elven was in recovery and taking his time to find Madds, because for as far back as he could remember, there was little to no media presence in Dupray.

It had been a big deal back when Max Barraso had shown up to put together his blog about the murders when Elven was a deputy. Well, about as big of a deal as it could be in Dupray. Other than that, they were left with Otis and Charlie running the little paper out of Otis's garage, though that was more of a hobby to cover up why the two men needed to spend so much time together.

And now here Zane was. This was no small paper, nor was it some overrated blog. This wasn't even written media. This was a real reporter, holding a microphone in front of the man while a camera recorded the whole thing. Some major strings had been pulled, favors called in, and probably more money than should have been spent changed hands.

To Elven, it was unnecessary fluff. The guy just wanted to make himself look bigger and better than he actually was. He'd dealt with plenty of men like him in the past, but rarely was there ever anyone who had it in him to actually back it up.

Zane had money, sure. Business sense, yes. Was he charming to the point that he could talk to large groups of people and not get booed? Probably.

But Elven was much better than Zane was at all of it.

Of course, that wasn't the reason he was there. He was there to bring him in for questioning. It might just be an added bonus that all his supporters, along with the reporter and the rest of town, would learn that he was a person of interest.

Word got around fast in Dupray as it was, but to have a news story like this? The chatter would be almost instantaneous.

Elven's boots crunched underneath him as he approached the crowd, Tank close behind him. It was like walking a runway, one that was lined with campaign signs, all for Zane Rhodes. Line after line, pun after pun, all based around Zane's last name.

TAKE THE HIGH RHODE, VOTE ZANE RHODES
ALL RHODES LEAD TO ZANE
VOTE THE RHODE LESS TRAVELED

It was so overwhelmingly stupid that Elven had to admit he was becoming almost giddy to bring Zane in, like a kid waking up on Christmas morning.

And all the while, Elven felt inadequate. Jealous, even. Maybe he should have taken this election a little more seriously. He had no campaign signs, no slogan, no interviews. All he had was his history and reputation, but was that really enough? Especially after all that had happened?

After this, he really needed to take his mother's advice and work on his campaign with her. He never would have thought that working with Victoria was the solution, but then again, a lot of things had changed.

Elven stood in the back, deciding not to barge through the crowd and into Zane's interview. The crowd wasn't large, probably a little smaller than when he had first seen Zane in the parking lot where the farmers' market took place. This wasn't in the center of town, after all. It was on the side of the highway, between town and Jake's Feed and Speed. Not much around here at all, so all the less reason for people to be in the area.

But that didn't seem to bother Zane. He stood confident while speaking to the male reporter holding the microphone in his face.

"And how is this business different from your coffee shops you have already opened in other states and counties?" the reporter asked. Elven didn't recognize him, but he wasn't much for televised news. For all Elven knew, it was some YouTube reporter who had his own little channel. But the truck with the large antennae atop the roof made him think otherwise.

He was too far away to see what channel was on the side of the van, and he wasn't all that interested. But he was curious what Zane's answer would be. This was some ground-breaking ceremony, but what kind of business would thrive out in the middle of nowhere?

"This isn't just another coffee shop," Zane answered. "I mean, don't get me wrong, there will still be our customer-favorite coffee, but this is a multipurpose stop for trucks. And, really, any families on the road."

Elven could tell Zane was presenting well for the interview. He was polished, but not too much. Dupray wouldn't handle someone well who was pristine. A little rough around the edges was what people liked, but not too rough, either. There was a fine line for what the county could tolerate.

"A truck stop?" the reporter asked into his microphone, then shoved it back toward Zane.

"In the simplest of descriptions, yes. Dupray isn't well-known for being a destination, really, anywhere in the county, but we are prime for trucks driving through right along this highway. They go through to Monacan and beyond, and come back here as well. The plan is to create an oasis of sorts for all those drivers to come to, refresh themselves, and in doing so, who knows? Maybe more people, more of a boost to the economy, and then it's all up from here for Dupray."

Elven wasn't sure what to think of that. Zane wasn't wrong about the trucks driving through, but to suggest that they'd ever be here for more than passing through seemed like a stretch. And Elven had seen Dupray in its heyday when the mines were open. Even then, it hadn't been much to look at.

"And look at this! Even the sheriff is here to see the announcement," Zane said, motioning toward Elven.

"The very sheriff whose job you're trying to take?" the reporter asked.

"Aw, you know how it is in politics," Zane said. "I have great respect for Elven Hallie, and clearly, he can see the progress I'm working on here."

Elven grumbled. Zane was already trying to spin his presence there. And he didn't like it.

"Sheriff Hallie, care to comment?" the reporter asked, gesturing for Elven to approach.

Elven did just that, the small group of people letting him through. But instead of addressing the reporter, he spoke to Zane. "Zane, I actually have a few questions for you."

"Sure thing," Zane said with a chuckle. "But if you want to work out a law enforcement discount, you might be getting ahead of yourself." The crowd laughed along with him.

"Actually, it's about something else," Elven said. He was doing his best not to make a big deal out of it. Part of him wanted to make a spectacle, but the other part wanted to keep it professional. It all depended on how Zane responded next.

Zane furrowed his brows, breaking his public mask for a brief moment, but managed to keep a smile. "Well, Elven, can't you see I'm in the middle of an interview here?" he asked, his teeth clenched a little too tight.

"And I'm in the middle of a murder investigation," Elven said.

"Which is exactly why I'm here right now. So, if you don't mind, I need to take you down to the station."

The reporter's eyes lit up as if he'd stumbled upon the story of the year. In Dupray, he actually might have. Considering the lack of media presence in the county, it wouldn't take too much to achieve that. He motioned toward the cameraman to pan over to Elven and Zane.

"Murder investigation?" the reporter asked Elven. "Is Zane Rhodes a suspect in this?"

Elven ignored his questions, not even giving him a cursory glance. He kept his eyes locked on Zane.

Zane tried to laugh it off. "Already trying to pass the torch and get my input on a case? Didn't want to wait until the election?" Sweat had broken out across his forehead. He wiped at it with his sleeve. "How about we just step aside, and I can clear up whatever it is you need help with?" Zane suggested, his volume loud enough for everyone else to hear him.

"I think it's best we do this at the station," Elven said. He glanced across the way to Tank, who was ready if he needed him.

"Am I under arrest?" Zane asked, lowering his voice now.

"Depends on how you wanna do this," Elven said, not caring about his own volume. He pulled his handcuffs out from behind him.

"I'd like to know what this is about," Zane said.

"Alright, then," Elven said, his voice raising in volume. "I need to ask you questions about a murder. Right now, all evidence is pointing to you."

Gasps and whispers followed Elven's statement. He was sure the news would reach the other side of the county in no time.

The reporter no longer cared about asking Zane or Elven any questions. He was just trying to pick up whatever he could on camera and audio.

Zane took a deep breath and looked around. His core group of supporters didn't seem too happy about Elven being there. "This is ridiculous, you know that?" Zane asked. "Trying to ruin my reputation this way isn't a good look."

"And neither is murder," Elven said. "Now, you coming, or do I need to make it more formal?"

CHAPTER THIRTY-THREE

"This is what you have?" Zane demanded, sitting in Elven's office.

There wasn't an interrogation room in the building, and Elven didn't think it necessary to put Zane in a holding cell, though the thought had made him smile. But he was sure Zane's lawyer would have thrown a major fit if he did.

And Zane was no dummy. He made sure to mention his lawyer as soon as he sat down in the back of Tank's truck.

Donald Jenner sat in the chair next to Zane right in front of Elven's desk. He wore a suit, which was too much for Dupray, but then again, Donald wasn't from Dupray. He held himself in a way that told anyone around that he was from the city. Which city? Well, that was up for debate, and Elven didn't even ask. Zane had connections from all his businesses outside of Dupray.

Elven would have expected Donald to be an older gentleman, what with his name being Donald. Plus, that's just what he was used to. Anyone worth their salt in the law field seemed to have a lot of mileage on them. That's what his father had always led him to believe, anyway.

But Donald? He was younger. In fact, he looked even younger than Zane from what Elven could tell. Maybe even closer to his own age.

But he sure scowled like he was older. Because right now, listening to why Elven had brought Zane in for questioning, why he had threatened to arrest him, and why he was making a big fuss to connect Zane to the murder, he was wearing the biggest scowl Elven had ever seen.

Elven sat in his cracked leather chair behind the desk, looking at each of the men. "That's correct," Elven said, finally answering Zane's question. "I want to know why you were offering to buy Robin Sullivan's land and now she's dead."

"Seriously, Elven, I figured I was leaning hard into you being inept with your casework, but now I see I wasn't pushing hard enough on it," Zane said. "This is so damn thin that you're practically writing this out on tracing paper."

"I'm still waiting on an explanation," Elven said.

Zane shook his head and threw his hands in the air. "Yeah, I offered Robin money for her land. She said she was going to think about it—"

"That's not what I was told," Elven said.

"If you'd let me finish."

Elven gestured for Zane to continue.

"Then she said no, she couldn't sell it to me because it wasn't enough to make it last. She wanted to put a house, or trailer, on the land and live there. I guess her rent was becoming a problem," Zane said.

"And you didn't like that," Elven said.

Zane shrugged. "I honestly didn't give a damn. Sure, it would have been more convenient if she sold it to me, but the property wasn't all that big in the first place. It's right next to where I was breaking ground today. I was more doing her a favor by buying it, with the added benefit that we *might* need the extra space. It wasn't a big deal to not have it."

Elven considered that for a moment, letting the silence sit until it felt awkward. He hoped that Zane would add more detail, potentially implicating himself further, but he gave up nothing else.

"Seems odd that you brought in a lawyer when we just had some questions for you," Elven remarked. "Not a good look for someone innocent."

"Now you're just grasping at straws," Donald said, holding a hand up to keep Zane quiet. "And if there is nothing else—"

"It's called being smart," Zane said.

Donald's eyes widened. "Zane, I—"

"It's fine, Donald," Zane said, then directed his gaze toward Elven. "You're the one who is accusing me of murder—"

"I ain't accusing—"

"Insinuating, then," Zane said. "You've got no evidence of it, otherwise you would have brought that up by now. Hell, this is the first I'm hearing that the poor woman's been killed. All you've got is me making an offer for her land. And what now? She's dead, so you think that means I automatically get the land?" Zane scoffed. "I don't know who her next of kin is, and her land will probably go into probate for all I know. You know how much time that takes, and what kind of hoops I'd have to jump through? My business will already be up and running, probably have all the kinks ironed out, and I'll be looking at expanding to a second location by the time the land even became available. I would have just offered her more money if I was that hard-up for it, but news flash, Elven, I'm not!"

Zane's face was now red, and he was taking some deep breaths. Elven wasn't sure what to think, and now something was telling him that he was barking up the wrong tree.

Of course, he wasn't going to admit that now. He was in it this far, so he had to see it through to the end.

"If this is all you have, then we're leaving," Donald announced, standing up. "My client and I are willing to answer whatever questions you have, but right now, I'm not sure you even have any. So unless you're holding him for some reason or charging him with something, perhaps—and I'll tear through whatever thin attempt you make—we'll be on our way."

Elven stood. "I'm not fin—" A knock on the door cut him off. He sighed. "Yeah, what is it?"

The door opened, and Tommy poked his head into the room. He looked nervous. "Sorry to interrupt," he said. "But Elven, I need to talk to you."

CHAPTER THIRTY-FOUR

"What is it?" Elven asked, closing the door behind him. "It better be important since I've got Zane trying to get out of here. I don't have much to hold him, so if you've got something, I'm all ears."

Tommy shuffled around, like he was stalling. Tank stood in the hallway, towering behind him. "Tommy," Tank said, "just tell him."

Elven sighed. This didn't sound like it was going to be in his favor. Especially if Tommy needed Tank to help him break through his hesitation.

"This morning, we got a call," Tommy began. "It was from Lenny. You know, the shop owner who found Robin Sullivan dead in the parking lot?"

"Sure," Elven said, his patience growing thin.

"Well, uh, Lenny found something last night," Tommy said. "He called it in, so I went down there."

Elven could hear Zane and Donald speaking from his office. He wondered what was going on, but Tommy wasn't getting to the point. "What was it?" Elven asked.

Tommy cleared his throat. "I figured I would see you this

morning to tell you. Didn't think it was a big deal to call you right away or anything like that," he said, continuing to ignore the question.

"Alright, so what is it?" Elven asked.

"I mean, I had no clue you were onto Zane for this. Or anything, really," Tommy stammered. "If I had—"

"Tommy," Elven barked, clapping his hands. Tommy stood straight up. "What. Is. It?" He didn't want to jump down the man's throat, but time was something he couldn't waste right now.

Tommy swallowed hard. He held out a piece of paper to him. It had dried blood soaked into it. But there was something else, words scribbled on it. They weren't written in blood, but from a marker.

And the handwriting looked very similar to other handwriting he'd seen. But the problem was, the handwriting it resembled wasn't the scribblings on the receipt with Zane's offer to buy Robin's land. It matched the handwriting they'd found on the papers in the mouths of library victims.

The note read: *Wouldn't know love if it hit her in the face.*

Elven closed his eyes for a moment and took a deep breath. Tommy had been holding onto this the whole time. And instead of telling him, he'd let Elven go to Zane's and pull him in, right in front of all his supporters.

If Zane was guilty of something, it would do Elven a ton of good in the election. But this case, now linked to the library murders—the one that Zane had absolutely no connection to, as far as Elven could tell—meant the opposite.

This was not going to look good at all for Elven.

"Tommy," Elven said slowly.

"Elven, I—"

"Go," Elven said. "Right now. If I open my eyes and you're still here, I—"

"He's gone," Tank cut in.

At least Tommy had the sense to heed his advice.

Elven looked to Tank, who frowned. "This doesn't mean anything," Elven said.

Tank bit his bottom lip and shook his head.

Elven sighed. "It does, doesn't it?" The question was rhetorical. He already knew; he was just throwing it out there, hoping it wouldn't be the case. But there was no denying it at this point. Even if Zane was guilty of something, they had nothing to connect him. So there was nothing to keep him at the station for.

Elven spun around and entered his office. He tried not to seem defeated, bolstering himself with confidence that he didn't have any right to have. Fake it till you make it, or something like that. He wasn't going to let Zane see through the cracks.

"You're free to go," Elven said. He left the door open and walked past the two men, still sitting where he'd left them. Elven made sure not to turn and face them right away, hoping they would just leave. But of course, Zane wouldn't make it that easy for him.

Zane and Donald stood up. Donald seemed ready to get out of there, but Zane needed to have the last word.

"That's it?" he demanded. "All this hubbub, and for what? Just to make me look bad in front of the cameras?"

Elven shook his head and turned to face the man. "I wasn't even aware there would be cameras there in the first place. You were the one who brought me into it when I was waiting for you to finish up."

"Sure," Zane scoffed. "Try to stick to the high road when you went dragging me through the mud just now."

"I'm sorry for any inconvenience," Elven said. "You answered all the questions we had. Thank you for that. It's an ongoing investigation, so if we have any more questions, we'll be in contact."

Zane scoffed again and walked toward Elven, past the desk. "Zane," Donald said, his tone warning his client not to cross the line.

Zane held up a hand to reassure Donald. He did, however, get right into Elven's personal space.

"This isn't over, you know that," Zane said. "You owe me what I'm due."

"And what's that?" Elven found himself asking. He kept his chin up, knowing he was in the wrong but not wanting to tip his hand to Zane.

"A public debate," Zane said. "And an apology."

Elven snickered. "You can see yourself out."

CHAPTER THIRTY-FIVE

ELVEN SAT AT HIS DESK WITH THE NEW PIECE OF PAPER THAT Tommy had given him. It was spotted with blood, but it was still clear enough to see the writing on it. Elven had put it in a plastic sandwich bag so as not to damage it any more than it already was. He considered sending it in for testing, but he knew the blood on it would return as Robin Sullivan's.

He turned his desk light on and pulled out the rest of the papers he'd collected from Phil Driscoll. It was clear that Robin's murder was linked to the library massacre. But he still had absolutely nothing to go on, other than these little papers. And they didn't exactly spell out who the killer was.

Each of them showed a different sentence or word, all negative in tone. At this point, it seemed personal to take the time to write these words on a piece of paper and shove them in the mouths of the victims after they were killed. Other than Robin, of course. Either there'd been no time for the killer to put it in her mouth, or she still wasn't completely dead when the killer inserted the paper, and it fell out.

He didn't think this was some serial killer thing. He wasn't equipped for something like that. He was no profiler. But in his little experience dealing with one in the past, they targeted individuals for specific reasons. They didn't generally go after large groups in one go.

No, this was definitely personal.

He sighed and leaned back when a figure stepped into the open doorway and knocked against the wall. Elven looked up to see Tommy standing there.

"Hey, boss. Is it okay to come in?" Tommy asked.

Elven frowned, then gave a single nod and waved him in. "Got more evidence you didn't share with me?" Elven asked. He was still a little irritated at Tommy for not sharing that note with him earlier. Actually, he was more than a little irritated.

"I'm sorry I didn't tell you right away," Tommy said. "I just didn't think—"

"And that's the problem," Elven interjected, standing up. "Had you thought about it, then you would have realized that keeping it to yourself was an asinine idea."

"I know," Tommy admitted, sounding even more sheepish than before. "I just didn't figure you'd be on to someone right away. If I was told that you were going to pull someone in for questioning right away, I would have. But I didn't see you this morning."

"Oh, so now I'm supposed to tell you where I'll be every moment of the day?" Elven asked.

Tommy bit his lip, considering what to say next. It was clear that he was battling something internally, but one side won out. And Elven was about to find out it wasn't the good side, either.

"Before, you never had to," Tommy said. "We could always find you holed up in that shitty motel room doing God knows what. The only thing I know you were doing was not helping us as we tried to pick up the slack of doing *your* job."

Elven glared at Tommy. Right or wrong, he wasn't going to have some deputy tell him this. He stepped into Tommy's face.

"I have been breaking my back for this county long before you were ever thinking about being a deputy," Elven growled. "You don't know a thing about what I've done or will do for it. I have bigger things to worry about than helping you catch some shoplifter. I figured you could pick up the smaller things so I wouldn't have to put my hands on every darn case that comes in. But I guess I was wrong," Elven said, finally taking a breath. "I don't know how they did things in Monacan—actually, that's not true. I know *exactly* how they do things in Monacan. And maybe I was wrong about bringing you into my county. Maybe you are much better suited for that place than here."

Tommy clenched his teeth as he stared at Elven. Part of him wanted Tommy to say something so he'd have a reason to go off on him again. But instead, Tommy took a deep breath, looking straight into Elven's eyes, and turned around, leaving Elven alone in the office without another word.

CHAPTER THIRTY-SIX

JOHNNY SAT IN THE SECOND ROW AT DUPRAY METHODIST Church, where Pastor Luke Magner was finishing up his sermon. It was night, and while he normally made it to Sunday morning service, he wasn't always able to make it to the midweek evening service. Since waking up from his coma, and no longer being a deputy who had to work all sorts of odd hours, he was trying to make it more of a priority to spend more time in church.

Bernadette, or Button, as he called her, was in full support of that. She hadn't been very involved when they'd first gotten together, but once they became serious, it felt like the right thing for them to do. He could tell they were at the cusp of settling in, maybe even putting down some roots. Did that include having kids? Well, he didn't want to jump the gun on that one. He needed to propose to the woman first.

But he was happy. And with being a part of the community and involved in church, like most of the county was, he felt like he was on the right path. Even though he was no longer a deputy, Elven finding him a place on the team meant a lot. He felt more at peace with his life these days.

Pastor Magner usually ended with a prayer and then released everyone. But this time, he asked the congregation if they had the time to stay seated after the prayer.

"I know this is a little different," Pastor Magner began, holding his hands up as if to say *don't shoot the messenger*. "And I clearly want nothing to do with politics in church, but since this is also where our community gathers, and the election and other things going on these days affect this community, I thought it best to allow the announcement."

Pastor Magner stepped aside, making way for someone else to stand. It was Zane Rhodes. Johnny hadn't had many words with the man—or really, *any* words—but most people in Dupray knew who he was. He might be just as recognizable as Elven Hallie himself. But where Elven came from money, Zane was a self-made man, acquiring money. That was something that a lot of people looked up to, even dreamt of, in Dupray. And Johnny was one of them.

It didn't mean that he was voting for the man, of course. Elven was his friend, and a darn good sheriff.

"Thank you, Pastor Magner," Zane began, his words firm but kind. He spun to face everyone. He wore a button-up shirt tucked into pleated slacks. He wasn't wearing a tie, instead opting for an open collar, but he still came off as put together. Respectful in the house of the Lord.

Johnny wasn't big on reading between the lines, but even he could tell this was calculated on Zane's part. Maybe working with Elven for so long was finally rubbing off on him. He smiled at the thought.

"I won't take up much of your time. I know that we're all here to gather and worship, so I don't want to take anything away from that now," Zane said, his arms waving along as he spoke. It made him look far grander than he actually was. He began to pace a few steps, almost as if he were an animated preacher in front of his congregation. "But being a member of this congregation, I needed to address something that happened the other day. As I'm sure you are all aware,

Sheriff Hallie brought me in for questioning about a murder investigation."

A bunch of rumbling and whispers occurred. Zane paused for them to continue for a moment before waving his arms again. "Now, I know how that looks," he said. "I'm sure that Sheriff Hallie knows how that looks, too. But I'm not here to talk about why he chose to do it so publicly, either. The fact is, I made an offer to buy some property from the victim at one point, so he had to follow up on every lead, which he did, and clearly there was nothing to it. Hence, why I stand here before you today.

"To make a long story short, it's all out of the way, luckily. And Sheriff Hallie has graciously accepted my challenge to debate at the town hall Friday night. So you can head down there yourselves to see us discuss the matters of the county there."

Zane scanned the congregation, his brows scrunched as he did. He even put his hand over his eyes for added emphasis. "I was hoping that Elven would be here to tell you himself, but it appears he isn't here. Come to think of it, I've noticed Elven hasn't attended much, or at all, ever since I started coming here. Does he?"

Zane waited for people to whisper amongst themselves again. Johnny could see what Zane was trying to do. In the past, he would just have accepted the man's words at face value, but now his manipulation tactics were obvious to him.

Johnny sighed, remembering when he was happy being ignorant of those things.

"Well, anyway, no matter. I'm glad to be a part of this community and congregation. Johnny here can attest that Elven's all signed on for the debate," Zane said, motioning to where Johnny sat. Everyone looked at him in the second row.

"Oh, uh," Johnny muttered, looking around. He could feel the heat in his cheeks.

"Right, Johnny?" Zane asked.

"Y-yeah," Johnny said. "Must be so, if you say it is."

"Thanks, Johnny," Zane said. "I can't wait to see everyone on

Friday who wants to come down. And with that, I'm all finished here. Thanks for giving me the time."

Zane went back to his seat, and Pastor Magner stepped into the front. He started talking, probably dismissing them or maybe leading them in another final prayer. But Johnny didn't hear any of it. He was too busy thinking about how he'd probably just messed something up real bad for Elven.

CHAPTER THIRTY-SEVEN

Martin's Bar wasn't too busy yet. But then again, church hadn't gotten out yet, from what Elven could tell. That usually happened around nine p.m. He hadn't been to a service in ages. Not that he had any issues with it; it just wasn't for him.

He had grown up attending Dupray Methodist from time to time, and he had great respect for Pastor Magner and what he did. And he was sure that the various other churches in the county were just as effective at connecting people with what they were searching for. There was always a place for God, or a higher power, in his life. He'd just never found it while sitting in a pew.

And either way, he didn't want to hear any of it right now.

One rough day would be one thing, but life had been trying ever since Johnny pulled him out of his motel room and he started working the library case. If he were being really honest, it had been rough before that. He'd been hiding away from all of it, claiming he was trying to find Madds.

But now he was back at it. Trying to step back into the role that he had done for so long, that he had been good at. Now it felt like he was completely in over his head, spinning his wheels on this case and making absolutely no sense of it.

He had each and every small piece of paper, individually sealed in plastic baggies, splayed out on the bar in front of him. After he had tried doing this at his desk when Tommy came in and interrupted, he figured getting out of the station might help. The air in his office had felt stuffy after he went off on Tommy, most likely burning that bridge. It had lingered in the room, leaving Elven unable to concentrate.

He had been too harsh on the kid, but it was done. He wondered how long it would be until Tommy turned in his notice. Was he going to try to keep the job until finding a new one? Or would he just never show back up at the station?

Elven sighed, trying to forget about it. He needed to focus and figure out what all of these notes meant. But all he could think about was how unfair he had been to Tommy.

He frowned, remembering back to when he was in Tommy's position. When he was the screw-up and Lester was the sheriff in charge. But instead of swinging the hammer down on him, Lester had given him some sage advice. Elven knew he'd been given far more chances than he deserved from that man. And it wasn't only accidents or slips of the mind that Elven had been scolded on. It was his entire attitude.

Tommy didn't even have that ego. He'd messed up, but he wasn't arrogant about it. Elven had been the opposite.

Elven knew he'd really messed it up today.

"Whoa there. Just making yourself at home now, are you?" Paige asked as she entered behind the bar from the back room, passing right where Elven had the notes all laid out.

Elven looked up from the bar top and set eyes on her. She was a little less frazzled today than the previous day when he first met her. She had on a tank top tucked into jeans. It seemed a little inappropriate for the weather, but then he saw the sweat on her face. She wiped it away with a towel before tossing it under the counter.

"Martin running you ragged?" Elven asked. It was meant more as a joke, but his tone came out far more serious than intended.

She lifted an eyebrow. "You gonna arrest him if I say yes?"

Elven frowned. Usually, he'd have some comeback or quip. Maybe it landed, maybe it didn't, but he would flash a grin and it wouldn't matter. But right now, he was running on empty. Between having no leads on the murders, how he'd treated Tommy, and Zane's interrogation blowing up in his face, he wasn't sure he had any right to try.

"Nothing like that," Elven managed.

"Oh, man," Paige said, pouring a glass of scotch and placing it down in front of Elven.

"I didn't even order—"

"Don't sweat it," she said. "It's on me if you can't afford it."

He furrowed his brow, never having been told that before. "I, um, you do know who I—"

She rolled her eyes and laughed. "Yes, I'm well-aware of the prodigal son Elven Hallie."

"I don't think that means what you think—"

"God, come on," she said, putting her hands on her hips. "You really must be in some gnarly funk right now. I know my humor isn't for everyone, but to land this flat is really depressing."

Elven pursed his lips. "Sorry," he said, knowing he was not great company right now. He looked down the way of the bar at the rest of the stools. Other than two men at the other end, they were all empty. "No Sterling today?"

She smiled, and he could see her picturing her son at that very moment. It was nice to see someone light up at the mention of someone they loved. "Fortunately, my neighbor was able to watch him tonight," she said. "Now he doesn't have to be bored around a bunch of drunk people."

"I'm sure it was the highlight of his week," Elven said. "Going to work with my dad was like that. Got to be proud of him, and he got to show me off. The attention was always nice."

"Oh, Sterling definitely liked the attention," she said. "But I bet your dad wasn't cleaning up puke off the floor at his job."

"You got me there," Elven said.

She leaned against the bar, still smiling as she looked off in the distance, her thoughts buried somewhere in her mind. "I just want better things for him than I had," she said. "He's so intelligent that he amazes me. And he's not weird, either. I mean, he's not awkward—he's weird in a quirky, funny way. When his father passed, I told Sterling I would do anything to keep him from having to struggle to get by. It hasn't been easy, especially since his father's income isn't here anymore."

"What did your husband do?" Elven asked.

"He used to deliver stuff in the hills. Picked up some odd jobs here and there," she said. "Nothing fancy, but they didn't like coming to the city."

Elven snickered. "The city," he said. Dupray was technically a city, but he would never refer to it as *the city*.

"Don't get me started," she said, rolling her eyes. "There's a lot of good people up there, but dammit if they aren't stubborn about staying put and thinking anything outside of their bubble can be trusted."

Elven didn't make it out to the hills too often, mostly because of what Paige had just said. The people there liked to keep to themselves, and in many ways, they governed themselves as well. Anytime he had to make a visit out there, he had to be cautious in what he said and how he approached them. They were more than willing to stand their ground—and they generally had the firepower to do it.

"What ended up happening?" Elven asked.

"What's that?" Paige asked.

"With the deliveries, I mean," he said. "Considering their trust issues, I'm sure you could have taken over."

"Oh, right," she said, shifting her weight. "I have here and there, but it's not like it was a lot of money. Not like they have a ton of cash, so an upcharge on top of the cost of goods is hard to swing. Slim margins."

Elven nodded.

"So what is this, anyway?" She pointed to the notes on the bar top. He was enjoying their conversation so much, he had almost forgotten about them.

"Part of a case I'm trying to figure out," he said.

She looked at the notes more closely. It was all evidence in the case, and he probably shouldn't have been sharing it with anyone else, but at this point, he didn't think Paige seeing it would hurt anything. "Part of the library thing?" she asked.

He nodded.

"It's terrible what happened. Back when I had some free time before Harold died, I went there thinking I could be part of the book club or whatever, you know? Like I'd be a part of the community, make some friends, read some books."

"But then you had to stop because he passed," Elven said.

"Oh, hell, no," Paige said. "I mean, yeah, if I kept going, I would have. But I stopped going after that first time I tried."

"How come?"

"Those people were miserable," she said. "Don't get me wrong, they didn't deserve what happened, but I never heard so many criticisms of a book. And half of the people said they liked the book we read, and then they still shit on parts of it. Not sure what happened to people just enjoying something for what it is without needing it to be the next greatest thing."

The door swung open. Elven looked over his shoulder, expecting the after-church crowd to filter into the bar. It was Johnny.

"Elven, there you are," he said. "I was rushing around, trying to figure out where you'd be."

Elven pulled his phone out of his pocket and looked down. There were no missed calls. He held it up and waved it at Johnny. "Not gonna call me?"

Johnny stared at it for a moment and sighed. "I didn't even think —whatever, you're here."

"What's up?" Elven asked.

"I think I might have messed up," he said.

CHAPTER THIRTY-EIGHT

THE NEXT MORNING, TANK WAS EXHAUSTED. HE WAS BURNING the candle at both ends these days. Having Tommy was a big help, but they were still short-handed by one deputy. Though having Elven back was great, Tank could feel that he wasn't quite fully back yet. Sure, he came into the station, worked the crime scene. But something just felt missing with him.

The sheriff was unsure of himself, which was saying a lot, considering Elven was the most confident person Tank knew. It could even be annoying at times. He went in full-force, and sometimes was completely wrong. But he was never one to second-guess himself when he made a decision.

Until now.

Tank was willing to pick up the slack for now, but he hoped that Elven would find his footing sooner rather than later. The shoplifter was one thing, but the library massacre was a completely different ballgame.

He was longing for a morning where he could just sleep in—as if that would ever happen with all the kids running around at home.

But for now, he was still pushing into the station as early as he could manage.

He sipped on his coffee as he sat at his desk. He was in the office, but he admittedly was hiding out, not wanting to jump right into the day unless something big came along. Maybe once the coffee kicked in, he could get his first wind.

He heard the phone ring from the lobby. Meredith answered it. Tank closed his eyes, hoping it was just a small complaint. Maybe it was someone wanting to know about the debate that Johnny had practically thrown Elven into. He just hoped it wasn't something like another murder. He would handle it, of course, but he sure didn't want to.

Meredith rapped on his office door, then turned the handle, not waiting for him to give her the go-ahead.

"Come right in," Tank said sarcastically, opening his eyes. "What's up?"

"I got a call about a break-in," Meredith said, holding a paper in her hand. She'd written down an address. "Residential."

Tank took a deep breath. That wasn't so bad. "Alright, I'll take it," he said, standing up.

"I figured I could give it to Tommy," Meredith said. "But he's not in. Neither is Elven."

"Elven is prepping for the debate," Tank said.

"Or just sleeping in," Meredith said, her tone indignant.

Tank held his hands up. It was out of his control. "And Tommy, well, I don't know. I think he might be regretting his decision."

"What decision?" Meredith asked.

"The one he made when he took this job," Tank said. He walked around the desk and snatched the paper from her hand. "Or maybe he's just having a bad day."

"What happened?" Meredith asked. "Did I miss something?"

Tank was already pushing past her and heading for the front door. "Nothing to worry about," he said, not bothering to stop. He knew Meredith would be fuming that he didn't fill her in. She loved office gossip, but he wasn't in the mood to share right now.

TANK STOOD in the living room of Robert Paul, the man who had called into the station about a break-in. He was younger, maybe in his mid-twenties, but something about him seemed peculiar. He was super-friendly, matching the energy of a golden retriever, but either he had the worst memory or he smoked far too much marijuana.

The skunky smell that greeted Tank when he walked into Robert's house tipped him off. Tank was actually impressed, either by the man's ignorance or stupidity.

But he wasn't there to make an arrest for possession. He was there to hear about this break-in.

The house was unusual. It didn't seem to fit the style of a twenty-something male. There were old, dusty curtains that seemed border-line grandma-ish. The couch was patterned and had accent pillows. And when Tank walked by the bathroom, he spotted a toilet seat cover.

It was clear that Robert hadn't decorated this place.

Robert had let him inside, telling him how he noticed someone had broken in this morning, but hadn't elaborated. Instead, he went off on a tangent about how he spent an hour last night trying to find a ride home, but instead, crashed at a friend's house.

"So, how do you know someone broke in?" Tank asked.

"Oh, easy," Robert said with a big, wide-eyed grin. "Because things aren't where I put them."

Tank pulled out a notepad from his back pocket. A small pencil was wedged in the spiral top until he fished it out, poised to take notes. "Alright, then, what all was stolen?" Tank asked.

"Stolen?" Robert asked. "No, no, nothing was stolen. They just weren't where I put them."

Tank furrowed his brow. "So you couldn't find them, and then did?" he asked, bewildered.

Robert shook his head. "It'll be easier if I just show you," he said, running to a different room while waving for Tank to follow him. "Come on, it'll make sense once you see."

Tank let out a long sigh. So much for the idea that this would be an easy call to respond to. He was still tired and didn't want to spend his entire day dealing with this. Maybe it would be easier if he just arrested Robert for possession.

He cracked a smile at the idea, knowing Robert would probably just claim that it was for medical use or something like that. Soon enough, it would be entirely legal if it weren't already. Things were changing so fast that Tank couldn't remember if or when the law had changed.

He supposed he should just follow the guy into the next room and see this supposed evidence.

"See right here," Robert said, pointing to the box fan next to the window when Tank walked in. It was Robert's bedroom. The unmade bed with the empty beer cans atop the nightstand tipped him off.

"It's a fan," Tank said.

"Yes, but I put it here," Robert said, pushing it flush against the wall. He had moved it three inches at most. "But it was here." Robert pulled it back to where it created an acute angle from the wall.

"That's it?" Tank asked.

"Of course not," Robert said as if Tank were the idiot in this situation. "This, too." He walked to the other side of the room and showed him drawers that were fully closed. "I never close these things."

"So you called because things were moved out of place?" Tank asked. "Nothing is missing? Nothing is broken? Just kind of moved a little?"

Robert clapped, a big grin spreading across his face. Tank thought he was about to jump up and down like he'd won *The Price Is Right*. "Yes, now you get it! Someone was in here."

Tank looked around, trying to figure out what to say. The place was messy, but so oddly decorated. "You married?" Tank asked, though it felt like a stretch to even ask. "Maybe your wife, girlfriend, or even a roommate came—"

"No, I live alone," he said.

"Of course you do," Tank said. "And all this is yours?" He motioned toward all the random furniture and decorations that didn't fit with Robert's demographic.

"Well, not like *mine* mine," he said. "This is my aunt's place. She's letting me stay here since she got a new place. She let me keep a lot of this stuff, probably to move it to her place when she wanted it, but it's here for now."

"That explains a lot," Tank muttered. "Did you remember to lock up? Was there any sign of a break-in that you found, other than things being out of place, I mean? Broken window, forced-in door? That kind of thing."

Robert slowly shook his head. "Not that I could tell."

Tank rubbed his hand over his face. "And what about your aunt?"

"What about her?"

Tank lifted an eyebrow, really hating to have to ask the obvious, but he guessed he needed to. "Does she still have a key?"

Robert opened his mouth, then paused, lifting a finger. "She does," he said, almost like it was a revelation, but Tank could tell he wasn't quite there yet.

"Could she have let herself in, possibly to look for something she wanted to come back for?" Tank asked.

Robert was deep in thought, his eyes darting back and forth like he was processing a lot of information all at once. "I mean, shit," Robert said. "That would make sense, wouldn't it?"

"If there was nothing broken or missing, then that's probably it," Tank said. "I would double-check all your locks to be safe, but call your aunt. I'm sure she'll tell you it was her."

Tank would write up a report just to put something on file and follow protocol, but the case was closed as far as he was concerned.

He just wished he could say that about the murders. And until Elven finished up his debate tonight, he knew it would have to be put on hold.

CHAPTER THIRTY-NINE

It had been a while since Elven had to address the entire community in a town hall setting. In fact, the last time he could remember was when Oliver Meeks had set one up without Elven's approval, committing him to answer questions about Sophia Hawkins, who was found dead in the river. He had felt so confident before standing up in front of them. He remembered telling Madds that this was what he was good at.

Only to have it all blow up in his face. And Hollis Starcher, of all people, had settled down the crowd.

That felt like an eternity ago at this point. And while so many things had changed since then, somehow he had found himself in front of everyone once again. Not having agreed to it himself, but rather, been forced to show up.

Of course, he didn't *have* to show up. But how would that look if Zane Rhodes publicly called him out to a debate and he didn't appear? Elven supposed he deserved it for pulling Zane in for questioning in front of a crowd. He probably could have handled that one a little better.

But what's done was done, and now here he was.

Elven actually felt good about it. He'd spoken to his mother briefly, who had come up with a number of talking points. She had even put together a few phrases to turn attention away from Elven's shortcomings and back to his successes. Not to mention, there were a handful of things Elven could bring up about Zane not having lived in Dupray for long. Zane might not be a complete outsider since he originally hailed from there, but it was close enough. And Dupray wasn't big on outsiders.

Right up until Elven had to go up on stage, Johnny was apologetic. Over the top about it, too. Elven had told him it was fine, even if he still felt irritated about it. He knew Johnny meant well with everything he did, and if there was anyone to place blame on, it was Zane Rhodes. The man had read Johnny like a book, which wasn't necessarily difficult to do, but Elven hadn't been aware that Zane knew him at all.

Elven didn't like that. He knew someone else who could read people like that. Someone who was no longer in town because Elven had managed to put him behind bars.

The hall was packed full of people. Apparently, a sheriff debate was the biggest form of entertainment in town right now, though the room itself was small. He figured the town was pretty split between the town hall and Martin's Bar right now, considering it was Friday night. But if they were expecting a show, Elven would surely give them one.

Zane Rhodes approached Elven, wearing a suit. Elven had debated wearing his uniform or dressing up, but his mother convinced him to match Zane in attire. Something about being on the same playing field or whatever. Fashion wasn't Elven's forte, so he'd listened and put on a suit. It had been a while since he'd worn it, but the last tailoring still fit him well. He still worked out to stay in shape, making sure all that time in the hospital and in recovery hadn't ended up on his waistline.

"Elven, looking sharp," Zane said, holding his hand out.

Elven couldn't tell if he was mocking him, but he seemed genuine enough, so he decided to take it at face value. "Thank you," Elven said, taking his hand in a firm shake. "Can say the same thing about you." Elven stared up at Zane, trying to get a read on him. He hated that he was taller than him, that was for sure.

"Wasn't sure if you were gonna show," Zane said.

Elven grinned. He didn't even want to address it with a remark. They both knew why Elven had shown up.

"Gentleman, if you're ready," Willard Marks said from the front row. He was a small man with beady eyes and thick-rimmed glasses. He was acting as moderator tonight, which seemed like more of a formality than anything else. Elven figured the two of them could moderate themselves. "We'll start with Sheriff Hallie."

There were two podiums on stage. Elven took the one to the right, while Zane stood behind the one on the left.

"Thank you, Willard," Elven said, staring out at the people. He smiled, trying to muster up all the charm he had in him. Lately, it felt like he was lacking in that, but he was hoping it was like riding a bicycle. "I'm glad I could be here to discuss things with Zane today. The job has me very busy right now, but I felt this was important. Zane being here is a bit of a shock to me. His campaign came out of nowhere, mostly considering that although he might come from Dupray, he hasn't resided here for very long. Not even a year, as far as I can tell. Not sure how well an outsider would do stepping into a role that needs a longtime local in its place."

Zane grinned, but it wasn't the type that was happy. He looked like a shark when Elven looked over to him. He knew he'd hit him where he was most vulnerable, but he expected him to spin some story to make it look not as bad as Elven was making it sound.

"Thanks for that introduction, if that's what you can call it," Zane said. "I'm glad that Sheriff Hallie could make it. Like he said, he's a busy man. Cases have been piling up these days, and not a single one solved."

"Cases take time to solve," Elven countered. "A lot of evidence, a lot of leads, people to interview."

"Fair enough," Zane said. "Like when you pulled me in for questioning during my interview in front of all those people at my groundbreaking ceremony?"

Elven nodded. He knew this would come up at some point, he just hadn't expected it to be right away. "Yes, just like that," Elven said. "An inconvenience, sure, but time was of the essence. Every second wasted puts us further behind. I'm glad that you were able to clear some things up for us."

"But it wasn't really me clearing anything up, was it?" Zane asked, but he wasn't waiting for a response. Elven started to speak, but was quickly cut off. "I answered your questions, but it was some new evidence that made you let me go. Which, I might add, means that I was being held rather than helping to clear up some things."

Elven wasn't sure how Zane had heard about the evidence coming in, but then again, he had connections. And that lawyer of his certainly seemed crafty enough. "I don't know how any of this is relevant to what we're doing here right now," Elven said, trying to change the subject.

"Oh, it's very relevant," Zane said. He came out from behind his podium and started to walk the stage. The joke of a moderator didn't seem bothered. Instead, Willard was smiling as he looked up at Zane. To Elven, he had made his vote already.

"You say that I haven't been here long, and that's true," Zane said. "Sure, I grew up here, but I left for business. Well, I'm back now, and in the short amount of time I have been here, I've seen enough to tell me all I need to know."

"I don't—"

"I said earlier you pulled me in for questioning but threatened to arrest me," Zane said. "To me, I would think you had something big enough to charge me with, but all you had on me was that I knew the victim because of my business dealings. Isn't that right?"

"I—"

"To me, either that's an abuse of power because I'm running against you, or you just take the smallest connection and blow it out of proportion. And if that's the case, then you fall for every red herring that comes across your desk, like you're a detective in a book authored by a hack writer who capitalizes on clichés," Zane said, chuckling at his own joke.

To Elven's dismay, the crowd laughed along with him. "From an outsider's perspective, I can see how you would have jumped to that conclusion," Elven said. "But—"

"Speaking of *outsider*," Zane said. "Let's talk about that."

Elven glared at Willard, who did nothing other than look transfixed by Zane. "Sure, you want to tell us how you're trying to buy your way into this position, saying you're boosting our economy, but really, you're just trying to make a buck off of the good people of Dupray," Elven said.

Zane frowned. "I've already committed to donating to multiple charities and foundations in the community. I'm even setting one up for kids from broken families."

Elven bit his tongue. How had he not heard of that? He probably should have done more research on Zane before this debate, but then again, it had been sprung on him last-minute.

"I'm talking about how connected to the community I've been through the church," Zane said. "I am a good Christian, a family man. My wife Charlotte is here with me today along with our son. I've met so many of you while worshipping and serving our community. It's been a pleasure. I just want to serve as your sheriff, and be a tool for the Lord to use."

This time, the crowd clapped and cheered. A couple of "amens" were thrown out.

Elven sighed. This was one thing he knew would be an uphill battle. The people of Dupray—and the people of West Virginia, for that matter—loved church. Elven wasn't one to attend often.

"And in that time," Zane continued, "I've learned about all of the happenings in Dupray. Like when you thought it best to go in to catch a murderer with no backup and a broken foot, which ended up with three people killed that didn't need to be. Or how you let one of the biggest criminals in the state infiltrate your team."

"Allegedly," Elven said, closing his eyes right after saying it. What was he doing now, sticking up for Hollis? It was a low blow, but wow. He felt like an animal backed into a corner right now.

"You arrested him," Zane said. "Now you wanna play the innocent until proven guilty card?"

"I—I—" Elven blinked as he stared into the crowd. The faces all blended together. He was lucky he didn't go straight into a panic attack—he was finally willing to call it what it was.

Instead, he swallowed, trying to come up with an answer that didn't sound as desperate as he felt.

And this was just the beginning of the debate.

CHAPTER FORTY

ELVEN SAT BEHIND THE SMALL AUDITORIUM WHERE THE TOWN hall debate had been held. He felt like he had gone ten rounds in the ring without any training. In a way, that wasn't too far from the truth. Zane had prepped so many points in his favor, and even more points against Elven. Elven had absolutely nothing on Zane.

And maybe that was part of the problem.

But the thing was, a lot of what Zane said made sense. Maybe not everything he said about Elven, but what he planned to do for the community. If he were in the crowd with no skin in the game, Elven was pretty sure he'd be voting for Zane.

He hated himself for thinking that.

The night air was cold, and he had taken his jacket off. Sweat rings were under his arms, and not because it was hot inside. He'd never been so nervous and on tilt as he was tonight. And that was saying something, considering the person he once shared a bed with had turned out to be a mole for the enemy.

When the debate ended, Zane went down to speak to people in the crowd who had questions. Elven overheard some of them telling Zane they just wanted to say that they were big fans, that they couldn't wait for the truck stop to open. And that before, they weren't so sure about who to vote for, but they had now changed their mind on things.

Elven was sure that even though he had lived in Dupray his whole life, being a Hallie was still a hard sell for some people. But maybe it was more than that.

Was he really doing the best job he was capable of as sheriff?

Elven sighed, wishing he had a drink. But there was no way he was going to Martin's right now. He was certain that people would see him there, maybe rub in how awful the debate had gone. Maybe some would even offer their condolences to his career at this point. The last thing he wanted to deal with was someone angry with him. Or worse, someone who pitied him.

He heard footsteps just behind him, creaking along the wooden deck. Elven didn't bother to look as he sat on the first step at the top. But then a mason jar of moonshine was held over his shoulder, just next to his face.

"You look like you could use it," a male voice said.

Elven grabbed the jar with a smile. It was like he'd manifested the drink. Now if only he could have manifested winning the debate instead. But he wasn't going to look a gift horse in the mouth.

Then he turned and saw who it was. Lyman Starcher. Elven sighed.

"You here to rub it in?" Elven asked, unscrewing the top and taking a swig from the rim of the jar. It was rough but delicious at the same time. The Starchers were known to make the best moonshine in the area. Probably the *only* moonshine in the area due to Hollis's ability to chase off the competition.

Elven held the jar to Lyman, who took it and did the same.

Lyman popped a squat next to him on the step. "Nah, I saw what happened. I ain't gonna kick a man while he's down." Humor laced his words, but Elven knew it was the truth.

"Thank God for small favors," Elven said. "Not that I'd know anything about that since I don't attend church so often." It was hard to hold back the sarcasm at this point. "So what're you here for?"

Lyman passed the jar back to Elven, who took another swig and passed it back again. "Just wanted to make sure my friend is okay," he said.

"You still think of me as that? A friend, I mean? 'Cause if so, I've been a pretty crummy one," Elven said.

"Well, I wouldn't put it that way," Lyman said.

"That's nice of you," Elven said.

"I'd say you've been a *shitty* friend," Lyman said with a sly smile.

Elven let out a boisterous laugh. "I guess I deserve that."

"So, really, you okay?"

"I just stood up there in front of everyone and had my backside handed to me. It was so bad that I started defending your father because he isn't technically convicted yet. The man I was determined to put behind bars for so long." Elven grabbed the hooch from Lyman, taking a big pull from the glass. "I don't even know what that makes me."

"Human," Lyman said.

Elven looked over at the man he had once called his best friend. He'd been so busy being angry about Madds and Hollis that he had forgotten all about Lyman. He was stubborn, and that had cost him a lot.

"I'm sorry I've been such a terrible friend to you," Elven finally said. "I've been defensive. Let down. I don't even know what anymore." It was hard to admit, and he couldn't sum everything up in a few words, but at this point, he had nothing else to lose.

Lyman shrugged. "You have every right to be. It's not like I was innocent in all of this." He turned to Elven. "And that's not me admitting that I knew of any crimes happening that my father was involved in or that—"

"Oh, shut it," Elven said, shoving the moonshine into Lyman's chest. "I know the score, and you're right. I can't hold his sins against you. I'd lose too many friends if I did that. And if they did that to me."

"Well, either way, I'm sorry how it came about."

Elven nodded. He was happy to be talking to Lyman again. It was one thing to be angry, but another to cut the man out completely. He didn't deserve that. "You been to see your dad?" Elven asked.

"Yeah, I make it out there when I can," Lyman said. "The business isn't going so well—the cars, I mean. Corbin was always the better mechanic, Wade the businessman. I guess I got lost in all of that, never really picking up part of the trade."

"Maybe that's for the best," Elven said. "They might have picked up those things from Hollis, but they also picked up the criminal aspect. You and your sister—" Elven paused, thinking about Penny for a brief moment. "You and your sister were more like your mother, I think."

Lyman lifted the corner of his mouth in a half-smile. "Now they're both gone," he said, his tone sad but laced with happiness from remembering better times. "Now all I have are the criminals in my family."

"And you've got me," Elven said.

Lyman turned to Elven. "You sure about that?"

Elven nodded. "After what just transpired tonight, I'm not sure I have any right to be picky."

It was Lyman's turn to let out a laugh. "Glad to be your bottom of the barrel," he said. He waited a moment, then spoke again. "You know, the last time I went to see Hollis, he was asking about you. How things were going for you now, that kind of thing."

Elven nodded. As much as he wanted to put Hollis behind bars for what he was, and what he had convinced Elven to do, he still had an appreciation for the man. "You tell him I'm doing fine," he said.

Lyman shoved the jar of moonshine toward Elven. "Maybe you should tell him yourself," he said.

CHAPTER FORTY-ONE

ANOTHER DAY OF WAKING UP TO THE HOT, RANK BREATH OF YETI in the motel room. He didn't even look down at Yeti, just reached out and petted him behind the ears and along the back of his neck. He stared up at the ceiling, remembering how bad the debate had gone. Not even his head throbbing from all the moonshine could get him to forget that trainwreck.

He wondered if he could just lay around all day, playing hooky. Of course, that wouldn't do him, nor the community, any good. But he was sluggish, as was his M.O. these days.

He didn't like it. But he also didn't want to do anything to change it.

A rut. A funk. Depression. Whatever someone wanted to label it, he was in the thick of it.

He turned his head, seeing the wall of pictures. Madds, front and center. Being surrounded by one of his greatest failures probably wasn't doing him any good, either. But that was another thing he couldn't let go of.

Before he could go deeper into his existential crisis, his phone rang, startling both him and Yeti. What surprised Elven the most was that it wasn't on silent. Maybe that was a step in the right direction.

He rolled, reaching over Yeti, and grabbed his phone.

"You got Elven," he said, his voice gravelly from waking up.

"Elven, hey, I called this time." It was Johnny, and he sounded more excited than he should have been for whatever time in the morning it was. Elven used to be a morning guy, sometimes waking up before sunrise and waiting for it to crest over the tree line. That felt like an entire lifetime ago.

"And I answered," Elven said almost sarcastically, but quickly caught himself. The last thing he needed to do was snuff out Johnny's light. "What's up, Johnny?"

"The author's agent, or publicist, or whatever they are called us back," Johnny said.

"Author?" Elven asked, wiping the crust away from his eyes.

"The one that was on that video call with the library."

"Oh, right. What did they have to say?"

"They said the author, Mike Lindsay, has been busy, but he is going to call us back. They'll do a video chat with us," Johnny said.

Elven couldn't tell if Johnny was excited because he had gotten somewhere with the case, or if it was because he was going to do a video chat with an author. Either way, Elven was glad to hear it.

"Great work, Johnny," Elven said. "So, when can we expect this call?" He was a little annoyed that the author thought himself too busy to help with a murder investigation and would grace them with just a video call, but he kept that part to himself.

"That's the thing," Johnny said. "He said he had an opening in twenty minutes."

So much for getting a ride to the station. He was going to have to take his truck. "I'll be there as soon as I can. Stall the guy until I'm there if I'm running behind," Elven said, shooting up from bed.

"You got it," Johnny said.

Elven hung up the phone and stared down at Yeti, who didn't

seem like he wanted to get up and moving any more than Elven wanted to.

"Sorry, bud, but we don't have time," Elven said, rushing to the bathroom to get ready as quickly as possible.

CHAPTER FORTY-TWO

Elven managed to catch Marcus just after he had woken up to start his own day. The man was more than happy to keep an eye on Yeti while Elven went to work. He even told Elven he'd take him for a walk during his downtime. Elven knew the entire day was downtime when it came to the motel, but more than likely, Marcus meant when he was between his favorite television shows.

That was just fine with Elven. Yeti seemed to like snoozing in the lobby while Marcus reacted to whatever was on the TV behind the desk, but he would also be excited to get some outside time. It was much better than being cooped up in the motel room all day by himself. Part of Elven knew this arrangement wasn't sustainable, but until Elven decided to find a better place to live, it's what they had to do.

Elven pulled his truck straight up to the side of the station and rushed out. Getting ready, which consisted of brushing his teeth, running a moist towel across his skin, and throwing a uniform on, had been quick enough, but talking to Marcus about Yeti had eaten up a lot of time. He'd sped as fast as he could, breaking a few laws on the drive, and still managed to be ten minutes later than the twenty minutes Johnny had told him it would take.

He just hoped he hadn't missed the author altogether.

Elven rushed into the station in a flurry, heading straight past Meredith's desk. She looked up, cocked her head as she gave him a once-over, and sighed. "Rough night?" she asked.

He knew he wasn't his most presentable, but he didn't think he looked *that* bad. Whatever the case, he ran a hand through his hair, trying to smooth out whatever he imagined was the problem and continued on. "No time, Meredith," he said. "Did the author call?"

"In Tank's office," Meredith said.

Elven didn't stop, continuing through the lobby, down the hallway, and straight to Tank's office. The door was already ajar, so he didn't bother knocking and just pushed his way in. Both Tank and Johnny were there huddled together, staring at the computer screen. The one person he noticed was not there was Tommy.

"I've always wanted to write a book, I just never knew how to organize all the ideas," Johnny said.

"That's why not everyone can do it," someone said on the screen. "But the more you try, the easier it gets. I will say that."

"That's so cool," Johnny said, seemingly mesmerized by the author on the screen. Elven couldn't think of a time that he ever saw a book in Johnny's hand, so him wanting to write one was news to him.

"So... was there a reason I needed to call in?" the author asked. "I love talking shop, but I was told it had something to do with an investigation."

Tank looked up at Elven, his eyes telling Elven that he was grateful that he finally came in. "Perfect timing," Tank said, his voice strained. He turned to the screen. "Hey Mike, the sheriff just stepped in. I'm sure he can fill you in. Johnny, let's give him some space."

Tank pulled Johnny away from the screen by the shoulders, wheeling backward and leaving a gap for Elven to step into. Elven looked at Tank and mouthed *Tommy?* Tank shook his head and shrugged, as if to say he didn't know where he was.

Elven frowned, but quickly set his mind to the task as hand. He squatted down so that he was in frame of the little screen at the bottom. "I'm Sheriff Elven Hallie of Dupray County," Elven said before even setting eyes on the author.

"Elven, that's quite the name," the man said. "I don't think I'd ever pick that for someone's name. Unless I wrote fantasy novels, of course."

Elven had no patience for this. "Fair enough," he said. "So, Mike, is it?"

"That's what it says on the book's cover," he said, holding up a hardcover novel. It was red and depicted a spiral and the outline of a man, as if a person were falling into a pit of insanity. Elven saw the book's title was *Downward,* so the image made sense. The author's name was right at the bottom. Mike Lindsay.

"Alright, Mike, I'll try to make it as quick as possible so I don't take up your time," Elven said. "You had a video call a few days ago with the Dupray Library, is that right?"

"Sure is," he said. "The librarian, I think her name was Phylis, reached out. Said they were reading my book and asked if I could jump on and chat. I figured why not."

"And how did that go?" Elven asked. "Anything out of the ordinary?"

He shrugged. "They were some tough critics, but nothing I'm not used to. They liked the book as far as I could tell, except this one woman. Between you and me, she was a bit of a... well, I'll refrain from what I really want to say and just say she wasn't nice."

"Did you catch her name?" Elven asked.

Mike shook his head, swiping a loose strand of hair back behind his ear. "I try not to hang on to people like that," he said. "But I called in, answered some questions, they made some comments, and I was reminded why I hate interacting with people. I mean, don't get me wrong, there were some nice ones, but damn. I'm just glad I wasn't a new author."

"That bad?" Elven asked.

"At this point in my career, no. But if I were a first timer, I would have reconsidered my profession," he said. "I have a bit of experience at becoming a better writer, along with getting thicker skin."

"That was it?" Elven asked. "Nobody seemed off? Nobody came in that looked out of place?"

Mike pursed his lips and shook his head slowly. "I don't know exactly what would seem *off*, but it was a pretty average chat. So unless you want to tell me what exactly you're looking for, I don't—"

"Everyone is dead," Elven said. "The entire room full of people you spoke to, including Phylis the librarian, was murdered."

Mike opened his mouth and let it hang for a moment. He closed it and swallowed. He blinked a couple of times and shook his head. "Really glad I didn't just call that woman a cunt," he muttered, then looked back to the camera. "All of them?"

Elven nodded. "So, now you know what I mean when I say did anyone seem *off*? I'm sure you would have noticed anything like that, right?"

"Yeah—I mean, no, nothing like that happened as far as I know," Mike said. "Everyone was still alive when I got off the video call. They thanked me, we all said goodbye, and that was it."

Elven sighed. "Alright, I had a feeling. Would you be able to tell me who all was there?"

Mike let out a trill as he exhaled. "I mean, not really. I didn't get any names. I don't even remember how many people were in the room. I'm sorry."

"Had a feeling," Elven said, even more frustrated now than before. This was one big dead end.

"What did the other person tell you? Did they not remember anyone?" Mike asked.

Elven's ears perked up. "Other person? What do you mean?"

"The other person on the video chat," Mike said.

"Like another author?" Elven asked.

Mike shook his head. "There was this guy on the call. He was just a reader like the rest of them, but he wasn't in the room. I don't know if he was out of town, or what the reason was he was on video. He seemed kind of irritated. In fact, he seemed irritated with a woman in the room. She ended up leaving, and when she did, he got off the video call."

"Is that not something you would describe as seeming *off* to you?" Elven asked, impatient that Mike hadn't mentioned this already.

Mike shrugged. "I don't know, man. People get into squabbles all the time."

"When did this happen?"

Mike sighed. "Probably like halfway through the call. I talked for like an hour and a half in total."

"I'm guessing no names? How about a description?"

Mike made a noise that told Elven he had nothing. "I'm not great at paying attention to those things," Mike admitted.

"I can tell," Elven said. But while he might have been irritated with Mike for not remembering much of anything, he was glad to hear that they might have a new lead. They just had to figure out who it was.

CHAPTER FORTY-THREE

"So, what do you want us to do?" Tank asked.

Elven didn't have an answer to that just now. He only knew that they needed to find both the woman who left and the man from the video call and question them. It was a long shot, but maybe they would have an idea of who could have done this. But if Mike had finished the call before they were murdered, then they probably wouldn't have seen anyone come in.

There were so many *ifs* he could go over that he didn't want to think about them. It would be a waste of time until they could actually figure out who either of those people were.

Of course, finding them when the library didn't have a roster of people who'd attended the book club was going to be nearly impossible.

And when Elven looked at Tank, he could see that the deputy was out of his depth. He was clearly looking to Elven for the answer.

Elven's phone rang before he could reply. Perfect timing, given that he was at a loss for what to tell Tank.

Elven picked up the phone and put it to his ear. "You got Elven."

"Elven. Oh, good, you're up," Tommy said on the other end. His words said he was happy to hear Elven, but his monotone voice said the opposite.

"Tommy? Where are you?" Elven asked.

"I'm standing outside the prison in the parking lot," he said.

"What for?"

"Well, after I fucked things up the other day, I figured you had something on Zane, so I wanted to follow him," Tommy admitted.

Elven sighed. "And you followed him to the prison?"

"Yeah, he's inside right now," Tommy said. "I decided to call you before following him in. Want me to do that?"

Elven bit his lip. After ending up with nothing from pulling Zane in for questioning, and getting his backside handed to him at the debate, he had tried to push Zane as far out of his mind as he could. But now here Tommy was, saying that Zane was at the prison. It didn't seem like one of his usual haunts.

And then he remembered what his mother had told him. That Zane Rhodes was hiding something.

Could this be what it was?

He shot a glance to Tank, who still looked like he needed Elven to give him some direction. "No, I'll come meet you," Elven said to Tommy. "Stay put until I'm there." He hung up the phone. "I gotta head out. You and Johnny come up with something and run it by me when I'm back."

"But what—"

Elven spun around and headed out the door before Tank could ask him anything else. He didn't need to admit that he was just as lost as the rest of them right now.

CHAPTER FORTY-FOUR

About an hour later, Elven pulled into the visitors' section of the parking lot behind the prison. He didn't make it out here much when he wasn't transporting someone from the station, but he had stopped by a couple times over the years during his career. It was sometimes easy to forget that there was a full county jail in the area, with how far it was from the rest of the town. Elven's job was to put them there, not keep them there.

Dupray County wasn't much for appearances, but even they seemed to want to keep the criminals as far out of sight as possible.

Elven saw Tommy a few rows away from the visitors' entrance and parked his truck in a spot a few feet away. Tommy met him at the side of his truck and waited for Elven to get out.

"He still here? It's a long drive from the station," Elven said, placing his Stetson on his head once he was out of the truck.

"He already left," Tommy admitted. His body language was tense, like he was worried he would be scolded for not keeping better tabs on him. After their last interaction, Elven didn't blame the kid.

"Any idea where he went?" Elven asked.

Tommy shook his head. "I debated following him, but you said to stay put. Didn't want you to show and I wasn't here to tell you," he said almost timidly.

"Fair enough," Elven said.

"What are you gonna do?" Tommy asked.

Elven shook his head, staring at the entrance. "Guess I should go see if I can find out why he was here."

"Want me to come with?" Tommy asked.

"I think I can handle it," Elven said.

"You sure? I can—"

"Why don't you head back to the station, see if Tank needs you for something," Elven said. "There's a new development, someone we're looking for. He can fill you in."

Tommy deflated. "Whatever you say."

Elven headed toward the entrance of the prison. It was a chain-link fence that wrapped around the walls. A portion was on wheels and opened when he approached. He was greeted by a guard in uniform, who gave Elven a quick look and nodded. "Sheriff," he said.

"Thanks," Elven said, passing him and moving toward the door that led into the visitors' area.

He walked through the large metal doors and was again greeted by another corrections officer through a window. "Sheriff, here to see someone?" the officer asked, getting straight to business. He chewed gum while giving him a blank stare.

"Actually, I'm looking for someone that might have passed through. He—"

"Look, Sheriff, I appreciate that and all, and I'm sure you've got a job to do right now, but so do I. We do it by the book in here—visitation only. If you want to ask questions about who came through, that's above my pay grade. You gotta talk to the warden." The officer spoke in a monotone, like he was reading from a script he had long since memorized. "You want to see an inmate, I'm your guy. I give you the form, and you sign in. You leave your weapon with me, then do your thing."

Elven stared at him for a moment. He knew it would be so easy for the officer to give him what he wanted, but instead, he was being a horse's backside about the whole thing. And Elven didn't want to take the time to visit the warden. Not only would it take a long time, but they also didn't have the best relationship due to Elven's family being who they were.

That was something he really didn't want to get into.

"What's it gonna be?" the officer asked.

"Give me the form, then," Elven said.

"Who you here for?" The guard eyed him suspiciously, like he didn't believe him.

Elven hadn't been planning on making this little detour right now, but the name that came up was all he could think of if he was going to get what he wanted.

"Hollis Starcher," Elven said.

The guard lifted an eyebrow and smirked before sliding the clipboard with the sign-in sheet to him under the metal barrier that separated them. Elven picked up the pen and scribbled his name on the line. As he did, he scanned the form as quickly as he could, spotting Zane Rhodes's name only two lines up from where he was putting his own.

Next to it was the name of an inmate he'd never heard of. Glenn Sutherland.

CHAPTER FORTY-FIVE

After leaving his gun at the counter, Elven was led through a metal detector, where he was given a pass-over with a wand and, of course, a swift pat-down to make sure there was nothing he was trying to sneak in. Elven wondered how someone who wasn't law enforcement was handled when coming through. Either that, or the guards just didn't like Elven all that much. That was always a possibility, even in other forms of law enforcement. If someone resided in Dupray long enough, they'd have an opinion of him based on his last name alone.

He had been trying to turn those to his favor by doing the job, but even with that, he managed to make enemies. But at least they were his own and not due to the sins of his parents.

Once through security, he walked down the hall and to the room labeled VISITATION in yellow paint above the double doors. One door read IN, the other on the left, OUT. He had to give them credit —they ran a tight ship at the jail. Even the guests were herded around efficiently.

When he entered the large, open room for visitors, he remembered the first time he ever came through here. It was different than he'd thought. He'd expected a ton of security, maybe for the whole thing to be clinical. He'd been here a number of times, maybe not always as a "visitor" for an inmate, but he knew what to expect by now. It was still more secure than the psych ward, however. That place almost felt like a country club.

But this was neither that, nor what he'd expected for security. He imagined there'd be a counter and glass, speaking through a phone to communicate, but then again, this was still Dupray. They didn't spend money on frivolous things. Instead, they had small tables and chairs with lines painted down the center of each table.

On the outer edge of the room, guards stood at each wall. One right in the center, scanning over the entire room. They had tasers and batons, from what Elven could see. A few other corrections officers meandered about, scanning the room to make sure everyone stayed in line. He wondered how many people had tried anything in the visitation room.

But then again, what good would it do other than get someone more time inside? The only reason to do that was if there was a targeted hit on someone visiting. And that didn't seem very likely.

Unless, of course, it was the sheriff who'd put someone in here they wanted to get out.

Elven took a deep breath as he scanned over the room. There were a lot of people visiting, which was a surprise considering that the parking lot outside didn't look anywhere near as full as this room. Maybe a bus came out this way at the same time. Whatever the case, all of the inmates were focused on the people who came to see them, not on the uniformed sheriff who just walked in. That should have put him at ease, but for some reason, he found himself nervous.

He hadn't seen Hollis since the day he jumped in front of him, taking the bullet. By the time Elven was out of the hospital, Hollis had already been transferred here from the holding cell that Tank had placed him in at the station. It had all been so unceremonious, but that was fine with him. Even if he had been out of the hospital before the transfer, he wasn't sure he would have reveled in anything.

Taking down Hollis for real was nothing how Elven had expected it to be.

The air was thick with body heat, and it smelled of sweat mixed with the various colognes and perfumes of the visitors. Elven was too focused on making his way to table twenty-one to notice much.

He slid into the chair that was pulled out slightly. Right across from him, over the painted line, was another empty chair. He looked around while he waited, wondering who it was that Zane had come to visit. Was Glenn Sutherland still in the room now? But if he was, that meant someone else had come to visit him. Elven hadn't taken the time to scan the entire sheet to see if the inmate's name was elsewhere on the list.

At this point, he doubted Glenn was in this room. Elven had no idea who he was, what he looked like, or why he was in prison. He would have to do some digging when he got out of here.

He knew he could turn around right now and leave. This wasn't his original plan, just a means to find out who Zane had come to see. But after talking to Lyman, he thought that maybe he owed it to Hollis, and more importantly, himself, to come see him. After everything they'd been through, after everything Hollis had put him through, it felt like it was time.

The door buzzed from the back and opened up. A shadow spilled into the room. The room suddenly grew quieter. It didn't go completely silent, but the volume was noticeably lower.

Elven had almost forgotten how big Hollis was. He had always played the unassuming old man. Not feeble by any means, even though Elven knew his knee gave him problems, especially when it was cold. But he generally leaned into being seen as approachable by the community.

But in here, he looked different. No longer was he the country grandpa everyone loved. He was big, gruff, and intimidating. As Hollis circled around the various tables, making his way toward Elven, each table went silent. Once he was past, they started their conversations again. Some of the other inmates glanced toward

Hollis, but if he looked at them, they quickly returned their attention back to whoever sat at their table.

Elven didn't know what to expect when Hollis entered the prison system, but to be so commanding of respect—or maybe it was fear—in such an obvious manner, was different. Hollis's gray hair was neatly combed back, his beard cropped close to his face, and he had a twinkle in his eye. It was clear he was thriving in here.

Hollis plopped down on the seat in front of Elven and gave a big grin.

"Well, what took you so long?" Hollis asked.

CHAPTER FORTY-SIX

HOLLIS MIGHT HAVE CHANGED IN SOME WAYS TO FIT INTO THE prison system—or rather, to *command* the prison system—but when he sat and spoke with Elven, he was the same man Elven had known all those years ago when he was a teenager dating his daughter, partying with Lyman, and getting into squabbles with Corbin. Elven would never admit it to the man, but in some ways, he missed him.

Dupray definitely was not the same without Hollis Starcher. Sometimes that was a bad thing, but Elven liked to think that most of the time, it was a good thing. Of course, he had been too busy hiding from the world to really feel the full effect of Hollis's absence. But it *had* to be a good thing, didn't it?

"You don't return my calls," Hollis said with a sly smile. The wrinkles around his eyes deepened when he did, aging him by ten more years.

Elven couldn't remember any messages he'd received from the prison. "I didn't have any missed calls from—"

"Boy, I am just yankin' yer chain," Hollis said with a breathy laugh. "I know things ain't been the same since I moved residences, but hot damn, I didn't think things would be as bad as they are now. Where has your sense of humor gone?"

"Probably where my ability to trust went," Elven said dryly.

"Didn't even crack a smile when you said that," Hollis said.

"Because there's nothing funny about it. It's the truth," Elven said. He wasn't there to open up about how he felt. If he wanted to do that, he could find a therapist to listen to him gripe. But he wasn't going to sugarcoat anything, either. He was angry with Hollis, so he wanted him to know it.

Hollis nodded. "Hmmm," he said. He didn't elaborate, but didn't hold off on the issue any longer. "How's Lyman been doing?"

"Don't you know?" Elven asked. "He said he comes to visit you."

"Oh, sure, he comes in, gives me periodic updates," Hollis said, quickly raising a hand. "About how things are with the business and all, I mean. Nothing sinister."

Elven lifted an eyebrow, not needing the clarification. Anything coming from Hollis needed to be sifted through with a fine-toothed comb. But Lyman he trusted.

"But it's one thing for him to come in here, let me know how he's doing, and get eyes on him for a few minutes in the day," Hollis continued. "It's another to see how he's actually doing out there without me."

"Lyman's a grown man, so I think he can manage alright without you," Elven said.

Hollis chuckled. "One would hope," he said. He let the silence linger a moment as he ran his eyes over Elven.

"He's alright," Elven finally admitted. "Struggling with the garage some, but I think he's figuring it out."

Hollis nodded. "That boy never was the best mechanic in the family. He was always off running around instead of learning things from me or his older brother."

"I don't think you need to worry too much about him," Elven said.

"You boys still talking, then?" Hollis asked.

Elven shrugged. "A little."

"You keep an eye on him, you hear? Lyman has a good heart, something he got from his mother, but he still needs guidance sometimes," Hollis said. "And you're about the best person I know for that type of thing. Don't hold this whole thing against him." He waved his hand as if to explain. "Can you do that for me?"

"Now you're asking me for favors?"

"Oh, quit with all the hogwash. You look like hell, and from my understanding, you've been letting *my* county go to shit."

"What would you know about it?"

"Elven, my boy, I don't know why it is a surprise to you, but I've got eyes and ears all over Dupray, keeping me posted on what is and what isn't happening."

"Careful," Elven said. "You're close to venturing into illegal territory."

"Ain't nothing illegal about being told what's going on outside these walls," Hollis said. "You're reaching pretty hard on that one."

Elven lifted his eyebrows. He wasn't even sure what he was doing there anymore. "And what exactly is it that you heard?"

Hollis lifted a corner of his mouth. Hollis always loved knowing more than the person across the table from him. Elven let him have it. After all, he was the one who had a cold cell waiting for him after this conversation.

"I've heard that you can't get your shit together," Hollis said. He was no longer reveling in the knowledge but sounded genuinely disappointed, maybe even hurt. "That you got a thief running circles around you, a mass murderer on your hands, and you're on the verge of losing your career."

"I wouldn't say that—"

"From my understanding, this *Zane Rhodes* is pulling your ticket," Hollis said, leaning back and crossing his arms over his chest. "Now I am not there, clearly, but you have been hiding away. That doesn't seem like you at all."

"Things have gotten complicated," Elven said, defending himself. "My recovery and—"

"That's a load of horseshit, and you know it, Elven," Hollis said. "Look what you did. You arrested me, didn't you? All due to my shit-head cousin, of course, but I'll give it to you. You really pulled out all the stops." He pointed a finger at Elven as he leaned forward. "I was so damn proud of you for that."

"Wasn't my intention," Elven said.

Hollis ignored the comment. "Stop the *what ifs* or the *hows*. Maddie wasn't your fault."

"No kidding," Elven said. "I know whose fault that was." He stared daggers straight at Hollis.

Hollis raised a hand. "Never expected it to get to where it ended," he said. "I owe you an apology for that one. So I'm sorry."

Elven clenched his jaw. He didn't want an apology. He wanted it to never have happened. He wanted Madds not to be related to Hollis, not to have stabbed him in the back. But nobody could give him that. The apology was the most he could get, other than catching her.

"I take it you ain't heard from her since—"

"No," Elven cut him off. "You?"

"You and I know the same amount on her whereabouts at this point, which is diddly-squat," Hollis said. "And that's the truth."

"If you say so," Elven said, watching Hollis, knowing he had no reason to trust him. But for some reason, something deep inside that went way back in the history of their relationship told him Hollis was telling the truth.

"I do," Hollis said. He considered Elven a moment. "It's like Lyman."

"What is?"

"You coming in here. It's one thing to hear from people what's been going on, how you've been acting, but it's a whole 'nother thing to see it with my own eyes," he said. "I never would have believed it otherwise."

"And what is it you can't believe?"

"That you've lost your edge," he said.

Elven put his hands on the table and started to lift up. "Well, Hollis, this has been fun, but—"

"Sit back down," Hollis commanded.

The look on his face was stern, and while Elven didn't need to heed a single word from this man, he sat, anyway.

"You put me in here, so I expect you to take care of business. What happened to the Elven I know? The one who went in guns blazing because he knew he was better than whoever might have been on the other side of the door?"

"He got a lot of people killed and then was shot by his girlfriend while saving your life," Elven said.

Hollis smiled. "Sure did," he said. "Except the getting people killed part, that is. To me, you followed your instincts, stopped a killer, and got your big fish." He leaned in. "That big fish was me, in case you didn't figure it out." He gave a small wink.

"And what about those I couldn't save?" Elven asked. He hesitated to say it, but it would be the one thing that Hollis could truly understand. "What about Penny?"

Hollis took a deep breath, letting it out slowly. He rubbed his face with his hand once. "You can't save everyone, Elven," Hollis admitted.

"That's all you've got?" Elven asked.

"You know what your problem is?" Hollis said, leaning back and folding his arms across his chest.

"I'd love to hear it," Elven said.

"You get too attached," he said. "It wasn't your gut instincts that got people killed. It was your own hubris. You make things so damn personal."

Elven couldn't help but chuckle. "Figured you were gonna say I was too arrogant," he said.

"I'll take an arrogant, gut-instinct-following Elven Hallie over whatever the hell this is in front of me," Hollis said, motioning his hand up and down at Elven. "Now stop with the woe-is-me bullshit, stop getting chauffeured around by your deputies, follow your goddammed gut, and go catch the shit heel who is making a mess of *my* town. And maybe this time, don't try to do it by yourself."

Elven smiled. He hated to admit it, but Hollis might be right. "Thanks, Hollis," Elven said, although a little begrudgingly.

Hollis smirked. "I never did thank you for saving my life, you know."

"And I don't expect you to now," Elven said.

Hollis nodded. "Glad you came by, Elven. Unless there's anything else, I've got a book in my cell with my name on it."

Elven started to stand but stopped. "One thing, maybe," he said. "What can you tell me about an inmate named Glenn Sutherland?"

Hollis grinned. "What do you want to know?"

CHAPTER FORTY-SEVEN

"I REALLY DOUBT YOU'LL FIND ANYTHING," DENNIS SAID, sliding his key into Robin's unit and unlocking it. "Especially after you and your deputy did a sweep of the place. Robin being targeted doesn't make any sense."

"Don't mean to cause you any trouble," Elven said, waiting for the man to open the door. He didn't want to get into specifics about what he was looking for. Dennis was acting a little tense, maybe even shifty, trying to get Elven to agree not to search her apartment again.

All he could think about was what Tank had told him. He really didn't want to discover anything about Dennis, like him being a Peeping Tom or something else along those lines. He had enough on his plate to deal with, and he knew whatever might pop up wouldn't even be related to the case he was working on.

He just wanted to get in the apartment, grab what he was looking for, and get out of there.

"It's no trouble," Dennis said. "Just if you're gonna come in and out like this, maybe give me a little more notice next time."

"I'll keep that in mind," Elven said, trying to avoid any roadblocks.

Finally, the door opened, and Dennis held his arm out while still standing right in the doorway. Elven stared a moment, hoping Dennis would get the hint and get out of the way, but he didn't. Elven sighed and went through the doorway sideways, trying to squeeze by Dennis without brushing up against him. He made sure to hold his breath as he did.

Once he was successfully through, he turned to the stack of books that lined the wall underneath the window. Nothing had moved since Elven and Tank had last been there, which was surprising considering how Dennis had been acting about letting him in the place, but also a huge relief.

The book, *Hollow Hearts*, sat right there on the pile where he had last left it.

He opened the book and pulled the loose piece of paper out of it. He took a quick look over his shoulder, seeing that Dennis was watching him far more closely than he was comfortable with. He turned so his back faced the man and read the paper.

It was filled with Robin's notes, just as he remembered. Complaints about the pacing, about the plot, about the characters, but none of it was what he was looking for. It was all vague, and about the writing only. None of it was personal.

Finally, he flipped the paper over and saw the one specific thing he was looking for. It had been mixed in with all the other nasty things she had to say about the book and the author's writing, but it was there.

It was the same thing that had been written on another note. It felt personal, and it also said a lot, as it related to a romance novel.

The author wouldn't know what love was if it hit them in the face.

Elven had a feeling he knew who he was looking for. He closed the book and looked at the cover, reading the author's name.

Misty Rivers.

There was one way to confirm his theory.

CHAPTER FORTY-EIGHT

HOLLIS DIDN'T HAVE ANYTHING TO TELL ELVEN ABOUT GLENN Sutherland, but he did tell him that he would ask around, see what people said. Elven wasn't expecting much, but it was something. Elven would also do a quick search when he got to the station. But right now, Zane wasn't a priority.

Hollis was right. Elven had been making everything so personal that he had lost his edge. He wasn't trusting his gut, and instead, he was trying to make Zane fit the crime. It was a square peg in a round hole.

He was done with all of that. Now, he was going with his gut.

When this entire case started, he had thought it wasn't to do with Phylis the librarian, but more with the people who were murdered. He went with the more obvious choice since Phylis hadn't made any friends.

But then Driscoll had found the notes in the mouths of the victims.

Elven should have known right then and there what his gut was telling him to do. He just hadn't trusted it because he was scared.

And instead, he was putting more people at risk by playing it safe, though more realistically, he was playing it unsure.

He considered heading to the station, but he was too amped up and wanted to get straight to it. That call with Mike Lindsay had opened his eyes to the fact that there were more people at risk of being killed. And very possibly, finding the suspect themselves.

Of course, it wasn't as easy as just knowing who those people were. No, the author hadn't been able to name or describe anyone. But Elven had a hunch that he knew what to look for.

And if he were being honest with himself, he always knew it. It was right in front of his face, and he was just too scared to see it. If he was wrong, what would have happened?

At this point, if he didn't try it his way, it was just as bad as doing nothing.

He raced to the library as fast as he could and pulled into the parking lot. It was pretty empty, which, for being free entertainment, seemed to be unusual. He didn't make a trip there often himself, but either people weren't into reading much in Dupray, which was possible, or a lot of people were afraid since there had been a mass murder there.

Elven walked into the library and set eyes on the desk. The last time he'd been at this desk, a dead woman was lying on the floor behind it. This time, though, none of that was the case. The library was mostly clean, with a few rolling carts full of books that were waiting to be put away. Nothing was overturned, there wasn't a speck of blood in sight, and the only bodies he saw in the building were upright and breathing.

In fact, there was a familiar face behind the counter. Linda, the librarian who had found all of the bodies, was working. The sight of her there shocked Elven, remembering how upset she had been.

"Linda," Elven said enthusiastically. He immediately met with a *shushing* noise as she pressed a finger against her lips.

"Sheriff," she whispered. "You're in a library."

"Oh, right, sorry," he said, bringing his tone down. "I'm surprised to see you here."

"Short-staffed because, well, you know," she said with a frown. "Most of the other employees are afraid to come in."

"Understandable," Elven said. "And you're okay?"

"Doing the best I can," she said. "Honestly, I'm still happy to be working here. Not that, I mean, I don't know... it makes me sound like a terrible person. I didn't want Phylis to get hurt, but I love this job."

Elven nodded. "Don't sweat it," he said. "I get it."

"You're very kind," she said with a small smile. "What can I help you with today?"

"I know you said that you don't keep a log of who attends the book discussion, right?" Elven asked. "None of them?"

"I'm sorry, but no," she said, shaking her head.

"But I'm sure you do keep a log of who checks out a book, don't you?"

She nodded her head slowly. "Sure. It's all on the computer now, too. In the past, it used to just be written by hand, so it's a lot easier to search now," she said. "What book are you looking at?"

"What book was last month's discussion on?" Elven asked.

She cocked her head and pursed her lips. "Let me check," she said. She went to the computer and started typing rapidly. By the sound of it, she was at least twice as fast at typing as Elven was. Good thing his job didn't need much typing. "Oh, this book." She frowned.

"What's wrong?" Elven asked.

"Phylis was not very kind when she told everyone about this book," Linda said. "Some self-published trash, according to her."

"Why did they read it, then?" Elven asked.

"They picked it because it took place in West Virginia," she said. "Clearly, they didn't do their research because it looks awful. The cover alone is amateur hour." She spun the monitor around.

And there it was. The same exact book that he had seen in Robin Sullivan's home. The one with the paper inside with her notes. And by notes, he meant her critiques. The ones that, in so many words, said she thought it was awful.

Hollow Hearts by Misty Rivers.

"You don't happen to know the author, do you?" Elven asked.

Linda snorted. "I'd be surprised if it was her real name."

He knew he was on the right path. The paper, the one Tommy had brought to him after Lenny found it in the parking lot, read: *Wouldn't know love if it hit her in the face.* That was the same thing Robin had written down. Or at least, it was close enough to it.

"Who all checked out that book before last month's book club discussion?" Elven asked.

Linda did some more typing after pulling the monitor back toward her. When she was done, she flipped the screen back to Elven. The list was not too long, but there were enough names that could keep them busy. He scanned with his finger, making sure not to actually touch the screen as Linda watched him carefully.

"Do you have a pen and paper so I can write this down?" Elven asked.

"I'll do you one better," she said, pulling the screen back. She hit two keys, and the printer behind her fired up. Linda grabbed the paper, then set it on the counter in front of Elven. "We don't always get enough books in for people to read in time, depending on how long they take. Some people opt to buy a copy instead elsewhere."

"That's fine," Elven said, knowing this was what Robin most likely did, considering she still had the book in her house. A quick scan told him that she hadn't checked it out. "This is a place I can start. Do you happen to have the addresses for these people?"

"Of course," she said. "Where else do we send the bill if someone doesn't return a book?"

"Think you can print that out, too?" he asked.

She gave a short nod and did her thing, firing the printer up again and handing the page of addresses directly to Elven. She bit her bottom lip. "I don't know if this is something I am supposed to ask to see a warrant for or whatever," she said, and Elven wondered if he might start to have some trouble. "But after what happened, I don't want any hurdles for you to catch whoever did this. And you will catch them, right?"

Elven gave a nod. "Of course I will," he said. And this time, he was determined to make it the truth.

CHAPTER FORTY-NINE

ELVEN RUSHED INTO THE STATION, COMPLETELY REINVIGORATED by the list he held in his hands. For the first time in this case, he felt like he had a real lead to something. If anything, there were more people at risk of being next on the killer's list, which meant they had someone to protect. And by doing so, they could find whoever had murdered Robin and all the others at the library.

Meredith sat behind her desk, per usual. She took a glance at him, then pushed her chair backward as if she were stunned. "You have a little more pep in your step," she said. "This morning, you looked like someone forced you out of bed."

"Probably because they did," he said. "But I'm feeling good now." It was the truth. And now he was ready to work.

"Glad to see it," she said with a smile.

"Is everyone still here?" Elven asked.

Meredith nodded, then motioned to the hallway. "I'm pretty sure you caught them all before they left."

"Great," he said, rushing straight to the hallway. He wanted—no, he *needed*—to speak to all of them.

He made his way through the hallway, passing each and every open office door. "Give me a few minutes, I want to talk with everyone in the lobby," Elven said quickly as he leaned into Tank's office, then Johnny's. Both men raised an eyebrow at him, wondering what it was about. Elven would tell them soon enough, but he had to speak with Tommy first.

He stood at Tommy's office and leaned inside. The young man was standing, his back facing the doorway and his head hanging low. Elven spotted a small box on his desk, which immediately made his heart drop.

"Tommy," Elven said, his voice gentle. "You got a minute?"

Tommy lifted his head and turned around. His eyes were soft with sadness. Elven wondered if he was too late, that Tommy had made his mind up. Tommy lifted his hands, offered a shrug, and nodded. "Sure," he said. "What happened now?"

"Why don't you take a seat for a second?" Elven said.

Tommy sighed and pulled his chair out, plopping down. "I think I know where this is going," he said.

Elven moved the things on Tommy's desk so that he could have a space to sit. He sat down in front of Tommy, just like he would do at his own desk. It was a little tighter in here, but he still felt like the older, wiser counselor to the younger student this way. He hoped he could get his point across, because right now, Tommy seemed pretty deflated. Elven had firsthand experience to know it wasn't a great place to be.

"First, I wanted to thank you for tracking Zane to the prison for me," Elven said. "You clearly saw that I had a theory about him, even if the evidence may not have lined up, and took the initiative to see where it went."

Tommy lifted his eyebrows as if to acknowledge it. "Sure," he said, not seeming to care much. "Not sure what good it did, though."

"Me neither," Elven admitted. "Not yet, anyway. But that's alright, it was still a good follow-through."

"Is that it?" Tommy asked, shrugging off the compliment.

"No," Elven said. Tommy let out a grumble of disappointment. "I also wanted to apologize." This perked up Tommy's interest, and his eyes met Elven's.

"You're not firing me?" Tommy asked.

Elven frowned. "Of course not," he said. "You're a good cop. Me going off on you like that had nothing to do with you or what happened. That was a miscommunication, and while it would have been nice to know first thing, it wasn't on you that I went after Zane. I made that personal with him, and that was wrong of me. And it was wrong of me to say what I said. You don't deserve that."

Tommy took a deep breath. "Thanks," he said. Elven could tell that he wanted to accept the apology, but he was still upset while also teetering on the relief that he wasn't fired. He didn't blame the kid for it, either.

Elven sighed. "We've all made mistakes in this office. Some have been small, while others have been colossal screwups that, well, probably should have had some repercussions that may not have come. But the thing is, we learn and don't do it again. Lester, my predecessor, gave me plenty of second chances when I didn't deserve them. And on top of that, he never took it out on me like I did to you. So I'm sorry, and I hope to do better." Elven tapped his fist on the table next to him. "I just hope that you will stay on with me."

Tommy smiled. "I'm not going anywhere," he said.

"Bando's that bad, huh?" Elven asked with a grin.

Tommy laughed. "You could say that. Though for about ten seconds after you chewed me out, I actually missed the son of a bitch."

"That right there is enough to keep me from ever making that mistake again," Elven said. Sheriff Reed Bando was a downright prickly, spineless—well, he was a word Elven didn't really want to think. He hoped to heaven that Tommy was leaning into a joke.

Tommy stood up and held his hand out. "After working with you in Monacan, I saw the kind of man you are. And I'm seeing it here again, so I'm here for as long as you'll have me."

Elven hopped off the desk and shook his hand firmly. "Great, then let's get to work," he said.

CHAPTER FIFTY

ELVEN STOOD IN THE LOBBY OF THE SHERIFF'S STATION IN FRONT of all his coworkers—his friends. Each one of them played a pivotal role in the inner workings of the office, and nobody was more important than the other. There was Tank, Tommy, Johnny, Meredith, and, of course, himself. They had all been through the wringer when Elven had been shot, and then they'd picked up the slack while he was in recovery.

And now they were here, waiting for him to speak. To say something that would make up for the past months Elven had dropped the ball and didn't bother trying to pick it up. Until right now, that is.

Maybe it was too little, maybe it was too late. But he had to try. Somehow, they still counted on him. They still expected him to come through. And he would do anything to make that happen for them. And for the whole county of Dupray.

But most of all, for himself.

"I know it was touch-and-go when we arrested Hollis," Elven said, thinking about how he could word what he wanted to say. In the end, he knew it was best to just be upfront, say it like it was, and not have anyone try to interpret or read into anything. He cleared his throat. "No, it's more than that. After what happened with Madds—er, Maddison, I guess." Calling her by the name she preferred made it sound like they were still on good terms. "After finding out that she had been a mole the whole time, that she lied to each and every one of us, well, it stung. And I kept it to myself. That wasn't right of me."

He watched their faces. He knew that Tommy didn't have a lot of skin in the game when it came to Madds, but he had been in Monacan, helping Elven find her, so he knew how much she meant to him at least. "I should have been open about it all, asked for help with what to do, and not tried to do it all on my own. I made it personal."

Meredith was the first to speak. "Elven, honey, it *was* personal," she said.

Elven smiled, but it was painful. "I appreciate that, Meredith," he said. He wanted to make it through without being interrupted again, but he didn't have the heart to tell anyone to not interject. They had every right to say their piece as well. "Some of it had been personal, sure, but in the end, it was my job to handle the case the best way possible. And that, I did not do. People ended up getting hurt, and some killed. And then I just didn't handle it well, trying to find Maddison, trying to not make a mess of things again. And instead of succeeding in that, I ended up abandoning you.

"That wasn't my intention. So I wanted to tell you all that I'm sorry. For everything. The thing is, I got a little kick in the backside from someone earlier today and, well, I think it's time I stop acting a fool and do my job. So unless any of you have issues with that, how about we catch a bad guy?"

"It's about damn time," Tank said with a grin.

CHAPTER FIFTY-ONE

ELVEN WAS REJUVENATED, AND HAVING HIS TEAM READY TO follow his orders was a huge boost. He might have worried he was rusty before, but right now, it was like riding a bike. He slipped right back onto the seat and pedaled hard, not losing his balance now.

"Johnny," Elven said, pointing to him. Johnny perked up, standing up straight. He was proud to still be a part of the team, and Elven was proud to have him. "I need you to call Zane Rhodes."

"You think he had something—"

"No," Elven said. "Tell him we're having another debate."

Everyone around Elven exchanged glances. They were all aware of what had happened at the last one, but Elven hadn't been ready. He hadn't been himself.

All of that had changed.

"When?" Johnny asked. "The election is in two days."

"Tell him we're doing it tomorrow," Elven said.

"What if he says no? Elven, I don't know if I can convince a man like Zane to—"

"First of all, Johnny, stop second-guessing yourself," Elven said.

"You took down the most dangerous man who's ever come through this county. I think you can handle this."

Johnny took a breath and let it out, nodding.

Elven decided to give him just the slightest edge to use. "And if he gives you any trouble, trying to say he can't or doesn't want to, you tell him that I know who Glenn Sutherland is. One way or the other, I'll be at a town hall meeting tomorrow night, with or without him to debate."

"Who is that?" Johnny asked.

Elven shook his head. "Just tell him that, alright? If he wants to know more, he can meet me tomorrow. Can you do that?"

Johnny nodded, and Elven had all the confidence in the world that he could. "On it," Johnny said, turning to head to his office.

Elven smiled, waiting for Johnny to disappear before turning to Meredith. The last big case, he made the mistake of wanting to do all of it himself. This time, everyone was going to have their part. "To piggyback off of Johnny's task, I need you to look up Glenn Sutherland," he told Meredith. "Find out why he's in prison and what connection he might have to Zane Rhodes."

"Elven Hallie, Johnny's in there convincing Zane to debate you on a bluff?" she asked.

"Let's not let Johnny or Zane know that. I hope it's not a bluff for long," he said. "Just get what you can. I've got someone else trying to dig into it as well."

"Of course," she said, heading for her desk.

That left the two deputies, Tank and Tommy. Both had that little sparkle in their eye, telling Elven that they, too, felt rejuvenated. Ready to do the job now more than ever.

"I've got two addresses of who I think could be targets for whoever killed the people at the library and Robin. They were at the last book discussion," Elven said.

"You think they were targeted because they were at the book discussion?" Tank asked. "Seems extreme to me. What could have happened to make someone do this?"

Elven agreed with a nod. "I think they said some things that someone didn't agree with."

"About the book?" Tommy asked.

Elven nodded. "Those notes the killer left, the one for Robin matched something she had written down about the book," he said. "I have a hunch that all those things were said at last month's book discussion."

"So someone is mad that they didn't like the book?" Tank asked.

Elven pursed his lips. "It feels like it goes beyond that," he said. "As you pointed out, it seems extreme, but the notes were all so personal. And nasty. But not all of them were directed toward the story or the book. They were personal toward the author." He held up the copy of *Hollow Hearts* that he had taken from Robin's apartment, tapping on the name of the author.

"Misty Rivers?" Tommy asked. "Is that someone you guys know around here?"

"Never heard that name before this case," Tank admitted.

"So you think this person who writes as Misty Rivers did this?" Tommy asked.

"Or someone who really identifies with them," Elven said.

"So a crazed fan, or a crazed author?" Tank asked. "Over some words said? They turn into a mass murderer?"

"We've seen people do worse for less," Elven said. "You never know what's going on in someone's head. Right now, it's a theory, but my gut is telling me I'm on the right track. Best case, we find the killer. Worst case, we protect the killer's next targets."

"That's good enough for me," Tank said. "Where do you want me?"

Elven handed Tank the paper with one of the addresses written on it. "Katelyn Manner," Elven told him.

Tank looked at the paper, biting his lip. "I know this place," he said. "We got a call about a break-in the other day, so I went to check it out. But it wasn't a woman. It was a single male who lived there.

Robert, I think. Said his aunt owned the place, had just moved or something like that. Guy was a little strange."

"So maybe Katelyn is his aunt," Elven said. "Look her up, see if she's updated her address elsewhere. Otherwise, pay a visit to Robert. See if he can tell you where she lives."

"Got it," Tank said, heading for his office to look her up.

"You want me with him?" Tommy asked Elven, ready to follow Tank.

Elven clasped his hand on Tommy's shoulder to keep him there. "You're with me," he said. "I've got another person we need to visit. Lucinda Hall." Elven didn't know the woman.

"Cool," Tommy said, pulling the car keys from his pocket. "I'll go get—"

"Nope, I'm driving," Elven said with a smile.

"Anyone else on the list?" Tommy asked as he followed Elven to the door.

Elven shook his head. "Nobody that's still alive."

CHAPTER FIFTY-TWO

THE DRIVE OUT TO LUCINDA HALL'S HOUSE WAS OVER SOME very steep roads that curved at unexpected times. Elven was surprised they'd never received any calls out to this road. He could imagine a drunk driver or two spotting the bend in the road too late and their vehicle skidding off the side of the cliff. With no street-lights, Elven was having to take it slow himself, and he was completely sober.

How dark it got out there at night made things even more difficult.

But he also noticed that he never saw another house on the way to Lucinda's place. At least, not one that was inhabited. A handful of crumbling buildings were about it. The location was nowhere near town, nor any businesses as far as he could tell. So there was no reason to expand many properties up in this area.

He wondered why Lucinda had found herself living out all this way in the first place. He'd find out soon enough if she was home.

After a slew of sharp turns, he drove on a paved road that eventually tapered off into a dirt path. They passed an abandoned, decrepit house that he mistook for Lucinda's at first, but he finally found the correct house. It was in surprisingly good shape, and not at all what he expected.

"Wow. With the road we took, I thought this place would have been a dump," Tommy said, echoing Elven's own thoughts.

"Hidden nooks and crannies all over this county," Elven said.

The two men got out of Elven's truck and took in the building. Elven imagined that the parcel it sat on expanded pretty far out. But the house itself was quaint. Nothing extravagant, and more like a cottage. It had painted blue wood paneling on the side and a roof that told him it was two stories. But from the angle he stood at, he could see that the depth of the house didn't go far back. The home was built on a slab, so it was flat on the ground with no steps leading up to the door.

The two men walked straight on the gravel path that led to a concrete porch. There were hanging planters from the ceiling, a few on the railing in front of the loveseat that looked out toward the nearby trees past Elven's truck. Elven stood back while Tommy rang the doorbell.

They could hear the chime, followed by scrambling footsteps. The two men exchanged glances. Elven imagined they didn't get many visitors out here, but was it that unusual to warrant this kind of commotion?

Tommy stood to the side while Elven faced the door. There was no answer, and the footsteps stopped.

Elven cleared his throat and pulled the screen door open, knocking on the solid wood door behind it. "Lucinda Hall," Elven said. "Dupray County Sheriff's Department." His voice was firm and loud.

Tommy leaned over the loveseat and pressed his face against the window, cupping his hands around his eyes. He pulled back and shrugged. "Curtains are blocking. I can't see a thing," he said.

Elven sighed. He knew someone was inside because of the stomping. Either that, or they'd scared the dickens out of a very large cat. Elven opened the screen again, ready to pound on the door one more time, but then he heard the deadbolt disengage.

The door opened a crack, and he was about to step back to give the person on the other side of the door some space, but before he could, a glint of silver came at him. He looked down to see a shotgun barrel had been shoved through the opening in an upward angle, right at Elven's face.

CHAPTER FIFTY-THREE

TANK KNOCKED ON THE DOOR OF ROBERT'S RESIDENCE, WAITING for him to answer. Tank hadn't been able to find a different address listed for Katelyn Manner anywhere in their files, which were mostly out-of-date as it was. The DMV would more than likely have that information, but that was if Katelyn had bothered to update it. Since she technically still owned the place where Robert now lived, she might not have been in a big rush to do so. And of course, they didn't have any sort of electronic connection to the files at the DMV. Sometimes Dupray felt like the Stone Age when it came to technology.

Then there was calling Robert. That ended up being a dead end, too. When Tank had tried calling him, it went straight to voicemail without even ringing once. He either kept his phone off or it was not in service. That alone frustrated Tank, considering Robert had called the station just yesterday morning to report the supposed break-in. How was Robert expecting an update from the station if he didn't keep his phone on?

So, as things went in Dupray, Tank found himself on Robert's doorstep, hoping the man was home. If only to point Tank in the direction of Katelyn Manner's current place of residence.

Some days, working in Dupray was just one big day of driving all over the county to ask questions.

"Robert!" Tank pounded on the door again, his patience growing thinner and thinner with each knock. "It's Deputy Provost," Tank said, using his last name. He used it often enough, but it was never his favorite. Neither was his actual first name. So many people called him Tank since his days in the military that he'd gotten used to responding to it rather than his given name. But being professional sometimes called for formalities.

Finally, the light on the porch lamp flickered on. Tank heard a click at the door as the handle turned. The door creaked open, and a huge puff of smoke came out, smelling awfully skunk-like. As the cloud subsided, with Tank waving his hand and trying not to inhale, Robert's face appeared, complete with bloodshot eyes.

"Deputy," Robert said, his voice shaky. "What, uh, what are you doing here?"

For someone as high as Robert was right now, he seemed nervous. Maybe a deputy showing up at his door unannounced was the cause, especially considering his current state. Tank cracked a smile at the absurdity of the whole thing.

"Robert, everything okay here?" he asked.

Robert looked around, like he was expecting to see more than just Tank. "Yeah, everything okay with you?" he asked. The paranoia was clearly settling in.

"Any new break-ins?" Tank asked.

Robert shook his head slowly. "Is that why you're here?" he asked.

"I was trying to call, but—"

"Ohhh, yeah. I dropped my phone in the toilet," Robert said. "Don't worry, I stuck it in a jar of rice, but that's why I can't answer."

"You said this was your aunt's house, correct?"

"That's right," he said. "My Aunt Katelyn owns the place. I pay her rent, but she keeps it low since I come over and help her move shit around."

"Great," Tank said, not interested in the backstory. But he was glad that Robert had confirmed it was Katelyn. "So you know where she lives, then."

Robert scratched his head, nodding slowly. "It's pretty far from here. She said she doesn't like to be around a lot of people." He leaned out, looking around again as if others might be listening in. "Between you and me, she doesn't like most people. Always finds something to nitpick about them. She can be a real b-word, if you know what I mean." Robert's eyes went wide. "Oh, shit, don't tell her I said that, though. I don't want her to kick me out."

"Your secret's safe with me," Tank said. "As long as you can give me her address and phone number."

CHAPTER FIFTY-FOUR

"You better have a good reason for standing on my porch at such an hour," the small, bespectacled woman with blonde curls snarled from behind the shotgun.

Elven held both his hands up, his eyes darting toward Tommy, who stood to the side of the door. His deputy had his hand on his gun, ready to pull the trigger if needed. Elven didn't think they were at that point yet. This wasn't the first time a gun had been shoved in his face from just stepping on someone's property.

Sometimes it was a misunderstanding. Other times it was because they didn't like law enforcement and wanted him gone. There had only been a handful of times when gunplay had been required.

Elven swallowed, hoping he wasn't misreading the current situation. "Ma'am," Elven said, continuing to show the woman he wasn't armed. "I'm Sheriff Elven Hallie with Dupray County—"

"Oh, for Pete's sake!" she cried, pulling the shotgun back immediately. She propped the shotgun inside somewhere near the doorway. "I'm so sorry." Her eyes had gone wide. "You're not gonna arrest me now, are you?"

Elven smiled, his heart still racing inside his chest, but relieved that he read her intent correctly. "Not if you promise not to pull a gun on me again," he quipped.

She covered her face with both hands. "I'm so embarrassed," she said. She pulled her hands away, and Elven could see she was on the verge of tears. "We just don't get visitors out this way much, and, well, as you can see, if someone comes at me, there's no way I'll be able to fight them off. Plus, with what's been going on in town, well, to say I've been a little jumpy is an understatement."

"That's fair enough," Elven said. He pointed to Tommy, who still stood at the ready. "This is my deputy, Tommy Coast."

She looked at Tommy, offering a smile. "I'm so sorry," she said again. "What brings you all the way out here?"

"You mentioned you heard about what's going on in town," Elven said. "What can you tell me about it?"

"Lucinda," a male voice said from inside. It did not sound friendly. "Is someone out there?"

She poked her head back inside. "Abe, the sheriff and his deputy are out here. Go make yourself decent before they see you in your underwear." She turned back to Elven. "You boys want to come in for some tea?"

THE COTTAGE WAS JUST as cozy inside as Elven had expected. Lucinda had her own style, decorating the place with Hummel figures and other tchotchkes she'd collected over the years. Though Elven would never want to live in a place like this, something about it soothed him. It reminded him of being a kid, visiting someone's grandmother. It even smelled like she had something on the stove cooking away all day. The whole experience was like a giant, warm hug.

Lucinda had filled Elven in on what she knew about the happenings in town. She had gotten the gist of it right. The library had been shot up, leaving a lot of dead people, most of which she confirmed she knew from going to some of the book discussions. She even knew about Robin being killed in the parking lot by the thrift shop.

"She was *always* talking about that thrifting place," Lucinda said. "To be honest, it sounded like she spent more time on that drag than she did in her own home."

Elven spotted Tommy making notes, but he didn't think it was necessary. All of this was stuff they both already knew, and with how word traveled in Dupray, he wasn't surprised that Lucinda knew everything, even being this far out.

When the tea kettle squealed, she stood and headed into the kitchen. Tommy and Elven surveyed the room but didn't speak. There wasn't much to say other than Lucinda seemed like a nice older lady. She came back out with two tea cups on saucers. On each saucer were a couple of small cookies hanging over the edge.

"Not sure what you boys like, but I hope this is okay," she said, setting the plates down in front of them. "Like I said, we don't get many visitors so my stock is a bit low. Abe was going to head out tomorrow to stock up on some things."

"That's your husband?" Elven asked, not having seen Abe since coming inside. Apparently, he was still making himself decent.

Lucinda smiled wide, her eyes lighting up. "Yep," she said. "Married forty-three years in June."

"That's a long time," Elven said.

"Not to me," she said, still beaming. "Sure, looking back, it can feel that way, but it never feels that long when I'm with him. Marry your best friend, the one who you'd do anything for and would do anything for you. That's my advice."

Elven smiled. "I'll keep that in mind," he said.

Footsteps stomped around upstairs and began to grow closer as they took to the stairs. Both Tommy and Elven looked up.

"Oh, Abe's anything but a light-foot," Lucinda said. "I've gotten used to it over the years."

Abe came around the corner, showing himself for the first time.

Elven recognized him. He was in his sixties, his head shaved bald, and very tall with broad shoulders. It was then that Elven realized he recognized the man.

"I saw you at the library the other day," Elven said.

"Abe, you were down there?" Lucinda asked.

Abe didn't seem too happy to be called out about that, or maybe he was just sour all the time. Elven got the feeling it was both. Abe grunted. "I had to return those books," he said.

"Oh, that's right," Lucinda said. "I asked him to go down to return my books so I didn't get hit with a late fee. I sometimes forget to do that. That's when he told me about the commotion that was going on."

Elven thought "commotion" was downplaying it when it came to describing a mass murder.

"How long do you two plan on staying?" Abe asked.

"That's the thing," Elven said. "Could be quite a while."

Abe only stared at them like he was debating what to do next. Elven didn't really like the way Abe was acting, but it wasn't a crime to not like people coming to his door in the middle of the night, sheriff or not.

Lucinda, however, did respond. "What do you mean?" she asked. "Why would you stay?"

"Because we think whoever is responsible is going to do it again. We've narrowed down a list of potential targets," Elven said.

"Us?!" Lucinda shrieked, holding a hand to her chest.

"We're still trying to gather information, but right now—"

"This is horseshit," Abe said. "I can take care of myself and my wife. I don't need anyone else for that."

"Abe, it's alright," Lucinda said, trying to reassure him. Abe grumbled, but he listened to his wife, not protesting anymore. Instead, he turned around, went upstairs, and slammed a door.

Lucinda smiled apologetically. "Don't mind him," she said. "He puts on a big show, but really, he's a big softie. A romantic at heart."

"I can see that," Tommy said dryly. His sarcasm wasn't missed by Lucinda.

"No, it's true," she insisted. "That man would do anything for me. Here, look." She stood up and walked to a nearby bookshelf against the wall, pulling down a picture frame. She handed it to Tommy, who held it so he and Elven could look. It was an image of Abe carrying Lucinda, sometime twenty or so years before they hit their forty-third anniversary. It looked like they were competing in some sort of race, as each of them had numbers on their shirts.

"A marathon?" Elven asked.

Lucinda nodded. "Abe and I used to do these all the time. Drive around the country, enter races where we could. It was fun for us, but as you can tell, we got around to it when we were much younger than we are now." She smiled. "This race, in particular, I was gunning hard to finish, but I tripped. Abe had trained for this one for so long, and I was so proud of him for wanting to better his time and maybe even place."

"So what happened?" Tommy asked.

"I cramped up," she said, disappointment in her voice. "I couldn't make it the last mile. My body just gave out. I told Abe to keep going, but he wouldn't listen. He knew how much I was looking forward to finishing. So he picked me up and carried me the last mile."

"Wow," Tommy said. "That's a long way."

"Lucky for him, I'm lighter than most," she said with a smile. "But by doing so, it cost him his time and place. But he didn't care. He only wanted me to be happy. That's the kind of man he is. Giving up everything to help me. To take care of me." She took the picture from Tommy, then looked at it fondly, running a finger over it. "He just does so much for me that I wish one time that I could do something like that for him, you know?"

"I'm sure you do," Tommy said. "A relationship wouldn't last that long if it was one-sided, I would think."

Lucinda put the picture down. "I'm trying," she said. "So I guess you're right." She looked at them with a small smile. "So you said we're on your list of potential targets?"

Elven nodded. "How often did you attend the book discussion at the library?"

"Oh, well, being out here, it's one of the few times I actually get out to mingle with people," she said. "I try to make it every month. You think someone is targeting the book club?"

Elven nodded. "Were you at the last one? We spoke to the author—"

"Mike Lindsay," Lucinda said. "The book was very good. Thrilling, and I didn't see the twist coming at the end."

Elven didn't care much about any of that, but Lucinda was like an open book herself right now, so he didn't want to do anything to close it. He just needed to direct it more toward the information he needed. That would be easier to do if he actually knew what that information was. But for now, he could feel her out.

"And how about Misty Rivers?" Elven asked.

Lucinda shook her head. "Who?" she asked, but he saw a little tendon in her neck tense up for a split second.

"Oh, it was last month's discussion," Elven said, like it was just an afterthought. "All of the victims were at the discussion, along with two other people. You were one of them, I believe."

"And how do you know that?"

"You checked out the book."

She smiled. "That's some good detective work," she said. "And you're right. I was there, and so was that Katelyn Manner. I assume you already knew that, though."

Elven nodded. "Glad to know that I'm on the right track."

"You think that she's also at risk?" Lucinda asked.

"It's a possibility," he said.

"God help whoever tries something with Katelyn," Lucinda said, shaking her head.

"She's a tough one, I take it?" Elven asked.

Lucinda shook her head. "I guess you could describe her that way," she said. "I'd go with mouthy. I don't like to speak ill of people, but she might be the most miserable person I've ever met. To be honest, I was glad she wasn't at the last meeting. Though, saying that now has a double meaning, I suppose."

"But you were there?" Elven asked.

Lucinda sighed. "I suppose I wasn't all that honest, was I?"

CHAPTER FIFTY-FIVE

ELVEN SHIFTED, READY TO MAKE A MOVE IF NEEDED. LUCINDA just admitted she was there, but if that were the case, why wasn't she dead yet? Or at the very least, why hadn't she called in what had happened? He started to rise to his feet, feeling like this wasn't going to go over well.

But Lucinda stood herself.

"Abe and I like to go to the discussions together," she said. "But that night, he wasn't feeling well, so he joined in on a video call. He told me that I should go in. But ultimately, I could tell he wasn't feeling well. We kind of got into a little tiff, you might call it, so I left early."

"If you knew about what happened at the library, then why didn't you call us?" Elven asked.

Lucinda shrugged. "I don't know," she said. "I got nervous, I guess. I mean, I had been there, and if I stayed, then I would have ended up just like them. I didn't want to draw any attention to myself, thinking if I just played dumb, I wouldn't be a target." Her eyes widened in realization. "Oh, you can talk to that author fellow.

Mike Lindsay. He can tell you that I left early. I'm sure he'd remember it."

Elven rubbed the spot between his eyes. The story mostly matched up with what Mike had already told him, so there was no need to call him back up, especially since he wasn't great with the details. "I wish you would have just come forward," Elven said.

"I'm sorry," she said. "I just didn't know what to do. Abe will tell you I came right home, and then the next day when he dropped the books off, he told me what was going on. Then he heard all about it, and I just froze."

"And how about Abe?"

"What about him?"

"Was he home all night?"

She nodded. "Oh, yeah," she said, biting her lip. "I mean, he did need to run out and grab some Pepto. His stomach wasn't feeling great. I told him I'd bring some home, but he didn't want me stopping so he ran out to grab it himself. He's always trying to keep me in mind, even when he doesn't feel good."

Elven saw how nervous she was, and he couldn't blame her. He wanted to ask her more, but then Tommy's phone vibrated.

"Oh, sorry," Tommy said, holding a finger up and glancing at his phone. "Looks like Tank found Katelyn Manner's address," he told Elven.

"Where at?" Elven asked.

He began reading the text aloud. "It says, 'Hope this goes through to one of you, got no service when tried calling. Found Katelyn Manner's address. Three Thirty-Six West Birch Street.'"

"That's kind of out there," Elven said. It was on the other side of the county.

"I'm glad you found her," Lucinda said. "But tell your friend to keep an eye on her. I'm not sure what happened, but at last month's discussion, she was particularly upset about something. I don't think she agreed with what everyone said about the book. Most didn't like it. Since she didn't show up to this last meeting, I kind of thought she got her feelings hurt."

Elven pulled his phone out, not seeing any new texts on his phone. He tried calling Tank, but it never connected. He checked his phone again and saw he had no bars. "Do you have service?" Elven asked Tommy.

Tommy shook his head. "Not really," he said. "I must have found the right spot to get a message."

Elven nodded. "Do you have a phone I can use?" he asked Lucinda.

Lucinda frowned. "We only have a direct line for the computer. You can try to do a video call to your friend if you'd like," she offered. "Depends on his connection, of course."

"I don't think that'll work," Elven said. "Maybe I can get him on the radio out in the truck." He went to the door, motioning for Tommy to follow him.

"What's up?" Tommy whispered near the doorway.

"I'm gonna see if I can get ahold of Tank, but I want you to stay here. Keep an eye on Lucinda for me, will you?" Elven asked.

Lucinda had gone back to the pictures, looking up and smiling at the two men for a moment.

"You think she's...?" Tommy trailed off.

"I don't know. I just want you to keep your eyes peeled, okay?"

"You got it," Tommy said, popping a cookie in his mouth that he'd taken from the saucer. "I think I can handle this."

CHAPTER FIFTY-SIX

TANK MADE IT TO KATELYN'S ADDRESS, OR AT LEAST THE address that Robert had given him. He checked his phone before getting out of his truck, but there was no text or missed call from either Elven or Tommy. He didn't even know if his message had gone through.

At this point, he was on his own. Not that it was a big deal to him, but he liked to make sure someone knew where he was when on the job. The drive had been a haul, but he'd managed to make great time.

He made his way up the steps and onto the porch. The house was pretty bare as far as decorations went, and the light was off. The only streetlight was at the corner about a quarter mile down the road where he had turned off the main drag. He felt more secluded here than at Robert's.

He just hoped that Katelyn was home.

He knocked on the door, immediately announcing his presence with the sheriff's department. He waited a moment, then knocked again.

"I hear ya!" someone shouted from inside. "Gotta give me a second."

Tank stepped back, glad that someone was home. Finally, the door opened, and a woman stood in the doorway. She had long brown hair and looked to be in her mid-fifties. She wore sweatpants and held a glass of wine with what looked like a couple of ice cubes inside. She took a sip, looking Tank up and down.

"The hell you want?" she asked.

"I'm with the Dupray—"

"I heard you through the door," she said. "What do you want?"

She's rather pleasant, Tank thought sarcastically. "I'm here to ask about the library book discussion you attend," Tank said.

"How'd you get my address?"

"Robert—"

"My dumbass nephew," she said, rolling her eyes. "So what about it?"

"I don't know if you've heard, but there was a shooting inside. A lot of people died. I think you knew them. I'm sorry for your loss," Tank offered. He felt completely off his game with Katelyn. With how unfriendly she was, he found it difficult to believe she'd been friends with any of the victims.

She quickly confirmed his suspicions. "Hate to hear it," Katelyn said. "But they were just a bunch of assholes who I read books with. Most of the time, they had terrible taste. So, what of it?" She sipped her wine again.

"We're touching base with whoever might be at risk of being a future target," Tank said.

"So there's someone out there targeting us book readers?" she asked. "What has the world come to?"

"It's a little more specific than that," he said. "It has to do with what might have been said about a book. *Hollow Hearts* by Misty Rivers."

Katelyn snorted. "That piece of shit," she said dismissively. A smile crept over her lips. "Here's a question for you. You got any idea who did it? The murderer, I mean."

Tank took a breath, unsure how to answer the question. His silence was answer enough for her.

"Before you tell me some bullshit about how you're exploring every avenue possible," she said, "let me ask you. How do you know I didn't do it? You got no leads, right? It could be anyone. And now you're out here, all by your lonesome, with what I assume is jack shit for cell service."

Tank licked his lips, considering her for a moment. Katelyn was something else, that was for sure. "Do you have any ideas of who might have done it?"

Katelyn smiled, throwing her wine glass back and finishing the whole thing. "You really have no idea what you're doing," she remarked.

CHAPTER FIFTY-SEVEN

"CAN I GET YOU SOME MORE COOKIES?" LUCINDA ASKED.

Tommy had finished all his cookies, along with the cookies on Elven's untouched saucer. He slurped down all the tea in his cup and leaned back. He was stuffed. "No, I couldn't have any more," Tommy said with a smile. "I'll have to find out what brand those are, though, because they were delicious."

Lucinda smiled. "I'm glad you enjoyed them," she said. "I don't get a lot of time to entertain. Abe isn't big on having people over. Or making friends, for that matter."

"I'm sorry to hear that," Tommy said, unsure if that was the right response.

She waved her hand. "Don't be," she said. "I get by, and Abe is more than enough for me."

Tommy nodded, feeling the liquid catch up to his bladder. "Do you mind if I use your bathroom?" he asked. "Might have overdone it on the tea."

Lucinda chuckled. "Of course," she said. "Oh, but the downstairs one is broken, so you'll have to go upstairs. Second room on the left once you're up there."

"Great."

"Don't get lost," Lucinda said, throwing a wink in his direction.

Tommy smiled, making his way up the stairs. The stairwell was lined with pictures of Lucinda and Abe together through the years. He walked slowly, examining each picture as he did. It looked like they had a very happy life together. In each picture, Abe and Lucinda were smiling. Tommy hadn't seen a single smile from Abe since entering the home, though he had disappeared almost immediately after coming downstairs.

Tommy shrugged it off, thinking that some people were just introverted. From the way Lucinda spoke, Abe definitely seemed that type. Maybe even more shut in than a typical introvert, too. It wasn't Tommy's marriage, but he'd gotten a bit of a controlling vibe from the man during their brief exchange.

Tommy passed the first door at the top of the stairs, noticing how unusually narrow the door was. He continued down the hallway and stopped in front of the second door, finding it closed. He opened it and stepped inside.

He suddenly found himself in a room that clearly wasn't the bathroom. It was an office with bookshelves lining the walls. Right in the middle of the room was a desk where a computer sat. The monitor glowed, the screen white, open to what looked like a Word document. "So much for the second door," Tommy said to himself.

He was about to turn around, but something caught his eye. A copy of the book that Elven had been carrying around. The one that he thought was the cause of this entire case. *Hollow Hearts*. It was on top of a box sitting right under the desk.

Tommy went deeper into the office, picking up the book and flipping through it. It was nothing special, as far as he could tell, but it seemed odd to him. If they owned a copy of the book, why would they have checked it out of the library?

He looked down at the box and saw it was slightly open. He pulled the cardboard flap open and saw more books inside. They were all copies of *Hollow Hearts*.

"What the hell?" Tommy muttered. Now he was confused. That is, until he looked at the monitor.

It was a Word document, but it was the file name at the top of the window that alarmed him.

It read "HollowHearts2."

"The bathroom is the second room on the left," Lucinda called out from downstairs. "I always forget the closet door is there. Abe's office is the second door. He doesn't like it disturbed."

Tommy swallowed, realizing that the author of *Hollow Hearts*, Misty Rivers, was really Abe Hall. He quickly spun around, wanting to get out of the room and downstairs to tell Elven, but as soon as he did, he ran into what felt like a wall. He stumbled backward, catching himself on the desk. He looked up.

Abe Hall glared at him, holding a revolver in his right hand.

CHAPTER FIFTY-EIGHT

ELVEN OPENED THE DOOR TO HIS TRUCK AND SLID INSIDE. HE grabbed the receiver from under the dash, letting out a sigh as he did. It felt like this whole thing was a bit of a shot in the dark, but right now, it was all he had—a couple of people who might be at risk. Figuring out if one of them was the killer would be a tall order, considering there wasn't much evidence left at the crime scene to put them there.

But going with his gut was sometimes a shot in the dark. Generally, if he got out of his own way, he could hit a bullseye.

All Elven had was Lucinda admitting she was there before the murders took place. Did that mean anything? He couldn't be sure, but he could understand Lucinda being too scared to come forward. Plus, her husband seemed a little less than enthusiastic about much of anything. Lucinda might have talked him up, but Elven didn't see much.

He clicked it on, holding it to his mouth for a moment. "Tank, it's E—"

A gunshot came from inside the house.

Elven looked out the window to the house, as if he'd see anything different than the well-cared-for home that had the light on the porch with the flowers and decorations. It was all just as he'd left it.

There was a light on upstairs that he didn't remember being on before. Elven dropped the radio, exited the truck, and pulled his revolver off his hip. He ran for the house, barging in through the front door unannounced. He looked around, but didn't see anyone in the living room. Not Abe, not Lucinda, and not Tommy.

"Tommy!" Elven yelled out.

"Oh, my," Lucinda said, coming from the kitchen. She carried another saucer with a cup on top, fresh cookies on the side. "What is all that noise?" She looked worried as soon as she saw Elven holding his gun. "Abe!" But there was no answer from her husband, either.

"Tommy!" Elven yelled again.

"El—" he heard Tommy try to call for him, but he was suddenly cut off with a slam. It came from upstairs.

Elven spun on his heels and took the stairs two at a time, carrying his gun with both hands, his body swaying with each lunge upward.

And then he was at the top. The door to his left looked tiny, more than likely just a closet. The door following that was closed, but before he could reach it, a huge slam shook it and the surrounding wall.

"Tommy!" Elven shouted, grabbing the door handle with his left hand and pushing it in. It didn't budge. Elven pushed his shoulder into it. It gave way, then slammed shut again. Someone was on the other side, pushing against it.

"Yahhh!" Tommy yelled from the other side of the door. There was a loud tumble, then a crash. Elven kept pushing the door, and it suddenly gave way, sending him spilling into the room.

Elven's foot caught on something in the middle of the office, making him lurch forward. He tried to catch himself, but someone grabbed at his arm, the one that held his gun.

It was Abe. His nose was bloody, along with the corner of his mouth. It looked like the corner of his lips had been torn. But none of that was stopping him. He was determined, and he was angry.

He used Elven's forward movement to his advantage and spun him, sending him flying into a bookcase. Elven managed to hold onto his revolver, but the bookcase fell on top of him, flattening him to the carpet. Abe stomped toward him, but Tommy intervened by rushing Abe and tackling him against the wall.

There was a revolver across the room under the desk. It didn't look like Tommy's, so it must have been Abe's. Elven crawled out from under the bookcase, bringing his revolver up once he was firmly on his feet. But there was no clear shot. Not that he wanted to shoot, but at this point, Abe might not give them another choice.

"Abe, stand down!" Elven commanded.

But it was no use. Abe continued to wrestle with Tommy, both of them managing to stay on their feet. Tommy pushed against him, trying to get him pinned, trying to take him to the ground.

"Tommy, get out of the way," Elven barked.

Tommy tried to move, but Abe clutched him, twisting him as he did. "I'm trying," Tommy said. "Could use some—"

Abe slapped his hand over Tommy's mouth. Tommy bit Abe's hand, causing him to scream and release Tommy. Elven steadied his gun, but the men were too close. Hitting Tommy was too much of a risk.

Tommy broke away, giving a six-inch gap where Elven might have had a chance, but Abe was already closing it. He shoved Tommy, sending him falling straight toward Elven. But Elven was prepared, sensing something like that would happen. He took a huge step to the side and got out of Tommy's way. His deputy crashed into the desk, sending the monitor careening over the edge.

And then Abe rushed Elven. Elven pulled the trigger, but Abe had anticipated it. In spite of his size, he'd gotten himself under Elven's arms, pushing them into the air and making him shoot the ceiling. Abe shoved and grappled with Elven, the two of them flying through the open doorway, slamming against the wall in the hallway.

Elven's hands were still raised as Abe held them in position. Their faces were inches from each other. Elven could feel Abe's hot breath against his nose, and he inhaled whatever garlic dish he'd eaten for dinner.

"You're only going to get yourself hurt," Elven said through his gritted teeth. "Maybe even Lucinda. Now let go and put your hands up."

Of course, that didn't work, either.

Elven spotted Tommy climb up from the floor, shaking his head. He didn't look great, his face bloody and even scuffed. He spun around like he was looking for something. Then Elven saw that his gun wasn't in the holster. But who knew where it had ended up at this point with how trashed the office was.

When Tommy couldn't find it, he turned his attention to the hallway, where Abe had a small advantage over Elven. Elven couldn't get any leverage against the wall, so they found themselves in a standstill, trying to overpower each other to take control of Elven's gun.

Elven yelled as loud as he could, pushing with all his might. He gained a few inches away from the wall, reared his head back, and brought it forward as hard as he could, smacking Abe's face. He was going for the nose, but at this angle, accuracy wasn't at the forefront of his mind. He had to do something.

And it worked. Abe let go of Elven, grabbing at his own face. They were still very close, and if Elven brought his revolver down, he'd practically be handing it to Abe if he shot his hand out. Tommy was right behind Abe, ready to take him down.

"Get him down," Elven said, expecting Tommy to grab Abe's arm, maybe even kick at the back of his legs to bring him to his knees. Elven's goal was to put him in cuffs.

But maybe Tommy had taken too many blows to the head to understand, or maybe he wanted to win the fight, but whatever the case, he didn't try to subdue Abe. Instead, he let out a war cry and dove at Abe. Abe didn't expect it, and when Tommy hit him, his arms flailed to the sides, and the two of them crashed into Elven.

The three of them lost their balance, and they soon found themselves teetering over and down the stairs. Six legs, six arms, and three heads all in a ball, toppling down the thankfully carpeted stairs.

Elven hit his shoulder, his leg, his ribcage, and the side of his head on the way down. But he was still coherent, and now he was angry.

His gun, however, was no longer in his hands.

The three men all managed to get to their feet, but they were all panting, exhausted from the fight. Elven was covered in sweat. His body was screaming at him, adrenaline on the verge of running out. Somehow, he was the only one who wasn't bleeding. Tommy was in bad shape, but Abe looked in even worse shape.

The three of them looked at each other. Elven groaned, knowing that this wasn't over.

And then the sound of a break-action closing drew all of their attention.

"Stop all this nonsense right now," Lucinda commanded, pointing the double-barreled shotgun at the three of them. It looked massive against her small stature, but her face told Elven she was serious.

"Lucinda," Elven said, holding his hand out. "Put down the gun before someone gets hurt."

Lucinda wasn't listening. "Abe, get over here," she said. "I don't know what's happened, but we can talk it all out."

"What happened is your husband attacked me," Tommy groaned.

"I'm sure you did something—"

"Yeah, I found out that he's the author of that shitty book," Tommy said. "Misty Rivers."

That was news to Elven. He thought they'd be looking for a woman, if anything, but that was an assumption that he shouldn't have made. A pen name could be anyone.

"Abe?" Lucinda said. "What is he talking about?" She still held the shotgun firmly, but now her attention was on her husband more than anyone else.

Elven spotted his revolver. It was only two feet in front of him. He eased down, but not too far. This whole situation was a mess, but if she didn't lower that shotgun, he would have to do whatever it took. One slip of her finger, and all three of them could be dead.

"Lucinda, let me handle this," Abe said.

"I don't understand," Lucinda said. "What does writing a book have anything to do with this?"

"Lady, he killed all those people because they said nasty things about him, and he didn't like it," Tommy said, boiling it down to a simple sentence. And like Tank had said, it sounded absurd when said out loud. But it was also the truth.

"That doesn't make sense," Lucinda said, frowning.

"People have done a lot worse for a lot less," Tommy said, echoing what Elven had said earlier. But Elven was glad Tommy was talking so he could keep her occupied. The less attention on him, the better.

Elven inched closer to his revolver and glanced toward Abe, who now was looking right at Elven with gritted teeth. He could see something in Abe's eyes. They went from Elven, then to Lucinda.

Abe put his hands up and stepped out between the shotgun and the other men. He sighed. "He's right, though," Abe said. "Lucinda, put the shotgun down. I don't want anyone else to get hurt."

Lucinda stared at Abe, still processing what he was saying. "Abe, you can't—"

"Lucinda, put it down," he commanded. He turned to Elven. "That won't be necessary." He was well-aware that Elven was trying to reach his gun. "I give up. Take me in."

"I don't understand," Lucinda said, her hands shaking.

"I killed those people. It was me, alone," Abe said.

"No, you didn't!" Lucinda screamed, her eyes wide in shock. It was clear that this was news to her. Abe had just dropped a bomb on his wife.

"Lucinda!" Abe shouted.

Elven looked at Lucinda, who still held the shotgun. He wasn't going to make any sudden movements until he knew it was safe. Abe looked over his shoulder, then gave a nod to his wife.

Lucinda swallowed and set the gun down. "I'm sorry, I just—I don't understand what's happening," she said again. Tears welled up in her eyes.

Tommy went to Lucinda and grabbed the shotgun so she couldn't reach it again in case she changed her mind. That's when Elven grabbed Abe, pulling his hands behind his back and securing the handcuffs around his wrists.

"Please," Abe said. "Don't arrest her for trying to defend me. She didn't know and was just confused."

Tommy stood next to Lucinda, biting the inside of his cheek. Elven could tell he was on the fence. After a moment, he turned to Elven, his eyes soft.

"Alright," Elven said, letting Tommy off the hook from having to arrest the lady. "Let's get him in the truck."

CHAPTER FIFTY-NINE

ELVEN STOOD BEHIND ABE IN THE JAIL CELL BACK AT THE station. The man was big, and even just standing behind him, Elven felt slightly intimidated by his size. But he hadn't put up a fight once he'd been arrested. There was no squirming in the cuffs, no mouthing off, not even a hint of trying to make a run of it from the moment he was put in cuffs to right now.

"You're not gonna give me any trouble, are you?" Elven asked, pulling his keys out.

"No, sir," Abe said, polite as ever.

Elven sighed as he gently uncuffed Abe's wrists. Abe rubbed the skin there, but he didn't turn around. Elven stepped back so he was outside of the cell and swung the gate closed, locking it up right after.

"You're set," Elven told Abe.

Abe slowly turned around and offered a sheepish smile. It confused Elven. It was a complete turnaround from the man he had been introduced to back at the house. How had this man been able to kill all those people? Well, he knew how, but he just didn't understand it. Because they had made fun of his book? He supposed some people couldn't take criticism.

But he was sure there was more to it than that. This might have just been the straw that broke the camel's back.

Tank cleared his throat, pulling Elven's attention to where he stood in the doorway. Elven lifted his chin in silent acknowledgment.

"Lucinda wants to speak to her husband," Tank said. "What do you think?"

Elven glanced back to Abe, who'd perked up at the mention of his wife's name. Elven nodded. "I think it'll be alright," he said, then gave a long yawn.

It had been a very long night. So long that he could have sworn the sun was peeking up when he dropped Tommy off at Driscoll's before taking Abe to the station. His deputy looked worse for wear, and considering the amount of blows to the head he'd taken, Elven figured it was best to have him looked at.

"Go ahead and bring her in," Elven said. "I'll stay here while she talks. You mind pulling the truck back around to the front?"

Tank shook his head. "Sure thing," he said. "But don't stay too long. You're gonna need some sleep if tonight is still on."

Elven knew it. As soon as he walked through the door to the station, Abe in tow, Johnny told him that Zane Rhodes had agreed to the debate. Johnny told him he didn't even need to mention Glenn Sutherland, but he did, anyway. And as soon as that name came up, Zane's whole attitude shifted. He seemed shaken, according to Johnny.

That was good, but it didn't mean Elven had it in the bag. He still had no idea who this guy was, other than what Meredith had told him about his rap sheet when they came into the station. But that still didn't connect him to Zane. At best, it told Elven he was on the right path. But he still needed to be on top of his game if he was going to win the debate.

"Thanks, Tank," Elven said.

Tank knocked on the doorway once, gave a nod, and disappeared down the hallway. Almost as soon as he left, Lucinda took his place. If Elven thought Abe was sheepish, Lucinda was the entire flock. She shrank down as she walked through the doorway, lifting her eyes to meet the sheriff's gaze.

Elven nodded. "Come on in, it's alright."

"I just didn't want to get in trouble or cause problems," she said. "I think I've already done enough of that."

Elven thought about saying that she couldn't cause any more trouble than Abe had already done for himself, but refrained. It was a tense moment, and while Abe had a lot of explaining to do and come-uppance for what he'd done, Lucinda wasn't part of that. Finding out what her husband had done, along with processing the idea that he was going to get locked away for life—or worse—was enough for her to endure without him adding any jabs to it. He didn't fault her for the incident with the shotgun.

He motioned to the yellow line painted on the floor. The color was long faded but still visible enough that anyone coming into the room would get the idea. Maybe after the election, he could have it repainted. "Just stay behind the line," Elven ordered.

"I wouldn't hurt my wife," Abe stated.

"I believe it," Elven said. "But it's procedure, and you're lucky we're letting it happen." Elven walked to the corner and grabbed a free stool, plopping it down right in front of Abe, just behind the yellow line. "If you'd like to sit," he said to Lucinda.

"Thank you, Sheriff," she said, hesitantly sliding atop the seat. She looked to Elven, not saying anything, but it was clear she was uncomfortable.

"I'll be just over here," Elven said. "It's the best I can do right now."

He walked to the corner of the room, not wanting her to be alone with Abe just yet. He was willing to let her talk with him before they were thrown into the craziness of the legal system. He felt bad for Lucinda, and figured he could offer her that little bit of kindness.

"Thank you," she said again, watching Elven tuck into the corner of the room before turning back to Abe. From his angle, he could see the tears in her eyes, the hurt on her face, and the need for answers.

"I'm sorry," Abe said, leaning against the bars of the cell, looking down at Lucinda.

"Why did you do this?" she asked.

"Because you deserve everything in the world.".

"I already have that."

He shook his head. "Clearly not," he said. "I tried. I wrote that book for you."

"I know that, Abe," she said.

His brows knit as he tried to make sense of it. "When did you find out I wrote the book?" he asked. "I never told anyone."

She scoffed, but it came off as a laugh. "You think you can hide something like that from me?" she asked. "The moment I read it, I knew exactly who wrote it. Misty Rivers? What kind of a made-up name was that, anyway?"

He shrugged. "I didn't think it was that bad. But the things they said. About the book. About you—well, the character I based off of you. They were awful and nasty."

She sighed. "I know," she said. "I never wanted *you* to get hurt. They were awful."

They sat silently for a moment, staring at the floor like they didn't know what to say next. Finally, Abe smiled and lifted his head. "I need you to let it all go," he said.

Lucinda scrunched up her face, shaking her head as she looked at him. "What do you mean?"

"This," he said, pounding on his chest. "Me, I mean. Let it all go. Forget about all of those people, forget about the book, and forget about me. This is going to be too much for the rest of my life, however short or long it is. And I don't need you here for it. You have to move on, okay? Just let it all go and don't think about it again, you hear me?"

"Abe," she said. "I—I can't do that."

This time, he was the one crying. Tears ran down his face, and his chin quivered while he tried to say the next thing. "I'm giving you permission to cut ties right here," he said. "I love you so much. Please, let me at least unburden you the only way I can. Let me do this for you."

She shook her head, tears spilling down her cheeks. She didn't want to, but Elven could see that she was reluctantly resigning herself to the situation.

A light knock came against the door frame. Neither Abe nor Lucinda heard it, though. They were too focused on the mess that was their life now.

Elven turned to see Tank with keys in his hand. "You're all set," Tank said. "Let me hang out here. You should really go get some rest."

Elven didn't disagree. The last thing he needed was to turn his long night into an even longer day. He grabbed the keys from Tank, pausing before heading down the hallway.

"Just give them whatever time they need," Elven said. He still didn't understand how Abe could have killed all those people over some nasty words, but he could tell that he would do anything for Lucinda because of how much he loved her.

"At least this will be a good win for the debate," Tank said.

Elven hated to admit it was true. It would have been much better for everyone if the murders hadn't happened, but he might as well use them to his advantage since what was done was done.

CHAPTER SIXTY

THE SHOWERS WERE NEARLY EMPTY WHEN GLENN SUTHERLAND walked in. Only one other man occupied the farthest shower head, lathering up and keeping to himself. Glenn was completely nude, save for a small hand towel that he draped over his shoulder. He was muscular, had tattoos that covered over half of his olive skin, and had what appeared to be scars across the upper part of his back. He was in great shape for his age. He reached out and turned the water on, ducking his head underneath the stream.

"I'm sure that's an interesting story," Hollis said, staring at the scars that went from one shoulder to the next. Hollis sat in the shower on a little plastic stool just behind the pony wall, where he couldn't be seen upon entry. But while Glenn was nude, Hollis was fully clothed.

Glenn turned around, water flinging off his hair and landing just at Hollis's feet. Glenn stepped out from under the water and wiped at his face, trying to clear his vision. "What's it to you?" Glenn asked.

Hollis grinned as he grabbed the white tile of the pony wall to help him stand up. He still had that damned knee that gave him trouble, and no matter how much he tried to hide it and appear strong, he still had to be cautious of it. He'd lived with it for so long, it was second nature to work around it. It was mostly just an irritation now.

"I did some poking around and heard about you," Hollis said. "About why you're here."

Glenn sniggered. "Ain't gotta go through all that trouble to find out why I'm here," he said. "No big secret."

Hollis nodded. "Sure, everybody knows," he said. "About the bank robberies. About the partners that sold you out. Then there's the cops you killed when they came for you. And also the partners you hunted down after getting away." Hollis took a step here and there as he spoke, inching closer to Glenn. "There was some speculation about others that were found dead while you were in the area. Not a whole lot of proof to put on you, but from what I hear, it was nasty."

Glenn looked like he was proud of everything that Hollis was listing off, but it was clear that none of it was news to him. He shrugged. "Ain't gonna confess, if that's what you're after," Glenn said.

"No, no," Hollis said, shaking his head. "Nothing like that. A man's gotta take care of his own business how he sees fit. I get it." He looked over to the one other person in the shower who was finishing up. As soon as the inmate caught Hollis's eye, he took the hint and made a quick exit.

"Then why are you asking about me?" Glenn asked. "I ain't a fan of people that I don't know trying to get into my business." He stepped up to Hollis. "And I don't know you."

"I won't hold that against you," Hollis said. "I know you've been in here much longer than I have, getting popped as you were making your way through my county. So that means you don't know shit about what happens outside these walls."

"You're right about both," Glenn said. "So you must think because you were somebody out there, that makes you somebody in here. But I got news for you. Everybody in here knows to leave me be.

Otherwise, just like those bodies you mentioned, you'll find out first-hand how *nasty* I can be."

Hollis held a hand up. "I ain't interested in any of that," he said. "I just want to have a little chat with you. About your relationship with someone."

"This look like an ice cream social to you?" Glenn growled. "Fuck off before I get angry."

Hollis sighed. "Nothing's gonna happen if you just answer a few of my questions. Hell, we might even become pals after this."

A door opened from the side. A large inmate stepped in, dressed in the usual orange jumpsuit. He had a tattoo next to his eye and a scar along his cheek.

Glenn glanced at him and smiled. "You're really pushing it now," Glenn said to Hollis.

"Everything okay?" the man asked.

"Oh, all good here," Hollis said.

"Like hell it is," Glenn said. "Christopher, our friend here is confused and needs help finding the door."

The inmate made his way toward Hollis and Glenn. "This your man?" Hollis asked Glenn.

Glenn smirked. "I told you I ain't interested in questions or friends."

Hollis nodded. "And I told you that nothing would happen if you answered me. But now I guess we'll have to do it the other way." Hollis stepped into Glenn's face.

Glenn stared him down, standing his ground, which said a lot to Hollis. A man who could stand tall, willing to throw down right then and there while completely in the buff, was someone he wouldn't normally want to square off with. That type of person was confident as hell in their ability.

But Hollis wasn't worried. He puckered his lips and kissed the air, inches away from Glenn's face.

That's when Glenn took a swing.

But Hollis didn't flinch. The fist came right at him, but then Glenn's arm stopped in mid-air.

Glenn stared at it, confused. But then he saw that Christopher was holding Glenn's fist.

"Oops," Hollis said. "It looks like *your* man Christopher is *my* man Christopher."

"What the—"

Hollis swung his fist, nailing Glenn right in the face and knocking him on his ass under the flowing water. Blood poured from his nose, the water making it look worse, tinting the entire floor pink as it washed into the drain.

"Now, I may be a little too old to catch a fist, but I ain't too old to throw 'em," Hollis said.

Christopher stood there, backing Hollis up if he needed. But after the little show they just put on, Hollis didn't think it would be necessary.

"Fuck you," Glenn spat, grabbing his nose.

"I meant what I said," Hollis said. "I just have some questions. If you answer them right away or later is up to you. But one way or the other, you're gonna answer them."

CHAPTER SIXTY-ONE

"From what I gather, this information is coming at just the right time," Hollis said.

Elven held the phone to his ear, having listened to Hollis rattle off all the information he'd gathered on Glenn Sutherland. A lot of it he knew from Meredith's search through the records and finding out why Glenn was incarcerated. But there were some very large gaps that Hollis had just filled him in on.

And if Hollis was right, this intel would be more than enough to win the election.

"Is there confirmation on this?" Elven asked. "Are your sources reputable?"

Hollis chuckled. "Elven, you know I don't do anything half-assed," he said. "You can take my word for it. This is legit."

Elven heard sounds coming from the background, like muffled cries. He didn't really want to know what was happening over there, telling himself that if it was concerning, the guards would handle it. Deep down, however, he knew the kind of pull Hollis had wherever he went.

"Alright," Elven said.

"You make sure and win this thing," Hollis said. "After every-thing we've been through, I don't want some out-of-town yuppie coming in and taking over my county."

"I don't intend on letting that happen."

"Good. And Elven?"

"Yeah?" Elven said as he walked up to the lobby where the debate was to take place again.

"This ain't an ongoing thing," Hollis said. "I owed you, and now I don't. Feel free to visit anytime, but when it comes to owing favors, you don't want the roles reversed."

Before Elven could respond, Hollis hung up the phone. Elven stared at the blank screen and sighed. "I don't plan on it," Elven said to himself.

Zane had been walking around with this bit of dynamite, and now Hollis had practically handed Elven the light for the fuse. The only question was, when would he ignite it?

Elven made his way to the back of the building without entering the main meeting hall. He had rested up for this debate, and Hollis had pulled through for him at the last minute. And now he needed to prep for what was to come tonight.

Elven carried his Filson Twill briefcase that held all the notes he had made that afternoon, with a little help from a quick phone call with his mother. She had been surprising him throughout this whole election time, stepping up in a way he'd never expected. He felt more prepared than he ever had in his career for a meeting like this. He was used to winging it on his charm, but he knew this time, that wouldn't be enough.

He opted to wear his sheriff uniform rather than a suit like last time. He felt out of place and off his game in something that wasn't who he was. Sure, he had worn suits before, but after the last debate, he was going to be on his best game. And that meant being his most authentic self.

After all, if he played it all right in this debate, he would win this election. He'd caught the person responsible for all the murders, and he had the inside knowledge about Zane. So what if he hadn't caught the thief yet? That was small potatoes compared to everything else he had going into this debate. Besides, there were always robberies and more minor cases they were working on. That was just one of them.

"I heard you caught your killer," Zane said.

Elven turned around to see Zane leaning against the wall next to the doorway Elven had just walked through.

"I did," Elven said.

Zane nodded in approval. "And now you've finally decided to go mud-slinging to win this thing," Zane said. He wasn't jovial, but he didn't seem angry, either. If anything, he just seemed *resigned*. It was clear that Zane knew he was cooked.

"You mean because your father is Glenn Sutherland?" Elven asked. He looked around, making sure that they were both the only ones in the room. He didn't need anyone else to spill the beans before the debate. That wouldn't have the effect Elven was looking for.

"I don't even know how you scrounged that information up," Zane said. "I didn't even know it until a few years ago myself. Hell, his name isn't even on my birth certificate. My mother never did tell me growing up. But as soon as I found out..." He looked down. "Well, finding out the father you never knew was actually a mass murderer, bank robber, a sick-in-the-head type with no remorse... it does a number on you."

"But you still keep in touch?" Elven asked.

Zane shrugged. "I never knew him growing up. I never had a father. I wanted to know more. Can't you understand that?"

Elven nodded. "Sure," he said. "Learn anything?"

Zane snickered. "Only that I'm nothing like him."

"That's good."

"You know, I know I can do a better job than you at this job," Zane said. "You're too fast and loose, too attached, definitely too arrogant. And somehow, you still got the job done. But the one thing I never thought of you was that you played dirty. I didn't think you'd stoop to something like this. " He shrugged. "But I guess you want to win, so I don't think I can blame you. Congratulations. You might have won this thing after all."

"I think so," Elven said with a smile. "But not because of this."

Zane cocked his head. "Oh?"

"I know how it feels to be judged based on who your parents are. Nobody deserves that. And you didn't even know who he was for practically your whole life," Elven said. "I'm not going to use this in the debate or as some key to winning. Don't get me wrong, I'm going to win this election, but I'm gonna do it on my own accord and based on my accomplishments."

Zane smiled in disbelief. "Well, Elven, I stand corrected. You are a man of honor, and that's something I sure as hell can respect." He adjusted his suit and held a hand out. "Best of luck to you, 'cause you're gonna need it."

Elven grinned and took his hand firmly. "Maybe a lot less than you think."

CHAPTER SIXTY-TWO

THE STAGE WAS SET, METAPHORICALLY ANYWAY, JUST LIKE THE previous debate. Willard Marks was set to moderate again, though, as Elven had learned from the last time, it was just a position of formality. But Elven didn't mind. He was going to come out swinging during this thing, and once he had momentum, he planned to steamroll through any obstacles that came up. If that meant putting Willard in his place this time, well, so be it.

This wasn't going to be about how Zane wasn't as fit as Elven to be sheriff, because that argument was thin at best. It would center on Elven's history and how he was the best choice for the job. Running or not, nobody could stand up to his track record.

Elven had done his best to keep this county safe and turn it around from the crumbling mess it had become. Even with him being a Hallie, it was hard for anyone to argue against that.

Even Zane had said that Elven had succeeded in the job, and now he even thought Elven was honorable. What else was there?

He stood behind the podium, staring out over the crowd. It was even bigger this go-around compared to the last time they were here.

After word got out that Elven had caught the man responsible for the library murders, he figured a lot of people in town had something else to think about. But he wasn't out of this race by any means.

He smiled at the thought, knowing he could still win back the community. He hadn't lost them. He'd just wandered off for a bit until he could find the trail again.

He lifted his Filson briefcase from the floor and plopped it on top of the podium, opening the flap at the top and reaching inside. He pulled out what he thought were his notes, but instead was the book, *Hollow Hearts*. He had forgotten he still had it after picking it up from Robin's house to look at the notes she'd made.

He sighed, not wanting to relive the case at this moment, and pushed the book to the side of the podium. He reached inside the briefcase again, this time coming out with his notes for the debate. He flipped open the notebook, trying to give himself a quick refresh as he scanned all the points he'd written down.

"Gentlemen," Willard said, once again in the front row of the crowd. He wore a button-up shirt that was about a size too small. Whatever brand the shirt was sure made buttons that could handle stress, because the one right at the peak of Willard's belly was doing the Lord's work holding the whole thing together. Elven held back a smile.

"Are you ready to begin?" Willard asked.

Both Zane and Elven gave a nod, ready to start.

"Alright. Thank you, everyone," Willard said, standing up. "Let's quiet down and give both Elven Hallie and Zane Rhodes the opportunity to speak. The election is tomorrow, so I know this will be a very important moment for our community. I can see that the rest of you agree, considering how many more people are here today."

"Just start it already!" somebody shouted from the back.

This time, Elven cracked a smile and stole a glance to Zane, who gave a chuckle. Apparently, they were both thinking the same thing. The man in the audience wasn't wrong. Elven wondered if Willard just liked the attention.

"Alright," Willard said, holding a hand up. "I can take the hint." He turned around to face the metaphorical stage. "We'll go ahead and start with our current sheriff, Elven Hallie."

Here we go, Elven thought. He found himself just the slightest bit nervous, but nothing he couldn't handle. He knew what was on the line, but this time, he was confident. He had the notes. But most of all, he had his gut.

Hollis was a lot of things, but he was right about that.

"Thank you, Willard. Let's do it," Elven said.

"Alright. So first, I'm sure everyone has now heard that you have caught the person responsible for the awful tragedy that occurred at the library," Willard said. "Situations like this have happened before, and we would like to know how you plan on preventing them instead of reacting to them."

Elven smirked. Even when he had a win, people still wanted to twist it into something negative. Sure, people dying was a bad thing, but it wasn't like he could police everyone at all times of the day. The citizens' mental stability wasn't something that he could do much about, and he didn't think that telling everyone to be nicer to their neighbors would go over too well.

But that was okay. He could answer this, maybe even spin it in his favor. After all, he'd solved the case, even if it felt hollow in some ways because Abe had just confessed right away. But he wasn't complaining that his job had been easy in the end.

His mind went straight to the point about adding more patrols and deputies. It would be a hard sell, especially because people weren't beating down the door to be hired, but he had a plan for that, too. He grabbed his notebook and flipped it open again, looking for the bullet points before speaking. As he did, his hand brushed against the novel that still sat on the podium. It teetered on the edge until it finally lost balance and fell to the floor, its spine open.

"Excuse me," Elven said, bending over to pick it up. He slid a finger underneath it and flipped it over, seeing it had opened up to the dedication page. He reread the words, pausing as he did.

For my love. There's nothing I wouldn't do for you.

Elven grimaced, thinking of Abe now behind bars. And then he felt that pit in his stomach, the same feeling he would get as a kid when scolded for doing something wrong.

He was in trouble, but why?

Maybe it wasn't what he *had* done, but more so, what he *hadn't* done.

He stood up again behind the podium, a blank stare on his face as he looked at the book.

"Elven?" Willard asked.

Elven shook his head and blinked, clearing his throat. "Sorry about that," he said. "Can you repeat the question?"

"Sure," Willard said, but a hint of impatience laced his voice. He started to rattle the question off again, but Elven wasn't listening. Instead, he was focused on the sinking feeling in his gut. He was thinking about how Lucinda had told them that Abe had carried her to the end of the marathon, sacrificing his own race just so she could finish. It was a lovely story when she told it, but now, after everything that had happened?

Something was wrong.

Willard still spoke, but it was muffled. Elven looked up from the book again and shook his head, lifting a hand to stop Willard. "I'm sorry," Elven said. "I, uh, I can't do this right now."

There were rumbles, mutterings, a few gasps, and a couple of scoffs from the audience.

"I'm sorry, but what?" Willard asked.

Elven didn't pay any attention. He gathered his things from the podium, focused only on getting out of there.

"Elven, what's going on?" Zane asked, true concern in his voice. He walked to Elven's podium, placing a hand down. "Everything okay?"

Elven slung the strap of his briefcase over his shoulder and gave a quick nod to Zane. Then he turned and walked down the aisle that separated the room into two sections of people.

"Elven!" Zane shouted. Now he teetered on anger, maybe irritation. Whatever the case, Elven wasn't stopping. "Elven! What are you doing?!" His voice carried all the way down to the end of the crowd, where Elven made his way straight to the doors.

"My job," Elven finally answered.

CHAPTER SIXTY-THREE

Katelyn sat in her overstuffed leather recliner with a glass of wine on the table. In her hands was a Sue Grafton novel. She was somewhere in the middle of the series, catching up on it between books that the discussion group at the library chose to read. Of course, she wasn't really sure what would happen to the discussion group now, given that almost everyone was dead.

There had to be other people in Dupray who wanted to read, right?

No matter. Most of the people rubbed her the wrong way as it was. Maybe she was better off reading on her own, and if she needed some sort of discussion, there were plenty of chatrooms she could join online. She wasn't really up to snuff when it came to joining things like that on the computer, but her nephew could set her up. He wasn't good for much else as it was.

It was cold in the house, and she was wrapped in a throw blanket. She didn't care to turn on the heat until it got unbearably cold, but for now, the blanket and even the lamp above her head kept her content. The damn thing put out enough heat, which made reading during summer a bit uncomfortable, but it was perfect for the colder seasons.

She turned the page, then grabbed the glass of iced chardonnay while she started the next chapter. She took a big swig of it. One of the ice cubes had melted enough that she swallowed it down with the wine, chomping it once.

Just as she was settling into the next scene, the lamp above her head cut out completely. She looked up, as if the light would magically turn on if she did, but it stayed off. She set her glass down and reached up, turning the switch. It clicked one way, then the other. Nothing.

"You gotta be kidding me," she said. She set her book on the table beside the glass of wine and threw off the blanket. The drastic change in temperature gave her a shiver, and she rubbed her arms. She was pretty pissed now that she had to change the lightbulb.

She looked at the clock across the room on the old VCR, but it didn't show the time. Apparently, it wasn't just a lightbulb issue. The power was out.

"This better not be the damn power company," she grumbled. "If I have to call and bitch them out one more time, I'm gonna lose it. Bunch of idiots over there."

Katelyn walked to the kitchen and flipped the switch, which did nothing. She grabbed the phone on the wall and put it to her ear, hearing no dial tone. She let out a long, drawn-out sigh that turned into a groan.

She was going to have to go to the basement. She hated going down there at night because of how dark it was. The single light-bulb that hung from the ceiling barely illuminated anything outside of a four-foot radius, and a large set of shelves blocked the line of sight to the circuit breaker. She had been too cheap to pay someone to move them, and too lazy to ask her nephew to do it. Every time she thought of it, she figured he would find a way to mess the whole thing up and break something. Her opinion of him wasn't very high.

During the day, the hopper window near the ceiling let in enough light to see, but it was completely useless at night. It was either a useless window or a useless nephew, and at this point, she wasn't sure which one was worse.

She walked to the other side of the kitchen and went through the laundry room, where the door to the basement was. She opened the door and automatically reached to flip the switch on the wall to illuminate the steps. She was immediately reminded that the power was out when the light didn't come on. She grumbled to herself and went to the kitchen drawer, pulling out the flashlight. She clicked it on, and a weak beam shone out. It would have to do.

She went back to the basement door and shined the light down. The stairs lit up, but she could only see a few inches past the bottom step.

The stairs looked rickety as hell, like they were an afterthought when the house was built. She knew the creak of each one from the number of times she had to go down there since moving in. This wasn't the first time the breaker had blown, and she knew it wouldn't be the last. But each time she had to go downstairs, she hated it. The darkness unnerved her.

But she relented and took the first step, making sure the door was propped open with the cinderblock she kept against the wall. The last thing she needed was for the door to slam shut while she was halfway down the stairs, causing her to brown her panties like that one time a couple months ago. That was one of the few times she was glad she lived alone.

Of course, the fact that she hated most people actually made her happy about that most days.

She reached the bottom of the basement, having listened to the symphony of creaks from going down the stairs, and shined the beam forward. Normally, she'd be reaching out, waving her hand to find the pull string to turn the solo bulb on, but unlike earlier, she remembered why she was in the basement in the first place.

She wouldn't be made a fool twice over the same thing.

The beam searched around, hitting the shelving unit that blocked the view of the breaker box. She made her way to it, using a combination of the flashlight and her free hand running along the wall and shelves so she didn't bump into anything. She found the end, careful to remember that she had boxes on the ground so she wouldn't trip over them. Finally, she made it to the breaker.

Her biggest fear was that something had knocked out the power down the road somewhere. If that were the case, then this whole journey would be for nothing, other than to get her all fired up for when she had to call the electric company and chew them out.

After the power came back on, of course.

It felt colder down here for some reason, and she wanted to get back upstairs as fast as possible. She opened the panel, shining her flashlight on the various switches. It was only right then that she remembered when the breaker popped, it was always just one. It was never the entire house unless it was weather-related, and then, that wasn't due to the breaker.

But the odd thing was, the main breaker switch had been turned off. It wasn't jiggly or loose, but looked like it had been deliberately pushed to the off position.

She shivered at the idea that someone had turned it off on purpose. But that would be ridiculous. Nobody was in the house other than her.

She frowned, furrowing her brow. She reached up, pushing the switch to the on position. She heard the various things click on somewhere in the house, like the hum of the refrigerator coming from the kitchen. She wished she had gone ahead and pulled the string to turn on the light in the basement, because it was still so damn dark down here.

She shut the panel door, but it knocked into her flashlight, making it slip from her grip and clatter against the cement floor.

"Dammit," she grumbled, turning to see where it had rolled to. When she did, she saw the hopper window that was so useful in the day but useless at night. She hadn't noticed it earlier because it was so dark.

The window was wide open.

CHAPTER SIXTY-FOUR

ELVEN ALREADY HAD HIS PHONE RINGING AS HE EXITED THE lobby of the town hall meeting. He was trying to reach the station, and right now he had the best cell service. Once he was on the road, things would get dicey. Not that he would have waited. He had to act fast if his theory was right.

He worried nobody would pick up since Meredith had most likely left for the day—it was hours after her shift. But finally, someone picked up.

"Dupray County Sheriff's Department," Tank said on the other line.

"Tank! Thank heaven you're still there," Elven said.

"Hey, Elven, you alright? The debate over already?"

"Never mind that," Elven said. "Is Lucinda still there with Abe?"

"Nah, she left a little while ago," Tank said. He sounded exhausted. "Abe convinced her to go home and get some sleep. I agreed and tried to make her understand that she can't really come and stay here all day again."

Elven picked up the pace, running through the parking lot and around the various cars until he reached his truck. He fished his keys out of his briefcase, then unlocked the door and slid inside, throwing his bag in the passenger seat.

"Call Katelyn," Elven said. "Tell her to come to the station if she can."

Tank snapped his fingers in the background at someone. "Hey, Johnny," Elven heard him say. "Can you get ahold of Katelyn for me?"

"Sure," Johnny said in the background.

"Johnny's calling her right now," Tank told Elven.

"Good, let me know what—"

"It's not working," Elven heard Johnny say. "It's just giving me a busy signal."

"You hear that?" Tank asked Elven. Now he sounded concerned. "What's going on?"

"I need you to go to Lucinda's house and make sure she stays put," Elven said. "Can you do that?"

"Lucinda's? Not Katelyn's?" Tank asked.

Elven shook his head, then realized that Tank couldn't see him. "No, you're closer to Lucinda's. Make sure she stays put. I have some questions for her. I'll go to Katelyn's."

"You're kind of all over the place, Elven," Tank said. "What's going on?"

"I've got a gut feeling," Elven said. "And not a good one."

Elven fired up his truck and pulled out of the parking lot, flooring it as soon as he reached the main road.

CHAPTER SIXTY-FIVE

KATELYN BLINKED THREE TIMES, STARING AT THE OPEN window. A strong breeze blew through it, raising goosebumps across her flesh. Her mind was running through every single scenario of how it could be open.

She hadn't left it open—hell, she never opened the damned thing. Nobody had come to do work on her house recently, and her idiot nephew would know better than to leave something like that unlocked. He wasn't good for much, but he knew the kind of hell he would get if he did leave it that way. Fear was the best motivator for him.

She wasn't even aware that the hinges on the window still worked. She thought they had rusted shut years ago.

There were scratches on the side of it, like it had been forced open.

Her heart sank, and a lump formed in her throat.

Then she heard a shift somewhere to her left, deeper in the corridor where the shelves created a pitch-black pocket across from the breaker panel. It sounded like a foot sliding against gravel, or maybe a dirty cement floor.

Like the floor in her basement.

She dropped down, grabbing for the flashlight.

And just as she did, there came a blast so loud that she worried her ears were bleeding. A huge *whoosh* of air, or something else, whizzed just above her head as she grabbed the flashlight. The blast hit the circuit breaker with a loud *clang*.

Her ears were ringing so bad that she never heard the house go silent again. No more refrigerator hum, no more lights, no more power. Of course, seeing the scattered buckshot having blown the circuit panel full of holes told her enough.

She stood tall, taking one single glance toward where the blast came from, and that's when she saw the barrel of the shotgun pointed right at her. Behind it was a small figure in the shadows. She saw some golden curls of hair glint in whatever light was possibly catching it, but other than that, she had no idea who it was.

And she didn't care to find out.

Katelyn jumped back the way she came, toward the stairs just as another blast of the double barrel came. Another deafening ringing in her ears, but this time, she didn't come away unscathed. She felt the sting and bite in her leg as she hit the floor after stumbling on the boxes she'd left there. She grabbed at her leg, relieved that it was still attached to her body. It looked like she had just caught a stray pellet, either from ricochet, or she was just lucky enough to not take the bulk of it. She wasn't sure which hurt more, the wound to her calf or her hip where she had hit the cement.

She wasn't going to debate that right now, though. Instead, she climbed to her feet, rubbing her hip, trying to make the throbbing stop. She decided it was her hip that hurt more. She could deal with a pellet in her leg. It hadn't hit bone.

"Goddammit," someone, clearly a woman, said from behind the shelves. "Katelyn, you bitch, get back here."

Katelyn heard the shotgun pop open. Someone was digging out the spent shells, dropping them to the floor before shoving what

Katelyn assumed were a couple of new ones inside, closing the gun right back up.

"Lucinda?" Katelyn asked, recognizing the voice.

"Be a good bitch and stay put," Lucinda said, her voice twisting into something nasty.

Katelyn had never heard Lucinda speak this way before. In fact, Lucinda hadn't made much of an impression on Katelyn over the years. If anything, she'd just thought she was overly nice, which annoyed the hell out of Katelyn. A real cheese-dick type.

But now? Well, this woman clearly wasn't the Lucinda she'd come to know.

"Lucinda, what the hell are you doing?" Katelyn asked, though she'd pretty much figured it out already. Someone firing two rounds at you seemed self-explanatory.

"Oh, you know, just trying to kill a bitch," Lucinda said, sending another blast of the shotgun somewhere into the basement. Luckily, it was far off-target.

Katelyn made a run for it to the stairs and shot back to her feet. She worked her legs as fast as she could, ignoring the burning in her calf and the throbbing in her hip. Another blast, and this time, it was aimed right at the stairs. But she had already made it far enough up that it missed her completely.

Katelyn ran through the door and worked at the cinderblock, pushing it with her foot. She grabbed the door and saw Lucinda halfway up the stairs, reloading the shotgun. She slammed the door and stepped aside just before another blast peppered the door, sending fragments of wood everywhere.

Apparently, Lucinda had gotten quicker at loading this time.

Katelyn turned to the kitchen, but felt her side now searing in pain. A large piece of wood from the basement door had found its way into her. It had torn through her shirt almost in the shape of a small stake and stabbed right into her skin. She could see the blood soaking into her shirt. She hadn't been as quick to dodge the blast as she'd thought.

"Shit," she groaned, grabbing at her side. The damn wood hurt more than the buckshot itself.

She looked toward the other end of the kitchen, past the small table and to the drawer next to the fridge. That was what she needed to reach, because that was where she kept her revolver. She could picture it right then and there, the Kimber snub nose K6. It was small, but it was what she was used to. Anything bigger, and she would be useless with it.

Her nephew had gotten it for her and had even taken her out in the woods, setting up some cans for her. He'd shown her how to shoot them. Maybe he wasn't so useless after all. Of course, it had been his dumbass idea to keep the thing in the kitchen drawer. Still, that was probably on her for keeping it there.

Whatever the case, it was only a few steps away. So she pushed on, wincing as the piece of wood dug deeper into her as she moved. If that wasn't bad enough, her leg and hip decided to speak up, reminding her that she was in worse shape than she'd thought.

She grabbed the table and made her way toward the kitchen drawer. Running was out of the question now. She was lucky enough to still be standing with the amount of pain that kept stabbing into her side. She didn't even know how deep the wood went, but damn, it must have found the right nerve to make her want to buckle over.

And that she did as soon as she let go of the table, slamming against the linoleum floor.

She heard Lucinda fiddling with the door and stole a quick glance at it. The woman's hand had reached through the hole she'd blasted in the center. She blindly searched for the door handle, finding it and turning the lock.

Then the door opened, and Lucinda, small-little-annoyingly-nice-cheese-dick Lucinda, stepped into the laundry room. She held the double-barreled shotgun that looked about as tall as she was if she stood it up on its butt.

She turned her head, smiling as her eyes locked onto Katelyn. "There you are," she said.

Lucinda scrambled on her hands, trying to scoot closer and closer to the drawer. She was just below it, reaching up for it. Her fingertips dug underneath the drawer, inching it open.

"Katelyn!" Lucinda yelled.

Katelyn stopped working the drawer open and turned to face Lucinda. This tiny woman looked the same as before, except there was something else in her eyes. Something inhuman. Like a flip had been switched inside her. What it was, Katelyn didn't know. But she just hoped there was a way of flipping it back.

"Lucinda," Katelyn said, trying to not let her voice crack or stutter, though she still sounded frightened. "What did I do to you? I don't have a problem with you."

"It's not what you did to me," Lucinda said, holding up the shotgun, the butt against her shoulder. Her sights were lined up, one eye closed as the barrel pointed straight at Katelyn's head. It all seemed a little bit overkill, considering she was only a few feet away from her. When she pulled the trigger, Katelyn knew there wouldn't even be anything left of her to put in a casket.

"Please," Katelyn said, never the type to beg or plead. But here she was, asking this woman not to take her life. And unfortunately for her, it was just as she feared.

There was no flipping that switch back in Lucinda's mind.

Katelyn closed her eyes, just wishing that she could see her dumbass nephew one last time and let him know that she loved him and that he wasn't all that bad. She tensed, waiting for the blast to come.

"Lucinda!" another voice shouted.

CHAPTER SIXTY-SIX

"Lucinda!" Elven shouted. He had his Colt Python revolver pointed straight at her as he stood in the living room.

Lucinda stood in the kitchen in front of the open entryway, her shotgun aimed at Katelyn.

He could see Katelyn on the floor. She looked in bad shape. Her shirt was bloody with something jutting out of her side, her pants were torn, and blood had soaked through the fabric. She had hoisted herself on both hands, her butt on the floor, leaning backward. She was practically backed into the kitchen cabinets, cornered or close to it.

Elven didn't let his eyes stray far to scan the rest of the room, but he didn't think there was any other danger around. Whether or not Abe had actually been a part of anything didn't matter now. He was still locked up.

And honestly, Elven no longer thought Abe had anything to do with the killings in the first place.

When Elven had reached Katelyn's home, it looked quiet and undisturbed from the outside. Her car sat in front of the house on the side of the road, all by itself. Elven did a quick sweep around the front of the property and then around the sides as best he could without actually going into the backyard. There was nothing to suggest anything wrong was happening. That is, until he heard the shouting.

The voices were muffled, but it sounded like people arguing. The shrill voice sounded like a woman screaming something. He just couldn't make out what they were saying.

"Katelyn?" Elven called out as he walked back to the front of the house. There was no answer, of course.

He pounded firmly on the door, hoping it would swing open and reveal Katelyn on the other side. As much as he was trusting his gut that Lucinda had a lot more to do with the killings than she'd let on, he hoped to high heaven that he was wrong.

But then came the blast.

As soon as he heard it, he pounded on the door again. "Katelyn!" he yelled, this time straining his voice. There was no answer.

Another blast came, much louder than the last one. Like it had gotten closer to him, still somewhere in the house. He tried the door handle, but it was locked.

He had no time to lose.

He lined his body squarely against the door, pulled his revolver out of his holster, and braced himself. He kicked at the door near the deadbolt against the frame, hitting his heel against the wood so hard, he felt the frame crack. But the door didn't budge. He gave it another well-placed, firm kick with all his might, and this time, the frame splintered apart, flinging wood pieces in the air as the door swung inward on its hinges and hit against the wall on the other side.

Elven stepped inside the living room, gun in hand, hoping to still find Katelyn alive. As soon as he made it to the center of the living room, he lined himself up with the door and spotted Lucinda straight ahead. And that's how he found himself in the position he was now.

The barrel of his gun pointed right at the small woman, who

couldn't have weighed more than one hundred and ten pounds soaking wet. He was surprised that the shotgun hadn't sent her flying backward from the force of the blast.

"Lucinda, put it down!" Elven commanded.

Lucinda continued to point the shotgun at Katelyn. He was confident he could take the shot and put the small woman down, but her finger was on the trigger, and he didn't even want to assume the amount of pressure she already had on that trigger. There was no way he could take the shot without Lucinda taking her own. And she didn't need accuracy on her side.

"Sorry, Sheriff," Lucinda said. "She's the last of them."

"Of who?" Elven asked.

"The pieces of shit that can't keep their opinions civil," she said. "You should have seen my Abe's face when they said those nasty things about him."

"I never said anything about Abe—" Katelyn began.

"Shut the fuck up, you cunt!" Lucinda screamed, cutting off Katelyn. "You did. You didn't have to like his book, but you made it so personal. You got nasty! He didn't deserve any of it! Nobody does!"

"Lucinda," Elven said as gently as he could. There was a time for force, and then there was a time to pull back. He felt like right now, it was the latter. "Why don't we just talk it out?"

She didn't even look at Elven, keeping her eyes locked on Katelyn on the floor. "We can talk all you want—after I pull the trigger," she said menacingly.

"No," he said. "I can't let you do that."

If he thought she was at risk of going for it, he would take the shot. But he felt it in his bones that she was teetering on the edge. That meant he had a chance to bring her back to his side. But one wrong word would send her toppling to the other side. The one that ended with Katelyn dead and his own bullet in Lucinda.

He desperately didn't want that to happen.

"Why not?" Lucinda asked.

"Because you're a crazy bitch!" Katelyn shrieked.

"Katelyn!" Elven shouted, watching Lucinda tense up as she held the shotgun. This was it. If another outburst like that happened, well, he wasn't going to think about that. Instead, he was going to make this work.

"She isn't wrong you know, Katelyn," he said.

Katelyn looked confused, her eyes even leaving Lucinda and locking on Elven. Her face twisted as if offended by his words. The fact that she could even think that way with the pop gun trained on her said a lot about who she was.

"See?" Lucinda said to Katelyn.

"Not everyone can write a book, and the fact that Abe did is amazing," Elven continued. "To trash someone for wanting to create something, to tear them down, is an awful thing. And for what? Because they didn't like it? That's not right, is it, Lucinda?"

"No, it's not," she said, her tone calming a little. "They didn't see what it did to his spirit. What it did to his smile."

"But you did," Elven said. "And after everything Abe had done for you, you wanted to do this for him, didn't you?"

Lucinda nodded, and Elven saw a tear run down her cheek. "That's right," she said. "He's done so much over the years, and I've never been able to match him. I've dragged him through so much, and he stayed with me, encouraging me. So it's my turn to do that for him. And to not let anyone treat him less than he deserves."

"And you have," Elven said. "But you need to stop this. It's not what he wants. He told you to let it go, didn't he?"

Elven hadn't figured out what Abe truly meant when he spoke to Lucinda at the cell until now. Before, he thought Abe was just telling her to move on without him.

"Because he doesn't want to trouble me," she said, now full-on crying, tears dripping down her cheeks and landing on the linoleum kitchen floor.

"Because he doesn't want to see you behind bars," Elven said.

"He doesn't want to see *you* get hurt. That's why he took the blame for you."

She nodded. "And I didn't even ask him to do that," she said. "He had nothing to do with what happened at the library. He didn't even know I did, but when you came and told us you thought it was related to the book, he figured it out. That's why he attacked that young deputy. Abe has never been a violent man."

"I know," Elven said. "And if you put the gun down and come with me, I promise you that he won't take any blame for the murders."

Lucinda hesitated, still holding the shotgun, but he could see her grip loosening. It wasn't safe yet, but he knew it was working. He could do this.

"I don't know," she said. "I don't believe you."

"Alright, then how about this?" he said. He took his gun and pointed it toward the ceiling while he turned his other hand upward, his palm open. Then he slowly holstered the gun and showed both of his hands, now completely empty. "See?"

Lucinda slowly shifted her eyes toward Elven, then quickly brought them back to Katelyn on the floor. She was hesitating, and that was a good thing.

"I... I don't... you mean it?" she finally asked.

"Absolutely," he said.

She shook her head. "No," she said. "I need to do this for him."

"Lucinda," he said, taking a gentle step forward. He could see her recognize that he was closing in, but she let him do it. "I don't want to shoot you, but if you do anything to injure Katelyn any further, I'm going to have to. How do you think Abe will feel? You're his whole world, I can tell that. I read the dedication he wrote for you in the book. I saw it with my own eyes. He is willing to go to prison for life for you. Don't do this. All it's going to do is hurt Abe. You don't want that, do you?"

That was it. Elven could see he had finally gotten through to her as he watched her eyes widen in realization. Her finger slipped off the trigger. She took a deep breath and let it out in a long sigh, the tension from her shoulders leaving. She let the shotgun slip through her grip, the butt of the gun tapping against the floor. The barrel remained in her hand, but just so she could keep it upright.

Lucinda looked at Elven, her eyes glossy and bloodshot from the tears. "Okay," she said, nodding. She was giving up. "I don't want to—"

A gun blasted from behind Lucinda. Lucinda's chest exploded in blood. Her eyes went wide, and she looked down to where there was now a hole in her body. The blood was already seeping so fast into her blouse, her heart rate pumping it out faster and faster.

"No!" Elven yelled.

Lucinda dropped to the floor, hitting her knees before she toppled over on her side. The shotgun fell to the floor in the opposite direction. Blood trickled from her mouth as her head rested against the linoleum.

Elven rushed to her side and grabbed her, pulling her so that she lay flat on her back. His mind raced, trying to figure out what to do first. Apply pressure to the chest? Flip her over and apply pressure to her back? He needed to call Driscoll. He needed to get her to the hospital.

"Lucinda," Elven said. "Lucinda, we're gonna get you—"

He stopped talking as his eyes locked onto hers. She stared up at the ceiling, completely lifeless. The blood was no longer pumping out but seeping. Elven would venture to guess that the bullet had torn straight through her heart. There was nothing he could do.

As soon as the bullet hit her, she was dead.

Katelyn sat against the cabinets, taking short breaths, on the verge of hyperventilating. Her hands shook as she held the gun, and then she dropped it.

"I—I—I had to," she finally said. "She was trying to kill me."

Elven stared at Katelyn for a moment, watching her shake and contemplate what she had just done, what she had just been through.

He didn't blame her for her response. Lucinda had still had the gun trained on her, and Katelyn couldn't read the situation like Elven.

Finally, he turned his attention back to Lucinda. Her body lay on the floor, not moving. Her eyes were still glossy, and she looked sad. She hadn't even had the chance to make any sort of peace, if there was any to be had.

He shook his head, then dragged his hand over her eyes to close them.

CHAPTER SIXTY-SEVEN

LUCINDA'S BODY WAS NOW COVERED IN A BLACK BODY BAG THAT sat atop a gurney at the doorway of Katelyn's house. Elven had helped Phil Driscoll lift her onto it. Her body, though now dead weight, hadn't given them any trouble.

Someone so small doing so much damage was sometimes an odd thing to Elven. He knew that guns could level the playing field in that way, but Lucinda had been so small, so meek and feeble.

While the paramedics patched up Katelyn before taking her to the hospital, Elven and the deputies asked her about Lucinda. She replied that Lucinda had always seemed like a nice lady. Katelyn even seemed annoyed by the woman's innocent demeanor, shocking everyone all the more that Lucinda could be capable of something so destructive and cruel.

But Elven saw how personally she had taken things on Abe's behalf. One never knew what could be the tipping point for someone, and the reading group had found Lucinda's.

Unfortunately for them, they'd paid the ultimate price for being ignorant of it.

"You okay?" Tank asked Elven, having driven straight to Katelyn's house after arriving at Lucinda's empty house. He'd radioed Elven as soon as he got there, but Elven was too busy trying to talk the situation down.

Elven had called Tank after taking the gun from Katelyn, but he had no cell service, so Elven filled him in on everything as soon as he arrived on the scene.

"Jesus," Tank said. "I can't believe Abe was willing to go to jail for her. Hell, if this were a different state, he would have gotten the needle."

Elven didn't disagree, but there was no death penalty in West Virginia. Maybe that was why Abe wasn't worried about taking the fall. But he doubted it. The relationship they had, Elven was willing to put money down that Abe would have gone to the grave for her.

"We need to tell Abe," Elven said.

"It's gonna wreck him," Tank said. "We aren't letting him go, are we?"

Elven hadn't even thought about that until now. "He attacked Tommy and lied to us, so that's plenty for us to keep him."

"Good, 'cause he could be a risk for retribution," Tank said.

Elven nodded, but he didn't really believe that. Lucinda was gone because she couldn't let go of what they'd said about Abe. Was Abe a risk? Probably. But there wasn't anyone else's life other than Abe's that Elven thought was at risk.

"Book him for assault and obstruction," Elven said. He didn't want to do it, but Elven followed the law. And this is the only way he knew to keep the man alive. And at the end of the day, if Abe wanted to, he would figure out a way to end it. But Elven had done the job that was required of him. Anything outside of that wasn't his responsibility.

"I can do that," Tank said. "You should go ahead and get some rest after all this. I can break the news to Abe."

"No," Elven said. "I'll do that." He didn't want to, but this way, he could tell Abe that her last thoughts were of him. It wasn't much, but it was something. Even though Lucinda had committed a heinous crime, Elven still felt sorry for her, and for Abe.

"Alright," Tank said. They stood in silence for a moment, staring at the house from the side of the road. The two of them listened to the wind, the rumbling engine of Driscoll's vehicle, and their breathing.

Finally, Tank broke the silence. "I got a call from the grocery. The thief hit them, but they said they have some good footage."

Elven sighed. "Good to hear," he said. It was part of the job, but a smash-and-grab at a grocery store seemed like such a small thing compared to an attempted homicide that resulted in a death.

"I'll pick up the tape tomorrow morning," Tank said. "Unless you need it tonight, then I can—"

"Tomorrow is fine," Elven said.

There was another bout of silence between the two men until Tank found something else to say. "How'd the debate go?"

Elven let out a breathy laugh. It wasn't exactly funny to him, just absurd. Dealing with all this death and carnage, and all the while, putting on a show for the people so they could decide if he should keep his job or not. One more part of the job that just didn't seem so important compared to others.

"It went great," Elven lied. He'd completely forgotten about it until now.

"Good," Tank said, trying to be encouraging. "Election is tomorrow. I know who I'm voting for." Tank grinned, but Elven didn't match it. "You've got it in the bag. Especially after solving this one for good."

Elven didn't respond. Instead, he turned around to head to his truck. After tonight, he wanted to climb into bed and forget about everything for a few hours. But he couldn't do that just yet.

He still had to swing by the station.

A case might be solved. A killer might be taken down. But the job was never really finished.

CHAPTER SIXTY-EIGHT

"What are you doing here?" Paige asked, stepping behind the bar. She frantically strapped her bar apron around her waist and tucked her hair back in a ponytail. A few strands of hair still lingered around her face, but it didn't seem to bother her.

Elven took a look at his clock and saw the time. It was twenty-five minutes past the hour. He chuckled to himself. "I'm guessing your shift started twenty-five minutes ago?"

Paige offered a sheepish smile. "You caught me," she said, biting her lip. "Think you can keep this one to yourself? I've been kind of pushing it with Martin lately. I think he's regretting trying to help me out."

Elven waved her off. "Did you just clock in?" he asked.

Paige looked confused. "Yeah, why?"

"Then we're good," he said. "Just being late isn't a crime."

He smiled at her, not sure if the joke had landed or not. And he wasn't sure if he even cared. He just wanted to disassociate and not think about anything important right now.

"Well, that's reassuring," she said, leaning in. "So let's say I was having someone clock in for me? Then what? Would you bust me? Slap the cuffs on me and take me downtown?"

She was keeping it light and playful. Elven was happy to play along.

"Time clock fraud isn't really high on the priority list. I think I'd be the first sheriff in Dupray to bust someone for it," Elven said. "But don't try me, 'cause I'm not above setting the record for that sort of thing."

He grinned wide, and she smiled back before grabbing a glass from under the counter and slapping it in front of him.

"Hope you haven't been here long," she said.

"Define long," he said, watching her pour the liquor into the glass. She didn't even need to be told what he wanted, or she'd just poured him the wrong drink. He couldn't really tell since her hand covered the label. Honestly, he would drink it either way. "Service is kind of spotty here, ain't it?"

She smiled. "You didn't answer me," she said. "What are you doing here?"

He picked up the glass and took a sip of scotch. She'd gotten the drink right. "Having a drink. What does it look like?" he asked. In reality, he just wanted to avoid the job for the day. After last night, he felt like he deserved it. After sleeping in as late as he could, he'd spent the day dodging any and all calls from friends and family trying to offer their support.

"Isn't there somewhere better you have to be?" she asked. "Is there some sort of campaign party or something like that? I mean, they're counting the votes right now. Hell, they might even be announcing the results as we speak." She found a remote from under the counter and spun around, turning on the small television in the upper corner of the room behind the bar.

"No, wait," Elven said, but it was too late. She'd turned the news on, and he saw it all.

It went immediately to the local news, which displayed various graphs on the screen. It would cycle a few times through the different counties in the state. It eventually came around to Dupray County. Most of the bar graphs were heavily one-sided on who was winning. Some positions ran unopposed, while others were a landslide like everyone had expected. The biggest focus for Dupray, though, was the sheriff election.

And the bar graph for that was pretty even. They still had votes to count, though.

It was closer than he wanted, that was for sure.

Paige looked at him as he took another swig of the scotch. "I gotta say, I heard some stories about you," she said.

Elven lifted his eyebrows. "Don't believe everything you hear. Unless they're good things, of course."

"I heard you were an arrogant prick."

"Wow. Have you been talking to Bernadette?" Elven asked, thinking of Johnny's girlfriend. He wasn't her favorite person, but they'd come to an understanding. Still, he wasn't sure he'd put it past her to say something like that about him.

"Who?" she asked, then shrugged it off. "Well, whatever the case, I haven't seen that guy. Something is a little different in you now from when we first met, but even then, it's not that. It seems like you're avoiding the election right now. You really worried about it?"

He shrugged. "I'd be lying if I said no."

She smiled. "Well, I can tell you who I voted for."

"Zane's not the worst option."

She smacked him on the arm. "Shut up. You know I voted for you."

He couldn't help but chuckle. It felt nice to have some banter with someone again. To not have to be so serious all the time.

"I'm sure it was a tough decision," he said. He looked at the television for a moment, then back at Paige. It was busy in the bar, and she didn't seem to want to bother with the other customers. Might not be the best for Martin's business, but Elven was grateful for it. "After yesterday, it just didn't feel right to party," he added.

"I heard about that," she said, which didn't surprise Elven one bit.

His mother, Meredith, and Johnny all tried to get the word out that Elven had saved Katelyn's life, which was why he'd left the debate the way he did. "Want to talk about it?" she asked.

He shook his head. "Thanks, though."

"Good," she said, letting out a sigh of relief. "That kind of thing is above my pay grade." She looked over to someone who was pointing to their empty glass at the other side of the bar. She gave a thumbs up, then proceeded to fill a pint of beer.

Elven chuckled. "I did pick up some footage from the grocery out in Jolo earlier today," he said. "Saving a life one moment, running errands the next."

Paige grabbed the beer, ready to carry it to the man at the table, but suddenly stopped. "Footage?" she asked.

He nodded. "Apparently, they got hit by the infamous shoplifter," he said.

"What'd you have to do that for?" she asked, still holding the beer. "Couldn't someone else do that?"

He nodded. "They could, but I figured it would help be a distraction."

"How'd that go?"

He shrugged. "Other than matching the description we have, not much. Bearded guy in a hoodie caught on some grainy camera."

"Miss!" the man shouted across the bar.

Paige looked frazzled, like she'd forgotten what she was supposed to be doing. "Right, I got you," she said to him, then briefly turned back to Elven. "Sorry, be right back."

He waved her off, letting her do her job as he sipped on his drink. He threw it back, and just as he did, he caught the TV screen switch colors. A logo floated over the screen, saying BREAKING NEWS.

"Holy shit!" someone shouted from inside the bar. Everyone turned and watched the screen along with Elven. The news anchor in his suit was reporting something, but the volume was too low for him to hear. It didn't matter, though. The ticker underneath told him all he needed to know.

At the bottom of the screen, the words continued to cycle underneath.

DUPRAY COUNTY SHERIFF RESULTS: WINNER - ZANE RHODES

CHAPTER SIXTY-NINE

TWO MONTHS LATER

Elven sat behind his desk, leaning over the keyboard, staring at the monitor he had brought in. In the past, he'd liked to keep a clean desk, which meant he didn't usually like having a computer on top of it. It made for distractions when he needed to get work done. Not to mention it cramped up the area, so he had a hard time sitting on top of the desk when he needed to give sage advice to one of the deputies.

But those days were ending. For him, anyway.

He had brought in the computer not very long ago. There was even more footage that had been collected of this serial shoplifter they had on their hands. They had tried a number of different ways to bait the man into coming out, but they'd never lured him back the same way that Tank and Tommy had done at Jake's Feed and Speed.

After that experience, the thief had gotten a lot more careful. Not careful enough to not get caught on film, but despite that, they still hadn't caught the man over the last two months.

Elven had initially brushed the whole thing off, figuring that he would eventually get caught by some business security guard and call Elven up to come arrest him, but that never happened. Instead, it was just call after call from the various businesses with complaints about how they couldn't catch him, how they were losing money, and how Elven needed to do something about it.

It frustrated him to no end that he couldn't catch this guy.

So here he sat, rewinding, fast-forwarding, and pausing grainy videos from the handful of times the thief was shown on camera. None of it actually told him who it was.

At least, not on the surface. Something inside tugged at him, telling him that he knew this person.

He didn't recognize this man with his hoodie and beard at all. Elven didn't know everyone in town, but he figured someone would eventually come forward with information about who it was. They'd posted images printed from the video feed all over town.

And yet, nobody else recognized him, either.

For a small town like Dupray, where everyone knew someone who knew someone, it was mind-boggling. Elven was beyond stumped.

But now, something was different.

He zoomed in as best as he could, which only made the image more pixelated. On television shows, they always zoomed in and enhanced the image to create a clear picture. Elven wasn't sure if that was a real thing or not, but if it were, it had to cost a pretty penny for that type of technology. And this was Dupray. They were lucky they even had a computer to work with.

He went back to the footage. The man grabbed a box of what looked like some sort of food in bulk. Elven could check the records of what was stolen to confirm that it was food, but that wasn't what he was interested in. The thief turned at just the right moment, and he paused the video, staring at the image.

The thief looked up at the camera, and a light hit their face at an angle. At the edge of his beard, it looked odd. He couldn't quite place what it was, but it was like the beard was bigger in a spot. Or was it coming off his face? Clearly, a beard didn't just come off of someone's face, so Elven wasn't sure what it was.

The man had a thinner frame and seemed a bit on the shorter side. Nothing that looked unusually short, but he was clearly not someone who could ever lie about being six feet tall. And then there were his eyes. There seemed to be something... familiar about them.

He definitely recognized this person.

Before his memory could make the final connection, a knock came at the doorframe where Elven had the door fully open. He looked up from the screen to see Tank.

The deputy lifted his eyebrows. "What's that?" he asked, pointing to the monitor.

"Come here real quick," Elven said, waving for Tank to come around the desk. Elven rolled his chair back to give the man some space, which was still not enough since he was so large, but neither of them complained.

Tank took a look. "The shoplifter? This guy is like a fly that can't be swatted," he said, clearly not thrilled he hadn't caught him, either.

"Look at this right here," Elven said, pointing to the screen where the beard looked like it was lifting away from his face. "Does that look odd to you? The beard, I mean."

Tank leaned in close, squinting to get a better look. He spent a few seconds trying to decipher what he was staring at. Eventually, he shook his head. "A little, but the footage is so damn grainy. It's probably just a glitch in the video."

"I don't know," Elven said, but he didn't think Tank was right at all. He just didn't have any more proof to support his theory. Not that he even had a theory, just a gut feeling that something was off with the guy. "You still have that hoodie that was dropped at Jake's?"

Tank nodded. "Yeah, I think we stuffed it in the closet," he said. "Don't worry, Elven, we'll get this guy eventually."

"I have no doubt about it," Elven replied. He knew where this was headed.

Tank hesitated, his voice creaky as he debated his next words. "But you don't need to stress about it. Lucky for you, it's not your problem anymore." Tank tried to keep his tone light, telling Elven he was *lucky*, but in reality, they both knew it wasn't that.

Elven had lost the election, and today was his last day on the job.

"Zane seems like he'll be a fair man to work for," Elven said, sensing Tank's apprehension. Change wasn't something anyone really enjoyed. It came with a lot of unknowns, and sometimes it was better to deal with the devil you knew—though Elven liked to think he didn't quite fit that description. "He kept both you and Tommy on as deputies, and is letting Johnny and Meredith stay on," Elven pointed out. "I wouldn't worry about your jobs."

Tank nodded. "It's still Dupray," he said. "Not like there's a big pool to pick from as it is. Zane running was a big enough surprise."

Elven smiled. "It sure was," he agreed.

"It's not gonna be the same without you here," Tank said. "Johnny wanted to stay, but he was a mess."

Elven chuckled. "For Pete's sake, I'm not dying. I still live here.".

Tank shrugged. "Yeah, but you know Johnny."

"That's why we love him," Elven said. The two stood in silence for a moment, knowing that this day had to end at some point.

"So what's the plan now?" Tank asked, stepping back to the front of the desk.

Elven stood up and adjusted his shirt. It was going to be a big change of pace, having to actually decide what to wear every day. He took his badge, the one that said SHERIFF across it, and set it on the desk, lingering for a second to stare at it. He smiled softly.

"I have no clue," Elven said.

CHAPTER SEVENTY

Elven drove his truck to Martin's Bar, pulling into a spot. It was a lively night at the bar, judging by the amount of cars out front. There were hardly any open spots. It seemed every regular had decided to show up that night.

There wasn't anything special going on as far as Elven could remember. He sure hoped that all these people weren't here to celebrate Elven's career coming to an end. Zane hadn't won by *that* many votes. In fact, it was a lot closer than anyone had expected.

Except for Elven. He'd always figured it would be a close race. He'd just thought it would be in his favor, not the other way around.

But life was full of surprises.

In some ways, he was genuinely looking forward to the fresh start. He might not be chasing down bad guys for a living anymore, but he would land on his feet somehow. And it wasn't like he would be hurting without the income that came with being sheriff. Most people would be hurting living solely off the income that came with that job.

He hadn't been totally honest with Tank when he left the station. He wasn't fully lying when he told Tank he had no clue what he'd do next. The world had opened up for him to take on whatever it was going to throw at him. But he did have some errands to run right after leaving the station.

It took some doing, but he managed to get everything done with plenty of time to spend at Martin's before they closed.

Which played into what he had planned now.

He had something to attend to, and he wasn't even sure he was right about it. But after a certain someone had told him to get his act together, he was starting to trust his gut again.

And his gut was screaming that he was right about this.

Elven reached into the passenger seat and grabbed the wad of fabric, tucked it under his arm, and left the truck. He walked through the parking lot and straight into Martin's Bar, which was just as energetic as he'd expected. All the tables were taken. People were sitting around, drinking, laughing, and all around enjoying themselves.

Martin was in the corner, his hair pulled back into a bun as it usually was. He spotted Elven and gave a wave from across the room before going back to speaking with two gentlemen doing shots. The three of them laughed at something Martin said.

Elven scanned the room, smiling at the sight of the full, jovial bar. This was his town. It might be dumpy at times, it might drive him crazy, and some people may not like him because of his family name, but he would always come back to Dupray. It was home. He felt it in his bones.

"You gonna come sit and have a drink?" Paige asked, walking past him with an empty tray. She came so close, he could smell the beer she had spilled on herself, mixed with whatever conditioner she used in her hair. From the way she was sweating, he figured she'd been a lot busier with pouring drinks than usual.

Once behind the bar, she patted the counter right in front of an empty stool. Elven smiled and slid onto it. "This is something," he said, motioning a hand toward the room.

"You're telling me," she said, keeping her voice above the volume of the room. "Zane said drinks are on him. As long as everyone finds a D.D., that is."

Elven smiled. "He already won," Elven said. "As if people didn't like him enough. Maybe I should have done that before the election."

"Something to think about next time," Paige said, giving him a wink and a smile. "Drink?"

"Sure," he said, setting the black hoodie he'd carried in on the bar top.

"Must be cold out if you're wearing that," she said. "Doesn't seem your style."

He took a deep breath and let it out slowly. It was busier in here than when he ran the scenario through his head, but he supposed it was as good a time as any. After all, he'd done all the legwork to get here.

"Not mine," he said. "Figured you were missing it."

She laughed and twisted her face in confusion. "Don't think so," she said.

He held it up to her like he was sizing it up. As he already knew, it was a men's extra small. Paige might not have been extra small in women's, but in men's, he was willing to bet that it fit her just right.

He tossed it over the bar at her. She caught it with her free hand.

"Try it on," he said.

She frowned, looking a little put off. Then she held it open and looked down. There was still a dusting of flour on it from when Tommy had been covered with it. Nobody had bothered to wash it. Elven was surprised they still had it. Still having the evidence of the crime on it just made it even better.

There was a flash of something in her eye when she saw it, but she quickly shook her head, wadding the sweatshirt up and plopping it down on the bar.

"What are you doing?" she asked, her voice laced with irritation.

Elven cleared his throat. "Trying to return your sweatshirt," he said. "I know it's yours. You dumped it outside of Jake's Feed and

Speed a while back, though from the new footage, it looks like you went and bought yourself a new one."

Paige looked around nervously. "I have no idea what you're talking about," she said, shifting on her feet.

"Sure you do," Elven said. "When you stole all the goods at the grocery store."

She blinked a few times, like she was trying to figure out what to say next. "You're accusing me of stealing? From where?"

"Everywhere," he said. "You're the thief we've been trying to catch. And failing miserably, I will add. Until now, anyway." He gave her a sly smile. He might have been a little unsure at the start of this, but right now, he was on a roll and felt it in his gut that he was right.

"The thief whose pictures are posted everywhere?" she asked, and Elven nodded. "You mean the *man* with the *beard*? I don't know what's gotten into you, Elven, but maybe you need to get your head checked. And maybe you should find somewhere else to drink tonight."

"I know it seems weird, what with the beard and all," he said. "But what better way to slide under the radar than to slap a fake beard on and have us think it's a man we're looking for? I worked a case recently that reminded me of this. I thought we might be looking for a woman who wrote romance novels, but really, it was a man using a woman's name. A *nom de plume*, as they say in writing. I'm not really sure what it would be called in this situation, but it's the same thing."

"And you came to this conclusion because?"

"Because it makes sense," Elven said. "You're a single mom. You barely pick up enough shifts here to meet a grocery bill, let alone pay for an expensive private school tuition. Your late husband ran supplies up to the hills, but you said there wasn't a lot of margin in that. So, what better margin is there when supplies cost nothing? You still have the connections."

She licked her teeth, pushing her lip up as she did. He could tell he was getting to her. "That's it?" she asked. "I thought you were going to have some proof, but instead, you have this outrageous theory that's a bigger stretch than when I gave birth."

Elven considered her for a moment. "You know, people always tell me I'm a horrible liar. They can see right through me," he said. "I wonder if this is what they're talking about, because right now, you aren't doing yourself any favors."

"Elven Hallie!" someone shouted from behind Elven. He felt a hand clasp his shoulder and turned to see Zane Rhodes. "I'm glad to see you tonight." Zane held a hand out. Elven studied it for a moment, then grasped it firmly in a shake.

"Zane," Elven said. "Good to see you." Elven wasn't lying, either. He held no ill will toward the man. He had been wrong about the man from the beginning, making everything personal. Now he could see that Zane was a good man.

"Whatever you're drinking, it's on me tonight," Zane said, clearly having had a few himself. It wasn't alarming. He was just a little looser. "But you gotta get a ride home."

Elven smiled. "I appreciate it," he said. "Have you met Paige?"

"Briefly, but haven't exchanged many words," Zane said, offering her a smile.

"Oh, you really should," Elven said, narrowing his eyes at Paige. "She's a wild one. Very capable. But don't let her out of your sight, either. A real slippery one. She's full of secrets."

"Really?" Zane asked. "Sounds ominous."

Elven chuckled. "Well, I have this theory that I think we should run by you. We were talking about the th—"

"Elven," Paige said. "I haven't even poured you that drink yet."

Elven smiled. "No, I guess you haven't," he said. He could see how tense Paige had become. He turned to Zane. "Zane, enjoy your night, and thanks for the drink."

"Of course," Zane said. "And don't worry, the county is in good hands."

"I have all the faith that it is," Elven said, watching Zane wander off to another group of people.

Paige slammed her hand on the bar top and leaned in. "Okay, so what the hell is the point of all of this? You gonna arrest me?" she asked. "I just want what's best for my son. He's better than this place. You know what he is scoring on tests? The numbers are beyond me. No way in hell am I going to have him get stuck here like I am. And if that means—" She looked around the bar, making sure nobody was paying attention to them. "If that means I have to run circles around your deputies and do what I have to do to make that happen for him, then you better fucking believe I will."

Elven sat, listening to her. He wasn't sure what he'd expected when confronting her, but having confirmation felt good. "I get it," he said.

"But I'm also the only family Sterling has anymore," she said. "He needs me. I can't go to jail."

"Good news for you," Elven said. "I ain't the sheriff anymore. He is." He motioned with his head toward Zane. "There might not be proof, but I'm sure just the mention of who it might be would go a long way. There would be digging. Maybe he'd even put someone on you to follow you around. He doesn't seem like the type to let something like that go. Don't you think so?"

Paige did not look happy with Elven, looking daggers at him. "I was wrong about you," she said.

He lifted an eyebrow. "How so?"

"I see the arrogant prick that everyone complained about," she said, shaking her head. She turned away, staring off at nothing for a moment. Elven let her have it. Finally, she looked back at him. "What is this, anyway? Some sick game, or what? I highly doubt you need money, and nobody ever said you were into extortion. As if I even had anything to give. So what do you want?"

"I want to give you a job," Elven said.

Paige paused, her jaw still clenched like she had been ready to spout something nasty at him but was suddenly caught off-guard. "I don't understand," she said. "Work for you doing what?"

"That part I'm not really sure about," he said. "As you are well aware, I am currently between jobs. I have a lot of time, which means a completely new routine that I'm not used to."

"And what does that have to do with me?" she asked.

"I guess we can call you my assistant," he said. "The schedule is way more relaxed than having to be on time here. And you won't need to do any more of your, let's call it, side hustle."

"I can't just stop doing the deliveries. Those people depend on me.".

He nodded. "Then keep doing it. Legally, of course, like your husband did, by paying for the groceries."

She chewed on her cheek a moment. "Medical coverage?" she asked.

Elven smiled. Now it was a negotiation. "Done," he said.

"And so you'll just overlook everything I've done?" she asked. "Meanwhile, you hold it over my head and force me to work for you? Otherwise you'll turn me in? It's not really a choice anymore, is it?"

"That's not my style," he said. "There's nothing to turn you in for or hold over your head anymore. What you do next is completely up to you now."

"What are you talking about?" she asked. "You just said—"

"I paid for all the things that were stolen. Jake's Feed and Speed, the grocery, the other grocery, and all the other little things I could find reports of. Nobody is pressing charges anymore," he said. "I may have gotten a handful of teens off for stealing candy bars while doing it, too, but I wanted to make sure none of it had the possibility of being linked to you."

He grinned and lifted his eyebrows. He wasn't trying to be mean by tricking her. But he was sure having fun with it.

"And you have no proof that it was me, other than some theory? Because I need money?" she asked. "Like ninety percent of this fucking place needs money?!"

Before, Paige was angry because she thought Elven was extorting her, and now she was angry because he wasn't? He had to admit, she was kind of funny. Maybe even cute, especially when frustrated.

"So what—"

"Why?" she asked finally, no longer frustrated but looking more determined than ever. "I don't see how I'll make up the salary you're so determined to pay me. And you just want to do all this for me because I served you some drinks? That's not how the world works."

"It's how I work," Elven said.

"I'm not going to sleep with you," she blurted out.

He wasn't expecting that one, not because he was hoping she would, but because that hadn't crossed his mind. She was attractive, sure, but he wasn't looking for anything like that. He still felt very up in the air with how things had ended with Madds. Neither of them had said they were breaking up, but his being shot and her running off probably was enough for him to take the hint.

He wasn't even sure how to respond to Paige. He went silent.

"I'm sorry," she said suddenly. "I just didn't—"

"It's fine," Elven said. "But I know the effect I have on women, so try to resist the urge to come onto me."

"Oh, God, can we put jail back on the table?" she said, rolling her eyes. "What happened to the guy who used to come in here kind of glum, maybe a little unsure of himself?"

"Had to work out some things," Elven said. "And to answer your question, I can see something in you. The drive to help someone other than yourself, like your son."

"It's called being a mother."

"Well, you're a good one," he said. "And I want the same thing as you, to let Sterling have the best opportunities he can. That kid is special. Dupray has a tendency to keep people down who don't deserve it."

Paige gave a slow nod, her eyes drifting off. She began to frown. Elven could tell she was thinking about her son, and how hard it would be to get him out of here.

"I thought I'd have time to pay just before the school year starts, but they require it a lot earlier. Tuition is due in two weeks. I don't know—"

"I'll pay it," he said. "On top of your salary."

She swallowed. "I don't know what to say."

"Yes would be a good start."

She nodded. "Of course," she said. Elven thought he saw a hint of tears welling up in her eyes, but she quickly wiped at her face, and whatever he thought he saw was gone. "Yes, I'll take the job."

He smiled, holding his hand out. She shook it. "Glad to have you on board," he said. "Oh, one more thing."

"What is it?" she asked.

He smiled. "I hope you like dogs."

EPILOGUE

Elven decided not to close the bar down with practically the rest of the town. Zane was having his moment, and Elven didn't want to step on any toes. He'd gotten Paige to accept his job offer, which went just about the way he had expected. Sure, he was probably going to pay far more than what he needed, but why not?

If Zane was going to put his money into the community in big ways, then maybe Elven needed to figure out how to do that, too. Even with just this one small thing, he wanted to help make Dupray a better place for everyone in it.

Besides, he wasn't lying about starting the next chapter in his career, or life, even. He knew there were big things ahead for him. And it would shake up his entire routine. Paige being there to pick up the slack with whatever Elven had going was going to be a big help.

Now he just had to figure out what exactly this next chapter of his life was going to be. Because right now, he had no idea.

It was actually exciting.

He was willing to take on anything that life threw at him.

But he knew the very first thing he needed to do.

He stood in front of his motel room, staring at the door. He'd dropped off Yeti with his mother earlier that day before running all those errands at various stores, paying them off and convincing them to drop the charges. His explanation to them was to thank them for their patience and support while he had been sheriff. None of them seemed to mind as soon as he mentioned payment.

Victoria had played the reluctant part, but he could see the little smile that had slipped over her lips when she saw the white furball. She did her best to make it go away and pretend like she was giving in to Elven's request. And then as soon as Yeti walked in, she showed him to the bed she had purchased for him, along with a box of toys.

Elven had lifted an eyebrow, but Victoria just waved it off, trying to make up an excuse for why she had to buy all of it. He let her have her story, but knew she had a big soft spot for Yeti. He loved to see it.

Yeti would be fine with his mother for the night. In fact, the only thing he was in danger of was getting spoiled by her. Elven knew the dog was already spoiled enough as it was, but that was okay. He deserved to be. All dogs did, in his opinion.

He slid his key into the door and walked in. He didn't even bother turning the light on; he could see just fine. He stared straight ahead at the wall on the other side of his bed. It was still there, taunting him, telling him to fall back down the rabbit hole of trying to find Madds.

He'd kept it up the rest of the time he'd worked as sheriff, attending to it here and there but never giving it the entire focus he had before the library massacre. He thought having it up was something he should do, but at the same time, he knew what it would mean to keep trying to find her.

He had made it personal, which was admittedly hard not to do, but still, he had to let go of it. If he didn't, there was no telling what would happen to him. He wasn't sheriff anymore, so he had all the time to devote to the search if he really wanted.

A part of him did, wondering what had happened to her. Was it because he missed Madds, or was it because she had gotten away and he wanted to win? He knew there was nothing to actually win. In fact, he would just lose his own sanity that way.

It was like Lucinda. Abe had told her to let it go. But for whatever reason, she just couldn't. And now she was dead.

He wasn't going to go down that road.

Elven closed the door behind him and walked up to the wall. He went straight for the picture of Madds that he'd pinned to the wall. He removed the pin and pulled picture down, looking at it for a moment.

Would he ever see her again? Was she even alive? If so, where had she gone?

He supposed that it didn't matter anymore. He was done with it. He was done with her.

He crumpled the picture up and let go of it, letting it drop to the floor.

"Ouch, but I guess it's deserved," a voice said from behind Elven.

Elven's hand went to his side, muscle memory kicking in. He pulled his revolver as he spun around, pointing his gun at the source of the voice.

A figure stood in the bathroom doorway, but it was too dark to tell.

"You got one second to show your hands before I shoot," Elven said, his heart racing.

The bathroom light flicked on, and there she was, standing right in front of him. Her hair was shorter, her face leaner, and she wore flannel clothes that weren't her style. But it was her, alright.

"I guess that'd be only fair. After all, I did shoot you first," Madds said.

Elven didn't know what to think. His heart was racing at the sight of her. He'd been trying to figure out where she'd gone all this time, and now she was standing right in front of him.

Emotions flooded through him, overwhelming him. He never thought this would happen after so long, but here he was, battling between wanting to be angry with her and wanting to wrap her in his arms.

"Madds," he said, then paused, trying to find his words. "I could arrest you right now." A little less profound than he was hoping for, but it was the first thing that found its way out of his mouth.

"Is that so?" she asked. "'Cause it's my understanding that you're not the sheriff anymore."

She was right, and he didn't really have a rebuttal for that. When he had played this game with Paige, he was prepped for it. He could play with the idea that he'd tip off Zane when, in fact, he wasn't interested in that at all. But he'd been caught off-guard now, and he really wasn't interested in playing that game now. Not with Madds.

"What are you doing here?" he asked.

She hesitated for a moment, the two of them staring at each other. Her jawline tensed up, and from where he stood, her eyes looked sadder than he remembered. He wondered if she was looking him over the same way, trying to evaluate him.

Finally, she spoke.

"Elven, I need your help."

GET BOOK 8 in the Sheriff Elven Hallie Mysteries NOW!

AFTERWORD

Thanks for reading Carnage in the County, the seventh installment in the Sheriff Elven Hallie mysteries.

I feel like this book was an end to some stories, but the beginning of so many new ones! I hope you enjoyed reading it as much as I enjoyed writing it.

I had this idea working for a while, just waiting for it to take shape, so now that it's finally here, I'm so excited for you all to see what is in store for Elven next! Don't worry, there will be plenty of new cases for Elven to solve, even though he's on a major career shift right now.

Thanks to my wife Sara, my two boys, my editor Chelsey Heller, Lisa Lee for proofreading, and of course, all of you for reading and allowing me to continue with writing this series and do this full-time!

As always, being an independent author, I don't have a huge publisher's budget, so reviews are very important. If you have the time, please consider popping over to Amazon, or your favorite place to leave reviews, and post one!

To keep up to date and get some fun freebies, join my reader's list: http://drewstricklandbooks.com/readers-list/

-Drew Strickland

August 27, 2024

FORSAKEN IN THE FOREST

Get Forsaken in the Forest, book 8 in the Sheriff Elven Mysteries now!

ALSO BY DREW STRICKLAND

Standalone Thrillers

Last Minute Guest

A Secret Worth Keeping

The Carolina McKay Series

Her Deadly Homecoming (Book 1)

Her Killer Confession (Book 2)

Her Deadly Double Life (Book 3)

Poaching Grounds (Book 4)

Winter's Obsession (Book 5)

The Nameless Graves (Book 6)

Bury Her Twice (Book 7)

The Sheriff Elven Hallie Mysteries

Buried in the Backwater (Book 1)

Murder in the Mountains (Book 2)

Hunted in the Holler (Book 3)

Abducted in Appalachia (Book 4)

Secrets in the Squalor (Book 5)

Vendetta in the Valley (Book 6)

Carnage in the County (Book 7)

Forsaken in the Forest (Book 8)

The Cannibal Country Series

The Land Darkened (Book 1)

ABOUT THE AUTHOR

Drew Strickland is the author of the Sheriff Elven Hallie Mystery series, Soulless Wanderers: a post-apocalyptic zombie thriller series, and the co-author of the Carolina McKay thriller series and the Cannibal Country series, both written with Tony Urban. When he isn't writing, he enjoys reading, watching horror movies and spending time with his wife and children.

www.drewstricklandbooks.com

Made in the USA
Monee, IL
18 September 2024

66027820R00196